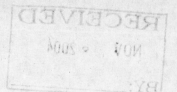

ALSO BY AMULYA MALLADI

The Mango Season

A Breath of Fresh Air

Serving Crazy with Curry

Serving Crazy with Curry

A NOVEL

AMULYA MALLADI

BALLANTINE BOOKS
NEW YORK

A Ballantine Book
Published by The Random House Publishing Group
Copyright © 2004 by Amulya Malladi

Reader's Guide copyright © 2004 by Amulya
Malladi and Random House, Inc.

www.ballantinebooks.com/BRC

Library of Congress Cataloging-in-Publication Data
Malladi, Amulya.
Serving crazy with curry : a novel / Amulya Malladi.
p. cm.
ISBN 0-345-46612-8
1. East Indian American women–Fiction. 2. Mothers
and daughters–Fiction. 3. Suicidal behavior–Fiction.
4. Women–India–Fiction. 5. Sisters–Fiction. 6. India–
Fiction. I. Title.

PS3613.A45S47 2004
813'.54–dc22

2003063774

Manufactured in the United States of America

First Edition: November 2004

9 8 7 6 5 4 3 2 1

For Søren and Tobias,

who eat all the crazy I serve

And

For my mother,

who taught me how to cook.

Acknowledgments

Without Søren, this book, or any other for that matter, would not have been written. I thank him for his patience and for always being honest, even when I slam the doors.

Matt Bialer's confidence in me helped me finish this book. I thank him for his advice all those years ago when he wasn't my agent and now when he is.

Allison Dickens, as always, with her impeccable insight, saved this book in many ways. I thank her for being a wonderful editor and for always listening to me when I need to vent.

Kelly Lynch and Jody Pryor read this book in its various incarnations and I thank both of them for their critique and guidance.

Dr. Mara Berkley and her husband, Dr. John Berkley, told me all I need to know about suicide and therapy, and in the process Mara even helped me solve a few personal problems. Though I used these wonderfully generous people mercilessly while I wrote this book, all mistakes made and liberties taken are completely and absolutely mine.

Suicide . . . brings on many changes,
And I can take or leave it if I please.

—MIKE ALTMAN AND JOHNNY MANDEL
THEME SONG OF THE MOVIE M*A*S*H

Eating is the great preoccupation of both primitive
and civilized man. But the savage eats from need,
the civilized man from desire.

—ALEXANDRE DUMAS,
LE GRAND DICTIONNAIRE DE CUISINE

Contents

Contents

Serving Crazy with Curry

The Beginning or The End

The DOW was down almost 600 points the week Devi decided to commit suicide. The NASDAQ also crashed as two big tech companies warned Wall Street of their dismal next quarter estimates. But the only reason Devi was half-heartedly listening to some perky CNN Sunday news anchor prattle on about the lousy week on the stock exchange was habit. A long time ago she'd kept track, listened eagerly, checked the stock of her company online on Yahoo!, but that was when she had stock options that could have been worth something. The last two start-ups she hooked up with hadn't even made it as far as the IPO.

After Devi was laid off (yet again) a week ago, it started to dawn on her that she was not going to be able to change her life. Everything she ever wanted had become elusive and the decision to end her life, she realized, was not only a good decision, but her only option.

As a good tactician, her mind laid down two categories on a spreadsheet: the reasons to die and the reasons not to die. After filling the columns she practically went through all the reasons, struck out those that didn't make sense, kept those that did.

REASONS TO DIE	REASONS NOT TO DIE
1. Have disappointed the father and grandmother who love me	1. Have a loving family (sort of, if mother and sister are not included)
2. ~~Laid off again~~	2. ~~Have my health~~
3. ~~Completely in debt~~	3. ~~Hmm . . .~~
4. ~~Can't pay rent~~	
5. ~~Have had only failed relationships~~	
6. ~~Slept with a married man~~	
7. ~~Had a relationship with a married man~~	
8. ~~Fell in love with a married man~~	
9. Lost a baby	

Ultimately, it didn't matter what the entries on the spreadsheet of her unbalanced mind were, because the decision was already made. She knew that the losses she incurred had eaten away everything joyous within her. In the past six months she went from being just slightly depressed to so sad and fragile that the passing of every day seemed like a wasted opportunity; an opportunity to not live through the day.

Devi's fingers moved over the remote control of the television and flipped through images, faces, and vacuum cleaners.

Wanting to delay her impending decision of death, she picked up the telephone and sat down on her sand-colored sofa (the one she couldn't afford), her Victoria's Secret white silk robe tightly secured at her waist. She'd been tightening her robe ever since she put it on at seven that morning, hoping it would settle her down, secure her mind and the uneasiness roiling inside her stomach. All night she had tossed and turned, going over the decision one way and then another. When finally sleep claimed her it was five in the morning and then sleep abandoned her again after just two hours.

Suicide was stressful business.

First, there was the question of how, which she'd pretty much decided on, but there were lingering doubts. Second, there was the question of when. Last night she thought she'd do it at night, in the quiet, but doubts kept her awake, alive. Now it was morning and even though there had been several such mornings in the past months that followed empty, contemplative nights, this morning was different. This morning nothing had changed with the break of dawn as it usually did. This morning her heart was as heavy as it was last night when she started to think seriously, once again, about death. And that's why she could feel that this was the day it would happen, the day she would make it happen.

Devi stared at the telephone and her fingers automatically tapped the numbers that would conjure up someone on the other end of the line at her parents' home.

She turned the television off as soon as she heard her father's hello. "Daddy, Devi," she said.

"What's going on, *beta?*" Avi asked in a groggy voice, like he'd just woken up, which he probably had since it was eight o'clock on a Sunday morning, too early for any of his children to call, definitely too early for party-all-night Devi to call.

"Just wanted to say hello," Devi said, tears brimming in her eyes. She desperately wanted him to say that everything would be okay, that the world would not collapse around her, but that meant asking him for help, and the way things were she was too ashamed to hold out her hand.

This was her life, she was responsible for it, and the mess she had made of it was not something he could clean up for her. As much as she wanted to be held in the secure circle of Daddy's arms, she knew that would just underscore her failure. At least in this, she wanted to succeed, not back out like a wimp who could neither live nor die.

"How's work?" her father asked next.

"Great," she lied instead of telling him that the company had closed its doors. She was out of a job again and this time there was no way around the facts. She was a loser. Had always been, especially compared to the successes in her family. Her father, Avi Veturi, had started a successful technology company with a friend and now was semi-retired, enjoying a privileged life in Silicon Valley. Her older sister, Shobha, was vice president of engineering for a software company. Her grandmother Vasu had been a doctor in the Indian Army, and retired as a Brigadier. Talk about overachievers, her family was loaded with them.

Her mother, Saroj, who'd spent her entire life in the house, had no solid successes to her credit and among all her family members, she was the only one Devi could compare herself to. That was a scary thought. Saroj never held a job, spent all her time in the kitchen cooking and pretending to take care of her family. She was a fairly good cook and a lousy mother. Her relationship with her husband seemed extra strained since he'd semi-retired a few years ago. Marriage to Avi had been Saroj's biggest accomplishment and now that marriage was also fading away, rotting in apathy and some disdain. If they were not Indian, Devi was sure they'd be divorced.

"G'ma," she told her grandmother, who lived in India, on the telephone just a few years ago, "they sleep in separate beds and now Daddy is talking about moving into the guest room, to avoid all the Hindi movies Mama watches at night."

Her grandmother had been honest as she always was and told Devi that some marriages simply don't work and they should be ended, but not too many people had the courage to do so. G'ma was not one of those cowards. She divorced her crazy husband when divorce was unheard of in India. She took that chance and so many others. She lived her life on her own terms and no one could ever call Vasu a loser.

Tears filled Devi's eyes again and regret flooded inside her. She wanted to be like her grandmother: strong, independent, and smart. Instead she was more like her mother: a complete failure at everything she ever attempted—life, love, children, job, relationships, finances, everything.

"Is G'ma up?" Devi asked her father. Vasu was visiting as she always did during the summer to get some relief from the scorching Indian heat.

"I don't know, *beta*. Probably not, we were up until three in the morning playing chess. But I can . . ."

"Who's on the phone, Avi?" Devi heard her mother call out.

"Do you want to talk to your mother?" Avi asked and Devi whispered an unsteady "no" and hung up quickly. She didn't want to talk to her mother, and on second thought she didn't even want to talk to Vasu. She felt she had said her good-byes the week before when the entire family met for dinner at her parents' house.

Girish, Shobha's husband, was unable to make it because of some "thing" at the university, but no one believed those stories anymore. Ever since they'd found out that Shobha couldn't get pregnant it had become more evident than ever that their marriage was not working, at any level.

For a very long time Devi had been jealous of Shobha; part of her still was. Shobha had it all. A vice president of engineering at a software company at the young age of thirty-two was quite an achievement. Marrying a Stanford professor and excellent man, Girish, was another one. Devi was perversely (and guiltily) glad that Shobha couldn't put down "perfect mother" on her list of achievements.

Just two years after marrying Girish, Shobha had surgery for endometriosis and was told that she could not conceive. Shobha was shocked that at the age of twenty-nine she couldn't have children.

"They have a billion people in India and I can't have a baby? Those crack addicts who can't take care of themselves get knocked up, so why the hell can't I?" Shobha demanded angrily. Even then angry. Not sad, not devastated, like the rest of the family. Shobha was angry, always angry. That was Shobha's trademark emotion, her way of dealing with the world at large. Anger, Shobha said, was not a bad thing.

"Fuck them who say . . . and yes, Mama, I can say *fuck*, I'm twenty-nine years old and barren, I can say *fuck* even if fucking doesn't get me anywhere anymore . . . so what was I saying?"

"You were saying that anger is a good thing," Girish filled in patiently. "Maybe you got endometriosis because you're so angry all the time."

Girish had been a broken man when he heard the news, and tried to convince Shobha that adoption would be the solution. She wouldn't hear of it. "If I can't have my own child then maybe this is nature's way of saying that I shouldn't have children. Not mine, not anyone else's." Their relationship deteriorated after that.

Devi wondered if she should call Shobha to say good-bye. They never really got along, not like sisters did in movies, in other people's families, in books. They were distant, and Devi had a strong inkling that Shobha genuinely disliked her.

She dialed Shobha's cell phone number, always a reliable way of getting in touch with her and the best way to avoid speaking with Girish, who could answer if she called their home phone. The fewer people she had to say good-bye to, the easier this would be. But even as Shobha's cell phone rang, Devi knew she was procrastinating. On the sixth ring, right before Shobha's voice mail would click in, Devi hung up, threw her phone down on the couch, and stood up. It was time, she told herself firmly. It had been time for a while now.

Devi was not the first person in her family to attempt suicide. Thirty-eight years ago Ramakant, Devi's grandfather, hung himself from the ceiling fan in his brother's house with one of his ex-wife's silk saris. Vasu never forgave Ramakant for killing himself just three months after the divorce. The blame fell squarely on her, and everyone merrily overlooked the fact that Ramakant was obviously unbalanced. Adding insult to injury was the suicide note, in which Ramakant took great pains to specifically explain how his ex-wife was not the reason why he was doing himself in and that he loved and respected Vasu very much.

Devi had decided in the beginning that if she ever killed herself it would be without a suicide note—no melodrama for the damned. This was a personal business, a private affair, no one needed to know why. Sure, her family may think she owed them an explanation, but that was an unreasonable expectation compounded by Devi's perverse desire to keep them guessing. Her parents may have brought her into the world (and that, too, without her permission), but it was her choice when she left.

She wanted to leave now.

It wasn't like she woke up one day and thought, *Oh, it's a good idea if I kill myself today.* No, it took several months before she reached this point. It started like a spark of electricity, something that happens when wiring goes bad. And once the idea popped into her head, she couldn't unpop it, no matter how hard she tried. No matter how hard she shook her head to clear it away, it stayed, and soon became a constant companion.

Everything seemed to be an omen, giving her the green, *go-ahead,* signal to die.

The computer crashed again. Damn, if only I was dead, I wouldn't have to deal with this.

I locked the car keys inside the car. Damn, if only I was dead, I wouldn't have to call Triple A.

It's a Friday night and I have no one to go out with. If only I'd killed myself in the morning then I wouldn't have to face this loneliness now.

So on and so forth.

Devi had it all planned, the method (this after some serious pondering), the time of day (though this kept changing), and the place. But in all her planning, Devi didn't account for one mistake she had made a year ago. She gave Saroj a spare set of keys to her town house in Redwood City. Saroj had virtually beaten the keys out of Devi when she'd rented the place; nagged the hell out of her until Devi relented.

"You have to give us a spare set of keys. If you lose yours you will have to pay your landlord all that money to get new keys . . . this way, everything will be nice and easy."

It hadn't been quite nice'n easy as the hair-coloring commercial promised. It had been a nightmare. Saroj quickly forgot her guarantee to Devi that she wouldn't enter Devi's house using the spare key and did exactly that. The first time was with a box of *ladoos.*

Devi was shocked to see her mother in the dining area putting a box of *ladoos* on the table while Devi struggled to cover herself with a towel and hold on to a baseball bat, convinced that someone had broken in while she was in the shower.

When asked why she didn't just ring the doorbell, Saroj splut-

tered something about having done that and then, having not gotten a response and seeing the driveway empty, used her key.

Devi reminded Saroj that she had a garage and therefore didn't
park her car in the driveway. Saroj just held up the *ladoos* and asked
peevishly, "So, you don't want the *ladoos?*"

Devi sighed and said it was okay this one time, but who was she
kidding, the visits soon became a habit. Sometimes Devi would
come home and there would be new Indian food items in her fridge
and a long message from her mother on her answering machine explaining why Saroj just had to use her set of keys to put the perish-
able food in the fridge.

So it would have been prudent of Devi to have set the deadbolt
from the inside that morning to prevent an unwanted visitor. However, new food hadn't appeared in her fridge for a whole month and
Devi had forgotten her mother's trespassing ways.

Devi sat down at the edge of the claw-foot bathtub, one of the
reasons why she'd wanted to rent the house despite the exorbitant
price the landlord was asking. She turned the delicate, antique brass
water faucet, her fingers caressing the water as the thick drops fell.
After a steady stream of cold water poured into the tub, wet heat
began to stroke her hand. Deciding that the temperature was right,
she rose and realized how insane it was to ensure the temperature
of the water was right when she was going to do what she was going
to do. How did it matter?

She tightened her robe one more time as her glance fell on the
beautiful ivory-handled knife she'd purchased in Chinatown several
years ago. She had bought it because it looked fancy and was expensive. She'd just accepted her first real job offer with her first
start-up and they were paying well. She wanted to buy herself something silly, something expensive, and the ivory-handled knife
caught her eye for all those reasons. At the time she would've never
thought how handy it could be, how the sharpness that surprised
and annoyed her would work to her advantage.

"Am I sure?" she asked herself and waited for a resonating answer in her mind.

She stood in front of the floor-length mirror, loosened her robe, and let it fall. Naked, she saw the small bulge of her tummy, a cause for dieting, her slight breasts, a constant cause of embarrassment, her curly, dark pubic hair that grew at a rapid rate, another cause of embarrassment.

"This is me," she said out aloud and removed the elastic band that held her shoulder-length hair in place. "I'm ready," she told herself with a small smile.

Compared to all that had slipped away like a chimera through her fingers, losing her life didn't seem too monumental. She sucked back the tears that were ready to fall on her cheeks. She wasn't going to cry. This was the right thing, the only thing, and she wasn't going to let any doubt enter her through those tears.

She dropped lavender bath beads inside the tub with some self-amusement. How would it matter how the bathwater smelled when soon, it would smell and look like blood? The thought and the realization that blood would be everywhere allowed nausea to creep in. She battled against it, just as she had the tears.

She lay down in the tub and took a deep breath before dipping her head in. The water soothed her, relaxed her, and she floated for a while, her mind empty of thought, her hearty empty of emotions. She held her breath for as long as she could under the water and then, when oxygen became vital, she pulled herself out.

Slowly, she rested against the bottom of the tub and raised both her hands up. They were wet and slick. She picked up the knife from the edge of the bathtub.

She ran her left thumb over the blade and felt the instant tearing of skin, gushing of blood. Carelessly, she washed the blood away in the lavender water.

She lifted her right hand and looked at the wrist carefully. This was the last time she would see it like this, unmarked. This was the last time for everything.

With the precision she'd always been known for, Devi took the knife in her left hand and slowly made a deep vertical cut on her right wrist, tearing open the vein that would lead her to death.

· · ·

Two things happened after the Devi "incident," as everyone in the Veturi household started calling it:

1. Devi completely stopped talking.
2. Devi started cooking.

Two things she did with such intensity and consistency that it drove her already shaken family up the wall.

Deeper Than the Deepest Sorrow

"She didn't want to talk to me?" Saroj asked Avi, annoyed and hurt that Devi hadn't spoken with her when she called.

"She wanted Vasu and then when I didn't know if she was awake, she said she had to go," Avi said, casually sipping his coffee. He drank it American-style, black with no sugar, made in that horrible, noisy coffee machine. Saroj always made coffee the old-fashioned, south Indian way, with decoction, milk, and sugar. How easily he had let it all slip away. He was still Indian, but he behaved as if he were American. Black coffee, with no sugar—ha!

"I am going to New India Bazaar . . . Raina said they have new mangoes," Saroj said, already plotting in her mind how she would visit Devi after shopping and confront her regarding the morning's phone call.

"Fine," Avi said, continuing to drink his coffee, not even looking up from the Sunday *Chronicle*.

"Do you want anything from there?" Saroj asked petulantly. He didn't want to be disturbed and because he didn't she wanted to disturb him.

"No," he replied tersely.

"I am making spinach *pappu* for dinner, is that okay?" Saroj asked. He didn't care what she cooked and had stopped making requests . . . oh, so many years ago.

"Sure."

"What about lunch?"

"Okay."

"Avi," Saroj cried out, and he finally looked up at her. "What about lunch?"

"We'll manage something. You can go," Avi said patiently.

"Mummy." Saroj called out for her mother, and when there was no response, she yelled again.

"Damn it, Saroj, can't you just walk up to her room and talk to her? Do you have to scream the house down?" Avi asked, annoyed.

"What?" Vasu called back, coming out from the guest room into the dining area where Avi was trying to enjoy his morning coffee and paper.

"I am going to New India Bazaar . . ."

"Then go, Saroj, why do you have to make a production out of it?" Vasu said condescendingly. "Just go and have a good time."

"I don't go shopping to have a good time. It is something I have to do because no one else in this house does it," Saroj snapped, feeling very close to tears. All she wanted was to be appreciated and they . . . they just . . . "What will you do about lunch? I am thinking about stopping for *dosa* at Dasaprakash. Do you want me to bring some back for you?"

"I'll make some *upma* for us. Don't worry, we won't starve," Vasu said, sitting across from Avi and pouring herself a cup of the American coffee.

Black, no sugar, Saroj noticed with a sneer. Her mother was a chameleon, Saroj thought angrily. She could change to blend into any surrounding. Vasu didn't live in America but fit in better than Saroj, who'd been there for almost three decades.

"Fine," Saroj said, flipping the *dupatta* of her *salwar-kameez* over her right shoulder.

Both Avi and Vasu said a farewell but didn't look up to see Saroj leave.

Who did they think they were? Saroj thought angrily as she slid the Mercedes out of the garage. She did all the work at home, took care of them, cleaned their clothes, cooked food for them, and they just took her for granted. One of these days she was going to leave and then they would find out how hard it was without her. She'd been thinking about leaving her family without warning for as long as she could remember, and each time she resolved to leave she realized that she had nowhere to go. Her friends could always go to their parents' home, or a sibling's home. Saroj didn't have any siblings, and she would rather be unappreciated by her husband than live with Vasu.

Saroj brought the car to a halt in the parking lot of the new, New India Bazaar on El Camino Real right next to the Bank of the West. Not too many people knew about the new bazaar and that meant shorter lines, at least until everyone did find out about it. The old New India Bazaar resembled a vegetable market from India; it was messy, full of people, and smelled like a combination of not-so-fresh vegetables, rice, wheat, and fried *samosas*.

Raina Kashyap, Saroj's neighbor, was right about the mangoes. They were ripe, beautiful, a sight to behold. Saroj took in the scent of a mango and sighed. Yes, they were from India, probably straight from Andhra Pradesh, straight from the homeland. It was at times like this that the pain of not living in India pierced through her sharply. It was coming here, to this white pit, that changed things between Avi and her. If they'd stayed in India, if only he'd wanted to stay, they would've been happy.

With bitterness bubbling through her she picked up nine mangoes, three for herself, three for Shobha, and three for Devi. Saroj was born in October, the month of the Libra, and that forced her to spread everything equally among herself and her children. Even when she went to India and bought saris and jewelry, she would buy three of everything, to make everyone happy. It confused and hurt her that neither Shobha nor Devi seemed to care about the saris or the jewelry she so carefully picked out.

Saroj's first stop was Shobha's house in Palo Alto. The traffic was moderate on 280 and Saroj could drive at seventy miles an hour all the way as she listened to the songs from her latest favorite Hindi movie, *Devdas*. Driving was one thing she thought was better in the United States than in India. Unlike many women of her generation in India, Saroj had learned to drive as a teenager on Indian roads. Vasu had insisted that Saroj be independent and ensured that her daughter learned how to drive a scooter and a car.

But now when they visited India, Saroj left the driving to Vasu or a taxi driver. The roads were poorly constructed and badly repaired. Traffic laws were nonexistent. Here, it was easy to drive. There was no livestock on the roads and people signaled when they changed lanes.

She didn't bother to call before she went to visit her daughters. She was always afraid that they'd make an excuse and not want her to come. To avoid dealing with that rejection, she just dropped by; if they weren't at home, she would be disappointed but not hurt.

"Saroj?" Girish said, his surprise evident as he stood at the threshold, responding to his mother-in-law ringing the doorbell. He'd probably just woken up. His jeans were hastily pulled on, his T-shirt crumpled, and his hair looked like it had been resting on a pillow just a little while ago. "Come on in."

"I thought I would come by, see Shobha and you," Saroj said, already looking past him to see if her daughter was at home.

"She's working this weekend," Girish said apologetically, barely suppressing a yawn. "Come in."

Saroj reluctantly went inside, her hands full of mangoes. If Shobha wasn't there, she wouldn't stay long. They both knew that.

"I got some mangoes. They were fresh in New India Bazaar," Saroj said, looking around suspiciously. The house always seemed to be in disarray, totally unacceptable to Saroj. But at least it was clean, thanks to the maid service that came in every week.

"You are at home?" Saroj asked uncomfortably. Girish usually worked on weekends, or that was the excuse Shobha made for him whenever Saroj invited them for Saturday-night dinner. "Shobha said you were *very* busy these days," Saroj said accusingly.

Girish shrugged with a smile. "I'm really sorry I couldn't make it to dinner last Saturday. Shobha told me that it was my loss as the food was excellent."

"You should come the next time," Saroj said and then handed him three mangoes. "Tell Shobha to call."

"Are you sure you don't want to stay for a cup of coffee?" Girish asked politely as he balanced the mangoes Saroj thrust at him.

"No, I am going to go see Devi," Saroj said, her back already to him as she started walking toward the door.

"How is she doing?" Girish asked.

"Good," Saroj said and then turned to face him, suspicion sparked inside her. "Why?"

"Well, I heard her company closed down and . . ." Girish stopped midsentence as if he realized that he shouldn't have said what he just did.

"What?" Saroj screeched.

"I'm sure I misheard. If she hasn't said anything to you . . ."

"That's why she called today! Early in the morning she called," Saroj said, blinking back tears. She was already overwrought after the scene with Avi and Vasu and now after finding about Devi she was ready to fall apart.

"I'm sure she's all right," Girish said uncomfortably. "Nothing to worry about, right? It isn't like this hasn't happened to her before. She's a strong girl."

"I have to go," Saroj snapped and walked out of the house. Concern and anger mingled, making her step on the accelerator of her car harder as she drove to Devi's town house in Redwood City.

Saroj had never really liked Girish. He was . . . not Indian enough, too much of an *angrez*, too British, too American, too much of a foreigner. He came from a very good family. Everyone knew the Sarmas and knew that they were a very well-respected and well-off Bay Area family. Srikant Sarma, Girish's father, had been a diplomat, traveling in all the right circles.

They were the right kind of people to associate with (even though Saroj thought they were a little too snobbish and oversophisticated). The problem was Girish. He was not the type to sit down for a cup of *chai* and chat. He didn't hang around Saroj's house with Shobha and tease his mother-in-law.

Saroj hoped for the traditional setup. A son-in-law who would be like a son to her, a man who would be her friend, stand up for her against her daughters, and tease Avi that if he didn't treat Saroj better someone would steal her from under him. She wanted a new friend; instead she got Girish. He rarely looked up to see her, and Saroj wasn't sure if he would be able to recognize her in a crowd. He was always donning those silly reading glasses of his and stuffing his nose inside a book. Even when they came for dinner or lunch, Shobha would chat, well, angrily display her opinions regarding everything, especially Devi's unproductive life, while Girish would talk to Avi, Vasu, and Devi but ignore Saroj.

When Saroj complained to Avi, he looked at her with a blank expression on his face. "Of course, he talks. What do you mean he doesn't?"

Saroj would try to explain and when she was unsuccessful, she would scream that Avi was insensitive to her needs.

Now, in all fairness, Saroj couldn't openly complain about Girish, as she had helped arrange Shobha's marriage to him. Avi had been furious that Shobha wanted an arranged marriage, but Saroj was delighted. The match just fell into their laps and the marriage was held with great pomp and show at the Livermore Temple, followed by a lavish dinner at the San Jose Reception Center.

The "boy" seemed perfect, so young, and a professor at Stanford, and then there was the prestige of marrying into such a good family. It was understandable that Saroj was swayed. How was she to know that Girish would be a stick in the mud, as British as his Oxford PhD accent?

Saroj parked her car in the driveway in front of Devi's closed garage. She was ready to confront Devi about the morning's phone call and about her being laid off, yet again. Why couldn't the girl find a decent job and stick to it? What was this start-up mania she couldn't shrug off?

Saroj knew that Devi wanted to be like her father and start a successful company, stay with it until retirement. Why couldn't the girl marry well like Saroj had and take care of her family instead?

Whenever Saroj used her set of keys to enter Devi's house, she snooped. She didn't look at it as a good or bad thing, but as concern. She was making sure her daughter was not doing drugs or associating with the wrong type (you have to be careful when you have an unmarried girl on your hands). And each time she snooped, she expected to find an unsuitable man lying naked in Devi's bedroom, or used condoms strewn around her bed, or worse, a naked woman in Devi's bedroom. Saroj had all sorts of ideas about Devi's lifestyle.

"These young Internet people," she would tell her neighbor, Saira Bhargav. "Always one thing after the other. This is her third start-up, God only knows if this one will make any money."

She knocked on the front door, loud and clear, and even tried the doorbell once for good measure. When there was no response, she got her key out from the small zipped pocket of her purse where she always kept a brass idol of Lord Krishna (with the crazy Californian drivers, you need otherworldly protection), her house keys, Shobha's house keys, and Devi's house keys. She never used Shobha's house keys without her knowledge, only when Shobha and Girish were on vacation and their plants needed to be watered, which was almost never. There really was nothing to see in Shobha's house. After all, she was a married woman.

Saroj went through Devi's living room into the dining room. She placed the plastic bag with the six mangoes inside the fridge. She would take three back with her when she left. No point in letting her mangoes get beaten by the heat inside her car. She didn't have to make any room, as the entire side-by-side refrigerator was empty except for a bottle of Smirnoff vodka in the freezer.

The girl lived on air and water. No food in her fridge, ever. Why couldn't she learn to cook like all good Indian girls?

All her life Saroj wanted to teach her daughters how to cook. They didn't even show a passing interest. Devi would watch and ask questions but never offered to cut vegetables, help out, or cook a meal. She did offer plenty of suggestions. Always wanted to put something that didn't fit in the food Saroj was preparing.

Why can't we add parsley in the *dal*? Devi would ask. Because Indians don't use parsley, only coriander, Saroj would say.

Why can't we make a duck curry or rabbit curry instead of a chicken curry? Do we always have to have the same kind of chicken curry? Devi would want to know. Because Indians don't eat duck or rabbit or deer or any of those other repulsive meats, Saroj would respond.

It was a constant battle whenever Devi would sit at the counter in the kitchen to watch Saroj cook. Saroj felt that sometimes Devi did it just to annoy her. Devi would tell her about all the restaurants she went to and how the food there was *so much* better than Saroj's. And the food was better because it was a mixture of cuisines. Plain Indian food was apparently boring. Saroj put Devi's queer sense of cuisine down to the burgeoning insanity that struck unmarried women her age.

Shobha didn't even bother to pretend to show any interest in cooking, despite being married. She believed cooking was for simpering housewives, not for smart, intelligent career women. She said that to Saroj ten years ago and Saroj had yet to forgive her for that remark.

Saroj hitched the leather strap of her purse onto her shoulder and looked around Devi's living room area for a moment before deciding to go upstairs. Just to check if Devi was maybe home and sleeping. She tiptoed up the wooden stairs and then peeked inside the guest bedroom first. Empty, except for the full-sized bed covered immaculately in a bright-yellow-and-dark-blue bedspread set. The entire room was in yellow and blue. Devi was good at that, adding those little coordinated touches casually, as if it were an accident that the lamp shade on the dark-wood bedside table was blue with a yellow lining, or the curtains in the room were yellow with thin blue stripes on them.

In this Saroj preferred Devi to Shobha, who didn't care what was in her house. Shobha's buying habits were random, and no thought went into what would look good with what. Shobha didn't decorate her home; she just threw things around in some vague order that made sense to no one, including, Saroj was sure, Shobha.

Devi was more like Saroj in this one aspect, always dressing the house beautifully, though Saroj would never openly admit it to anyone except herself and even then only quietly, in the closed walls of her mind. She didn't want to encourage Devi into spending money when she didn't have much. How could she? Devi ended up joining one failed start-up after the other. It was abysmal the way the girl always failed at everything she did.

Saroj hesitated just for an instant and then boldly stepped into Devi's bedroom. Here everything was in bright blue and mauve.

Feminine, but not overtly so, and it appealed to Saroj's aesthetic sense. Devi even had a mauve vase with some fresh blue tulips arranged perfectly.

Devi loved flowers, though she could never keep anything alive in the garden or even inside the house in a pot. If it was green and left with Devi, it would die. Shobha had a green thumb but no time for leaves and manure, as she would put it. Her garden was tended by some Mexican immigrant who spoke no English.

Saroj almost didn't go inside the master bathroom, but she had the sudden urge to pee, so decided to go in to use the toilet. But for her old bladder, Saroj would never have stepped inside the bathroom, never seen her daughter, naked and bleeding from her wrists, lying barely conscious in the white claw-foot bathtub.

The scream that ran out of her belly never made it to her ears as the blood roared and the world turned red in front of her. She stood rooted at the doorway, her eyes wide, horrified, her mind trying to wrap itself around the image. Denial sprang first; this couldn't be happening she thought surreally as suddenly her feet unglued from the floor and she flew to Devi.

Oblivious to the water and the blood, Saroj waded inside the bathtub and pulled Devi up, as her head bobbed precariously low inside the water.

"Devi, no, *beta,* no," she said as tears streamed down her face and she reached for her purse where it had slid down her arm by the bathtub. Even as she moved she held on to Devi, hugged her to her bosom. She could feel Devi's heart beat against hers as she dialed 911 on her cell phone. It was a small consolation.

"What do I do?" Saroj asked shakily, wanting to save her daughter until the experts arrived. Devi wasn't going to die, she told herself firmly, that wasn't going to happen. The skies would fall, but Devi wouldn't die. *No,* she kept yelling in her mind until all she could hear while the 911 operator spoke soothingly to her was *No.*

Saroj drained the water from the tub, snatched her *dupatta,* and wrapped it around Devi's right wrist. She used Devi's dark-blue-and-mauve towel, hanging on the railing by the bathtub, to wrap her left hand. There was blood everywhere, and Saroj could feel the scent of iron mingle with fear. She wanted to throw up, but her throat felt closed in as she dialed more numbers on her tiny Motorola cell phone as fast as she could.

"Avi, come now. *Now.* Our baby's dying, *now*," she cried out, hysteria filling her as she heard the paramedics rush inside the house, come up the stairs.

"Ma'am, you have to step away, we need to get to your daughter," a young black man, he was almost a boy, told her. A woman, a cop, put an arm around her and gently drew her away as the paramedics brought Devi's naked body out of the bathtub and laid her down on the floor.

"Is she okay? She's okay, right?" Saroj cried out to the paramedics working on patching up Devi's wrists and monitoring her vital signs.

"They're doing all they can, don't worry," the policewoman said and tried to get her out of the bathroom. "Why don't we go outside and you can call a member of your family?"

"I am not leaving my daughter and going anywhere," Saroj said, shrugging the policewoman's arm away. "I stay with her. You understand?" Even after more than three decades in the United States, her Indian accent was pronounced, and now in a time of crisis it came screaming through. "Not going anywhere," she repeated, "nowhere without my daughter. Okay?"

"Okay," the policewoman said patiently.

"She will be all right, okay?" Saroj said, her vision blurring because of the tears.

"Okay," the policewoman repeated patiently.

"She will not die, okay?" Saroj said, tears now staining her cheeks.

"Okay," the policewoman said, yet again.

"Okay," Saroj said as if agreeing with the policewoman, wiped her tears with her hands, and then with clear eyes watched over her daughter.

Hello, Reality

The image of her bleeding daughter was embossed in the eyes of her mind, stamped on her retina.

Forty-eight hours had passed since the paramedics rushed Devi to the Sequoia Hospital emergency room in Redwood City. They would release Devi, the doctor told Avi and Saroj, under family supervision.

"In cases such as these we feel the patient would be better helped by being around family. But we recommend you wait at least two, three days. One of you can always be here if you like," Dr. Feroze Shah said, his hand on Saroj's shoulder, a calming effect. "And we'll obviously need the resident psychiatrist to sign off on the release. I don't think it should be a problem."

The first day, Saroj sat at the hospital all day and all night, refusing to leave Devi's bedside even as Vasu, Shobha, Avi, and even Girish tried to persuade her into leaving, getting out of her blood-soaked *salwar-kameez*.

Two days later Saroj still shuddered as she stood under a hot shower, avoiding looking at the bathtub at the other end of the large bathroom. It would be a long time before Saroj could look at a bathtub and not see Devi lying there in her own blood.

The tears started slowly, mingling with the stream of hot water pouring from the shower, but the tears were hotter, heavier, burning in their intensity. Saroj tried to still them, stop them. She'd cried enough, cried too much, so much that she was afraid that her bedroom would flood with salty tears and she would float away in them.

Saroj didn't want to cry, what she wanted was to run away, have amnesia so that none of this would matter, none of this would hurt.

She came out of the shower, naked, having forgotten her towel. There are times in your life when your mind is blank except for one image and that image changes, turns, alters, but in essence remains the same inside your brain.

The relentless visual of seeing Devi in that bathtub haunted Saroj, and the world around her seemed encompassed with sorrow and shock. What could be more horrible, more terrifying than this? Would there ever be a pain that would be stronger than this?

"Saroj?" Avi came into the bedroom to find her standing naked, dripping on the hardwood floors. "Put something on, for God's sake," he said in a rushed voice as he grabbed a towel from the cabinet by the bathroom and wrapped it around her. "The AC is on, you'll catch a cold."

"We should give Vasu a break," Saroj said, tightening the towel around her. She wanted to lean on Avi to erase a part of the scary memory of yesterday, blur the image so secure in her mind.

She stood away from him, stiff, unable to make her limbs move.

"You're the one who needs a break," Avi said softly. "Vasu's just been there for three hours, and she wants to be there."

"Devi's my daughter," Saroj said possessively, snapping out of her blankness. She walked into their large closet to find some clothes.

"No one's saying otherwise," Avi said as he followed her in. "You need to get some sleep, eat something. I heated the *biriyani* Shobha and Girish brought last night from the restaurant."

"I am not hungry, Avi. Frankly, I don't know how any of you can even think about food," Saroj muttered, temper replacing sorrow. "She is dying and you are all pretending like it is a normal thing. She is lying in a hospital but we will eat *biriyani*."

"Oh, so you're the only one who cares about Devi, while we're all . . . what? Pleased that this happened?" Avi snapped. "Get off

your high horse, Saroj. Doesn't it get tiring always playing the righteous one?"

"Righteous? I am the one who sat with her all night . . ."

"No one asked you to. I wanted to, Vasu wanted to, damn it, even
Shobha wanted to, but you threw us all out," Avi exploded. "And
Devi is not dying anymore. She's fine, a little wounded, but alive.
Keep that in mind."

"Oh, I need you to tell me how my daughter is doing? Is that it?"
Saroj demanded as she pulled a *salwar* over her hips and tied the
string around her waist.

"No, what I don't want you to do is upset her when she gets here.
Is that too much to ask?" Avi said crisply.

"Upset her? Why would I upset her? I saved her life," Saroj cried
out as she picked up a matching *kameez* from a shelf. "I love my
daughter," she added, her voice muffled as the *kameez* covered her
face before sliding down and falling on her shoulders.

"You're not the only one who loves Devi," Avi said, his voice
falling, the fight leaving it. "We all love her and we're all hurting."

Tears filled Saroj's eyes as she saw the ones shining in Avi's. She
wanted to comfort him. So she took a step toward him, to hug him,
to hold him as she had several thousands of times, but he walked
past her to pull off a white cotton shirt from a hanger.

He had become adept at buttoning his shirt, all the way, even
without his right arm. He probably had always been able to button
his shirts and tie his shoelaces with one hand, but he used to ask
her for help. Being needed by him was as good as, and sometimes
even better than, being loved by him. But as need eroded, Saroj was
afraid that maybe even love had worn out. Through this tragic time
they couldn't envelop each other and offer comfort. Instead they
stood as adversaries, and bickered, from a distance.

"If something happened they would call, right?" Saroj asked as
a new doubt emerged. What if something went wrong while she
had been away, while her mother was at watch?

"Vasu has my cell phone," Avi said.

"Yes, she would call," Saroj nodded and then sighed. "Why? I
can't understand it. Shobha would never do something like
this . . . Devi . . . always so fragile, so . . . weak."

She watched Avi put on the white cotton shirt. Before he could get to the buttons, she took a step toward him and started slipping the white buttons into their buttonholes as she used to all those years ago.

She could feel the sudden rigidity in his body as she stood close, tension vibrating through him. What was wrong? she wondered. When had it all fallen apart? They had loved, loved so much, and now . . . nothing? The years had taken their toll. He'd worked hard, too hard, working late always, going away on business trips, always gone, to the point that when she was in labor with Devi, Avi drove her to the hospital via his office where he spent ten minutes and two contractions sorting out some matter. His priorities shifted and Saroj, whose place had been number one on his list, had slowly slipped to nonexistent.

They'd stopped communicating as he'd started spending longer hours in the office, and then when he semi-retired it'd been so long since they'd spoken that conversing was difficult, and after a few jerky and unsuccessful attempts they gave up. A promised second honeymoon to Paris ended with him meeting some clients and Saroj walking by the Seine alone, marveling at the Notre Dame, the outdoor cafés, the romantic city without the man she'd always wanted to see it with.

"Devi didn't do it because of me, did she, Avi?" Saroj asked, her fingers shaking as she slipped the last button into its little button-hole.

Avi took a step back, walked around her, and left the walk-in closet without answering Saroj's question.

They drove to the hospital in Saroj's Mercedes. When they were together, Saroj always drove. It was habit. It started when they'd just married, still in India all those years ago. They'd inherited Vasu's old white Padmini Premier and always, Saroj drove it when they were together. Avi was competent at driving even without his right arm. Nevertheless, it was Saroj who sat in the driver's seat.

The first time Saroj compared Shobha and Devi was when she was in labor with Devi. It was natural for a woman who had been in labor for more than thirty-five hours to feel some resentment toward the baby responsible for that mountain of pain.

Even now Saroj felt guilty when she remembered how she'd howled, complained, and in general made a fool of herself. She'd now forgotten the physical pain, but remembered the embarrassment of having Avi tell her how it was wrong to blame the child.

"Come on, Saroj, don't blame the child. You wanted a second child and so did I. Blame me . . . our child is without fault," Avi had said seriously while allowing Saroj to crush his hand as she rode through another contraction.

So it started then. Avi was always on Devi's side, always protecting her, no matter what her crime. Shobha and Avi had waged battles over the subject of Avi taking it easy on Devi, helping her become "a dependent loser."

Shobha was perfect as a baby. Born in the afternoon after putting Saroj through just five quick hours of labor, Shobha emerged with minimal pushing. A week after her birth, Shobha started sleeping for six hours every night, and within two months she was pulling eight hours a night. Saroj was surprised at how wonderfully easy Shobha was. All new mothers told her that she would be bleary-eyed, desperate for sleep, the first year of her baby's life, but for Saroj it had been easier than learning her ABCs.

And then, four years later, came Devi!

Well, she never really came out, rather had to be pulled out. After thirty-five hours of labor, Saroj finally dilated to the coveted ten centimeters and started to push, with hardly any energy left after so many hours of pain. After pushing for almost two hours, the doctor said that maybe it would be best to do a C-section. At that point Saroj wanted so desperately to get the baby out of her body, she all but shoved a knife into the doctor's hand.

Devi came out looking beautiful, not scrunched up by being squeezed through the vagina like Shobha had, and Saroj had sighed and told Avi, "This girl's going to be trouble."

And Devi was trouble. She was a colicky baby, screaming and crying every day for at least three to four hours until she was three months old. There were times when Saroj was sure that she would go deaf if she heard Devi cry anymore.

After colic, there had been the ear infections, one after the other. Devi was always crying in pain and even though Saroj's heart ached in sympathy, she wished that Devi was more like Shobha, who rarely fell ill as a baby.

As Devi grew up, her problems shifted from the physical to the emotional. She was in the fourth grade when Devi's teacher, a Mrs. Parson, invited Avi and Saroj for a small chat regarding Devi.

"My husband is a founder of a technology company, we have lots of money," Saroj blurted out when Mrs. Parson accused Devi of stealing money from a classmate.

Saroj refused to believe that either of her children was capable of stealing. Why would they steal? They had everything they needed and most of what they wanted. Hadn't Avi bought Devi that bicycle she nagged about? The orange-and-black dress (which Saroj thought was ugly and ill suited for Devi) that was hideously expensive?

"And she also hit a classmate, Lilly, very hard in the face. Actually, Devi broke Lilly's nose," Mrs. Parson further explained. "You have to understand, this is a very serious matter."

That information was digested by Avi and Saroj in icy silence. Saroj could barely form any words, she was so flustered. Her frail little Devi hitting someone? Breaking someone's nose? Impossible!

"We talked to her, but . . . she won't say anything. As a matter of fact, she simply won't talk, at all. The school counselor feels the problem might be that Devi is not getting enough attention at home."

Mrs. Parson could as well have said that Avi and Saroj were sexually molesting their child, Saroj was so horrified.

"What on earth are you talking about? My child has everything she needs. Are you saying we don't love her?" Saroj demanded. She stood up as she spoke, kicking her chair aside, towering over the teacher, her hands bunched into fists at her waist.

"Please, Missus Veturi," Mrs. Parson pleaded, but she was looking at Avi because it was obvious that mere words would not placate Saroj.

"Saroj, sit," Avi instructed, and Saroj had half a mind to throw the glass vase with the plastic roses on Mrs. Parson's table at him.

"You said your husband is a founder of a company and that probably means he's very busy, correct?" Mrs. Parson said in a questioning voice, and Avi nodded while Saroj shook her head.

By the end of the meeting Saroj was ready to pack her home and children, move back to India. "Here they are all crazy, Avi, and they are making our children crazy. Let us go home."

"This is home, Saroj," Avi said in his noncommittal tone as Saroj drove the car a little too rashly in her anger.

That afternoon both Avi and Saroj took Devi to task, but they couldn't pry a single word out of her. She just stood there, rooted, in silence. She didn't speak for a week to anyone, and then finally when Vasu called from India at Saroj's insistence, Devi spoke to her on the phone. But she didn't say anything about her little mishap in school.

Things went back to normal, but Saroj and Avi never found out why Devi stole one dollar and twenty-three cents and why she broke Lilly's nose. But they also never heard from any of Devi's teachers again.

Devi's problems didn't end there, though. There were many, many things that went wrong: there was the car accident without insurance, the dumped perfect-husband-material boyfriend (Indian boy from a good family), the kissing some black man in a public place for all to see, the speeding tickets, the layoffs from all her jobs, et cetera, et cetera. And each time something went wrong, Saroj thought how wonderful it would have been if Devi was just a little like Shobha who never seemed to have car accidents, unacceptable liaisons, or job problems.

Vasu once warned Saroj not to compare her daughters. "You will make them resent each other, and compete with each other. That is wrong. They are sisters, they should be friends."

"I have two children and if I don't compare them with each other, who will I compare them with? And Mummy, don't tell me how to raise my children. It's not like you did such a great job with me that you can tell me what to do," Saroj replied. A part of her could see sense in what her mother was telling her, but she couldn't bring herself to admit it. How could Vasu, the most irresponsible mother anyone could have, be right?

. . .

"Maybe if you had been a better sister . . . ," Saroj said angrily to Shobha, who was standing in the hallway just outside Devi's hospital room with her husband, Girish.

Shobha had just seen Devi, seen the bandages on her wrists, the paleness of her skin, and it had horrified her. The image still had the ability to constrict her throat, choke her. So she tried to make it fade away, to somehow replace the pain with anger. Anger was easier to deal with, pain was so difficult, almost insurmountable, and Shobha always avoided the difficult.

"What? If I was a better sister she would not have gone and slit her wrists?" Shobha demanded icily. "Did you hear that, Girish? Now I'm to blame for my insane sister's insanity. How about genes, Mama? Maybe she got it from your father. He hung himself, didn't he?"

Saroj's eyes filled, and Shobha shook her head in disgust. "So it's okay when you blame me for Devi's suicide attempt, but when I say something, you have to get all teary-eyed. Don't you ever get tired of the double standard?"

"Stop it, Shobha," Girish interceded and slowly let out a long breath. "We're all a little stressed, but it doesn't help to gouge each other's eyes out."

Shobha wanted to respond with something catty, something so Shobha-like, but the image of Devi lying in a bloody bathtub sailed through her mind. And because that imagined image shook her up so much, Shobha decided to give her mother some leeway. She didn't have any children, but she knew that nothing could be as painful as seeing what Saroj had seen.

"I'm sorry, Mama," Shobha said, which was a first. Shobha never apologized, never second-guessed herself, and never showed any weakness to anyone.

"She could've died. I had no choice but to drag her out of that bathtub," Saroj said, now indulging merrily in large tears. Shobha considered yelling at her again. Saroj just couldn't help milking this for all it was worth. Even at this time, she wanted to make this about her, show how she was affected by it all.

But Shobha didn't believe she had any right to criticize; at least

Saroj saved Devi's life. The last time Shobha spoke to Devi was a week ago at their parents' house and she'd told Devi that her life was a mess and not really worth living. It was said in the heat of the moment and Devi retorted right back with something about Shobha's useless and loveless marriage to Girish. It wasn't like Devi was washed in sacred milk or anything. She could give as good as she got. But Shobha could feel guilt eat at her insides despite all logical rationalizations.

After Saroj's panic-stricken phone call that morning, Shobha left work hurriedly and drove to Redwood City like an automaton. Parts of her brain simply wouldn't function. She couldn't even remember clearly what Saroj said. Disjointed words flashed in her head.

Devi slit her wrists.

In her bathtub.

Died.

Blood.

Even as she drove to Devi's house, Shobha knew that something was wrong. The rational Shobha was telling her that she had to go to the ER at Sequoia Hospital but she found herself stepping into Devi's town house all the same. The front door was open, and Shobha felt the first lick of fear race through her. What if she'd heard wrong? What if Devi was dead, lying in her bathtub here?

She sprinted up the stairs as panic set in. But before she could enter Devi's bedroom, a policewoman stopped her. "Ma'am, can I help you?"

Shobha looked past the policewoman. She could see blood streaming on the white-tiled bathroom floor from where she stood in the hallway. She couldn't see the bathtub, but bloody water was everywhere on the tiles.

"My sister," she whispered, her throat hoarse, her eyes blank. "My sister lives here," she finished shakily.

"Your sister's fine, she's stable. She's in the ER at Sequoia Hospital." The policewoman led her downstairs, gently, putting a firm hand on Shobha's elbow. "Would you like a patrol car to take you there?"

Shobha was too stunned to register anything. There was acid in her throat, a rancid taste in her mouth, and she rushed to the kitchen and vomited her breakfast of Noah's bagel and cream cheese into the sink.

The policewoman gave her a few paper towels from the roll in Devi's kitchen and Shobha turned on the faucet to wet the towels.

"I'm okay," Shobha said after she cleaned up and threw the paper towels in the trash. "I'm fine, thanks."

"Are you sure?" the policewoman asked. "I can drop you off at the ER. It's close by. And your sister is doing just fine."

"I can drive," Shobha said, taking charge of her emotions again. "I can fucking drive," she repeated but she was crying. "I can drive," she said again as tears streamed down her face. She hadn't cried this openly in such a long time and because she hadn't, the intensity of it shook her into doing something she'd never done before. For the first time in her life, Shobha turned to someone for comfort. The policewoman held her for almost ten minutes while Shobha sobbed for her sister who could've died.

But when she stood in front of her mother and her husband, there was no trace of the Shobha who'd cried in the arms of a stranger. It was vital to her that she not lose control, not show a chink in the armor. Her sister was alive and well, there was no need for melodrama or tears.

"If everything is A-okay, then I'll head back to work. It's the end of the quarter. We have numbers to meet," Shobha said casually.

"What?" Girish all but gasped, shock written on his face. It satisfied Shobha immensely that something she did finally needled him into a response.

Girish quickly replaced the visible temper and shock with his usual stoic, almost careless, calm. "Go," he said easily, quietly. "Do you want anyone to call you if something happens?"

"What could happen?" Shobha shrugged. "It isn't like she's going to find another blade to do any damage. But please, do call if something does happen. And I'll see you all at dinner?"

Shobha didn't want to be the hard-ass all the time, but with Devi perpetually screwing up, the onus fell on Shobha to lead the exemplary life. It was Shobha's job to be the better daughter, while Devi was busy playing the role of the prodigal one. No matter what Shobha did, her father always favored Devi.

Most children believed their parents loved them all equally, but Shobha knew the truth. Avi cared more for Devi than he did her. She was well aware of it and spent many years trying to change that truth before giving up. But just because she wasn't in the race anymore didn't mean she liked to lose.

Avi never said or did anything to blatantly show he loved Devi more, but Shobha could feel it in his different attitudes toward them. He held Devi's hand all the time, through all her troubles, while assuming Shobha could take care of herself. And Shobha was proud that she could take care of herself, but would it kill her father to show her some attention as well?

Even now when she was married, living the successful life, her father turned to Devi, gave her support. Shobha once told Girish how she felt but he didn't see things her way.

"She's not strong like you, Shobha. That doesn't mean he loves her more, just that she needs him more," Girish reasoned.

I need him, too, Shobha wanted to cry out. *I want my daddy, too. Just because I'm strong doesn't mean I don't need a father.*

But sometimes when you wore a mask for a very long time, it became your face. And Shobha had worn the mask of a strong woman for so long, no one, including her, bothered to look beneath it to see the fragile mess she was.

The hospital room reeked of cleaning supplies and the general medicine smell all hospitals emanate. There was a small buzzing sound coming from the outside, probably someone waxing the floor, though Devi wasn't sure of that. She could hardly hear anything beyond the voices of her family, which were loud and clear. She pretended she couldn't hear them and tried to concentrate on the buzzing from the outside instead.

There were a few facts she had to deal with despite the fuzz in her brain. The first, a hideous one: she was alive. And the second fact, worse than the first one, was she had been saved by her crazy mother. The irony of that was not lost upon her.

Damn it, if she was lying in her bathtub with her wrists cut to bits, it probably was because she wanted to be lying there the way she was lying there. That was her wish and she had a right to do as she pleased in the privacy of her own bathroom. Anger and resentment congealed within her, and she had half a mind to open her eyes and give her mother a piece of her mind. Death was supposed to have happened. She had chosen to die, but now she was alive, a survivor. What exactly had she survived? How was she supposed to deal with the failure to end her life as well as the failure of not being able to live it with any dignity?

They were whispering for her benefit. Shobha, her sister, had been in the room a while ago, was angry about having to deal with this at the end of the quarter. She had work to do, and the last thing she wanted was to hang around her dotty little sister, but there was a tremor in Shobha's voice and Devi heard her sister's tears even if she couldn't see them. Shobha was angry, but she was also devastated, just as everyone else was.

Her grandmother Vasu was the only one whose feelings Devi couldn't surmise. Vasu hadn't spoken a word, though Devi knew she was there. She could smell the Ponds talcum powder, which only G'ma used. Besides, even if Devi was half dead she'd know the hand holding hers for the past few hours was her grandmother's.

But it was her mother who annoyed her the most at this point. That woman had to use her key again, had to use her key on just the day she wanted to complete the business of living. Of all the shit luck she'd had, this one took the cake and the baker.

"Mummy, I will sit with her," Devi heard her mother say. Saroj had been in the room almost always, refusing to leave. When Devi heard her father tell Saroj to go home so that she could at least wash the blood off herself, Devi almost threw up. The jagged edge of adrenaline brought bitterness to her throat as she tried to forget yet again how Saroj saved her.

"No." Devi heard her grandmother for the first time. "You sat here all night. And Saroj, it is okay if someone else takes charge for a little while."

"This is not about who is in charge, this is about me wanting to be with my daughter," Saroj said indignantly. There were times when she sounded young, not like a woman over fifty, but like a petulant teenager. This was one of those times. The petulance usually entered her voice when she was speaking with Vasu. It was when Vasu was around that Devi saw Saroj as a daughter instead of a mother.

"Can't you be with your daughter while I am in the room?" Vasu asked patiently.

"Of course I can," Saroj said peevishly. "I am the one who saved her, you know?"

"And are you going to push that down the poor girl's throat for the rest of her life? If so, you would have done her a favor by letting her die," Vasu retorted.

"How dare you, Mummy?" Now she really sounded like a little girl, especially the way she said *Mummy.* "Do you have any idea what I have been through? How hard this is for me? There was blood everywhere . . . all over the . . ." Saroj's voice hitched and Devi heard a loud sob.

Oh, Mama, she thought irritably, *can't we do without the histrionics? Blood wasn't everywhere. It was only inside the bathtub.*

Devi was neat, tidy to the T. When she settled on the blade as being the best way to end her life she also decided that the bedroom was out of the question. Even if she was dying, the idea of soaking her mattress or the floor with blood was intolerable. The bathtub, teeming with warm water, was the perfect solution. The water would keep her warm and keep the blood from congealing on anything. And at the end of the day, all the landlord would have to do to clean the mess would be to drain the water and use a brush in the tub. He wouldn't even have to use her deposit of two thousand dollars to clean up.

Devi thought she'd contained the damage the best she could, though now she wished she had blown her brains out instead. So what if there would've been pieces of brain matter splattered everywhere, she would at least be dead.

And if she were dead she would not have to listen to this scene. Devi didn't want to open her eyes, didn't want anyone to know she was awake, alive. As long as she kept her eyes closed, she could shut the world away and at least for another delusional moment pretend that the problems of her life didn't exist.

"Why did she do this?" Devi heard her mother again, speaking through a voice full of tears and agony. Devi had no doubt her mother loved her immensely, but she had come to the conclusion that she would never reconcile her notion of love to her mother's. This was going to be just one of those things that couldn't be resolved and if she'd died it wouldn't have mattered. All those things she wanted to escape would've been eliminated, but now that chance had eluded her.

The real world waited with questions.

She hummed a small tune in her mind, a toneless tune that she used when she was sad to keep thoughts from entering and leaving her brain.

Slowly Devi drifted into sleep, letting the sounds of her family and the music in her brain lull her to sleep.

Genetic Coding

It was a given, Devi was more like Vasu, and Shobha was more like Saroj. It was unshakable. Vasu sincerely believed in it, but now, as she sat by her granddaughter's side, she admitted that there were dark crevices in Devi's mind she knew nothing about.

She only thought she knew Devi, but Devi . . . ah, but Devi was her own person, unique, like no one else. Vasu admired her spirit, her courage to try the unknown, seek out the strange and the un-usual. She wanted Devi to have inherited all those wonderful qual-ities from her. Now it looked like Devi was more like her suicidal ex-husband rather than herself, Vasu thought with a small laugh that quickly turned into a sob she needed to control.

The white bandages on Devi's wrists were evidence of Vasu's failure. On the surface, Vasu knew she could easily blame Saroj and her lack of compassion for this tragedy, but deep down Vasu knew that Saroj was not guilty. She knew inside her heart that Saroj stopped influencing Devi one way or the other, years ago.

Devi had been close to Vasu, had told her all the secrets, the first kiss, the first love, everything. Somehow Devi, who felt comfortable telling Vasu about her method of contraception, her years-older lover, had failed to mention her impending self-inflicted death sentence.

Oh, her heart hurt. Vasu put a hand against the pounding muscle inside her ribs. It was weak, maybe too weak to sustain this. Once again she stroked Devi's cool forehead and thanked God for sending Saroj in time to save Devi.

When her ex-husband, and he was always ex-husband, never just husband, killed himself, she'd felt myriad emotions, but they were a jumble. There was sorrow among the hate, the relief, the apathy, but it was buried, not like now, now there was only sorrow, gigantic, like the Himalayas, immovable. There was no comparison really.

Vasu married Ramakant because she was of marriageable age and his family proposed the arrangement. Then he worked in a bank and seemed normal. But once she started going to medical school, things went from bad to worse. Ramakant always reminded her that he was paying her way and how much money it was costing. He couldn't understand why she didn't want to just sit at home and be a housewife like every other woman he knew of. But Vasu had been determined. Even though she got pregnant in her final year of medical school, she persevered and didn't drop out as everyone expected her to.

Ramakant lost his job at the bank and Vasu joined the army. Her ex-husband never got over being fired from his job and made elaborate plans to sue the bank and/or steal from them. After that he started coming up with one get-rich-quick scheme after another. But it was when he started stealing money from home that Vasu decided to talk things out and tell Ramakant that he needed to start pulling his weight. The marriage that already hung precariously on mere legalities completely fell apart. The fights became intolerable. Ramakant would go away for weeks without telling Vasu and when he started hitting her, she decided enough was enough.

The divorce was a shock to Ramakant. He couldn't even imagine a woman would do something like this. But when the judge agreed with Vasu and gave her custody of Saroj, something seemed to snap completely in Ramakant. He threatened everyone, the judge, Vasu, even Saroj, and then moved in with his reluctant brother. Vasu wasn't sure what happened there but just three months after the divorce Ramakant killed himself.

Ramakant's brother called Vasu in Jaipur, where she was posted, to give her the news. He'd been very sincere in his apologies and very honest about why he thought Vasu should not come for the death ceremonies. "It wouldn't be proper for an ex-wife to come for the *puja*." Vasu assured him that she wouldn't want to even if it were proper.

Saroj hadn't subscribed to Vasu's notion in this matter, as she hadn't in so many others. She wanted to go for her father's funeral. She was just five years old, but precocious enough to hurt her mother by calling her a husband killer. Vasu couldn't believe her ears; her heart shattered and she began to slowly dislike her own child.

She'd always thought that mother and daughter were on the same team, fighting against Ramakant, whose moods changed like the weather did in Jaipur, from cold to hot, from pleasant to windy. There was yelling and screaming, even an incident with a butcher's knife and voices inside his head.

And most importantly, Ramakant was gone most of the time. He was always looking for a job, always coming up with a new scheme to make them rich. He never spent much time with Saroj, had no hand in raising her, yet Saroj thought of him as the "good" parent and Vasu as the bad one.

Saroj had blinders on, Vasu was convinced. She blamed Vasu for Ramakant's death. She held Vasu responsible for her father's tormented soul, as Saroj had heard from a friend that those who committed suicide got stuck in Trishanku—in limbo between heaven and hell.

Matters only got worse when Saroj started telling all her friends that her mother killed her father. Her friends told their parents and soon the entire army base at Jaipur knew that Captain Vasu Rao divorced her "good" husband, who then committed suicide. The few who'd known Ramakant were unable to stand against the advanced army rumor mill.

Vasu's commanding officer held a meeting with her. He wanted to know the truth and seemed to believe Vasu when she unwaveringly explained a matter so personal to a veritable stranger. But there was still a flicker of doubt. If Ramakant was abusive, how would five-year-old Saroj not see it? Because Saroj continued to claim her father was a nice man who brought her candy and dolls whenever he returned from out of town, no one ever completely believed Vasu.

But Saroj was just five years old, and Vasu was convinced that in a few years she'd forget about her father. That didn't happen. The rift that started when he died slowly got larger and deeper. Vasu sometimes was surprised that they even spoke to each other after all these years. Part of the reason they still continued to see each other was Avi, who kept the family together, especially after his parents died in a car accident in Delhi.

"You're the only grandparent Devi and Shobha have," he always said to Vasu when she worried about staying three months a year in his house. "You're welcome to stay forever."

It warmed Vasu that Avi said so, though she never took him up on the offer. It was one thing to visit, but to live in the United States? No, that just wouldn't do. She had friends back home in India. She had a home in India. Here, everything was too foreign, almost unlivable at times.

Maybe she should take Devi away with her for a while, just until she got better. A few months by the beach in Visakhapatnam would do the girl some good. They could even take a trip to Goa or go see the Ajanta-Ellora caves, the temples in Mahabalipuram.

Vasu dozed off as she started planning her Indian adventure with Devi.

Devi's eyes flickered open, her hands moved noisily against the sheets, and Vasu sprang out of her drowsiness. "Devi, *beta*, how are you feeling?"

Her eyes were like deep wells, filled with something intangible, and Vasu couldn't see past the brownness of her eyeballs. Devi could swallow herself whole into that vacuum, Vasu realized, and felt the pinch of fear that she may have lost her granddaughter even though she was physically alive.

Devi didn't say anything, didn't even look at Vasu, just turned her head away.

"Come on, Devi, you have to say something, anything," Vasu persisted when there was no response.

But Devi didn't nod or even move, just closed her eyes and drifted into oblivion again. Vasu wanted to shake her awake, kiss her noisily, jerk her out of this silent madness, but she did nothing, she sat down beside her granddaughter and held her hand as she had for the past hours.

"When will she wake up, Mummy?" Saroj asked later, perilously close to tears.

Vasu shrugged irritably. Saroj had the disgusting habit of crying every time there was any kind of stress. She probably even believed that crying could solve problems. How could she have given birth to a girl who was such a water tap?

Vasu never claimed to be a great mother. She knew her short-comings, and maternal, she was not. She realized now that she was one of those women who should never have had children. But now her child was grown and she even had grandchildren. Lives took their own course and she couldn't regret the part she played in creating her own little world. If she'd never had a child, wouldn't she have been lonely now? There would be no Devi, no Shobha, no Avi, no trips to the United States every summer. Life would be barren.

"Why did she do this?" Saroj asked, sniffling, tears rolling down her cheeks.

Vasu wanted to lay into Saroj and bring out every instance when Saroj had made Devi feel useless, but it was a pointless exercise. Saroj was convinced that she was the perfect mother, the perfect wife, and the perfect daughter. Saroj couldn't imagine being any-thing else. If her relationships with her daughters, her husband, and her mother were not working out, it was because something was wrong with them, not her.

"We'll know when she wakes up," Vasu said quietly but couldn't find it in her heart to take her daughter into her arms and offer com-fort. It was so easy for Vasu to hug Devi, cajole her friends, be playful with others. With everyone she was easygoing, but with Saroj, she was serious, unbending, critical.

"Avi thinks it's my fault," Saroj said bitterly.

"Did he say so?" Vasu asked.

Saroj shook her head. "But I can feel it. I can feel him accusing me every time he looks at me, even when he doesn't look at me. I saved her, Mummy, and he doesn't even mention it."

Vasu wanted to say something about guilty conscience but Saroj was doing such a good job of beating herself up, it didn't seem right to kick her some more when she was down.

Avi came inside the small white room with a beautifully arranged basket of white lilies, Devi's favorite flowers. Seeing the flower basket, Saroj burst into tears again and Vasu felt the desire to smack the woman across her face.

"She woke up once," Vasu informed Avi, not even stopping to think that she hadn't bothered to tell Saroj about Devi waking up. "But she drifted right back."

Avinash nodded and then sighed when he saw his wife sobbing. "Stop it, Saroj," he said as gently as he could, but the bite of irritation was there. "She can probably hear us, and do you want her to listen to this, to you crying? She's just sleeping. She isn't in a coma, she isn't dead."

"Did you talk to the doctor?" Vasu asked quickly before Saroj could say anything to Avi. She didn't want Devi to witness a marital scene while she lay in a hospital bed, forced there by demons no one knew about.

Avi nodded, ignoring Saroj. Her dramatics when overdone became too fantastic to pay any real attention to, and Avi had started ignoring his wife's meltdowns years ago.

"He says everything is fine, just that she might be tired. She should wake up soon enough," Avi said as he walked up to his daughter. He placed the lilies by Devi's bedside and stroked her hair. "He said a psychiatrist will talk to her and then, if they're convinced she isn't suicidal anymore, they'll release her to us."

"What?" Saroj said, biting her lip as a new wave of salty tears threatened to claim her. "Why won't they just let us take her home?

We are her parents. We can take her anytime we want, right? We don't need some mental doctor to tell us how she is. What do they know anyway?"

Vasu sighed loudly, but didn't bother to explain that even after Devi came home, she would continue to need medical help. She would need to speak with a psychiatrist, figure out why she broke down like this, and ensure it didn't happen again. This was an illness, and just like you'd go to the doctor if your head hurt too much, you sometimes had to go when your heart hurt as well.

Avi leaned closer to his daughter, kissed her cool soft cheek, and whispered, "You have to wake up, *beta*, time to go home. Devi, *beta*, are you awake?" Avi asked when he saw Devi's eyelids flutter open. "Are you feeling okay?" he asked.

Devi nodded.

"Ready to go home?"

Devi shook her head.

Saroj rose shakily and stood by Devi's feet, peering at her face. She wanted to say something nice, something comforting. "Why did you do such a stupid thing? Do you know what a scare you gave us?" she demanded, love and concern turned rancid, spewing out of her as anger.

Avi hissed and Vasu made a clicking sound.

Devi turned her head away from her mother and closed her eyes again.

"Oh, I am sorry," Saroj said immediately, guiltily. "I love you so much, Devi. The next time she wakes up, Avi, I will tell her how much I love her, how much I . . . the next time she wakes up . . . I promise . . ."

It is tiresome to see the ceiling at all times when your eyes are open. Even when you're alive, it makes you feel like maybe, you are not. But you know that you are alive and that the feeling of lifelessness is just a farce and that's when the tiresome part comes in.

Devi was tired of staring at the white crisp ceiling, the white crisp walls, the white-white-white everything of the hospital room.

She wanted to get up and around. Pop by and see who was in the room next door. Was anyone else here who attempted what she had? And how did that person feel? Guilty, cheated, desperate, angry?

As if lying there and having to put up with every member of her family was not bad enough, it really bothered her to have to talk to a psychiatrist. It was for her own good, her father told her as he explained why she needed to see a shrink. She wasn't exactly stupid and had watched enough *ER* to know that they wouldn't just release her into the general population before ensuring she was of sound mind and body.

It didn't make her resentment for the psychiatrist any less. She didn't want to be psychoanalyzed and she didn't want to give anyone any explanations.

"How are you feeling?" Dr. Mara Berkley began after she introduced herself.

Devi shrugged. How did she think she felt? Her wrists were sore, her head hurt, and her mother had not left her side for almost three days.

"Devi, I understand that as a child, you used to stop speaking during difficult times," said the doctor and waited to see Devi's expression.

Devi felt betrayed by her family. They'd told this woman, a stranger, about her life; it seemed like a violation. She didn't know if any of her emotions flickered on her face but the doctor continued even more soothingly, "Devi, it's important you let me know what happened so that I can help you. If you're uncomfortable speaking, would you write me a note?"

She spoke slowly, in a soft voice, and Devi felt ridiculous lying down, unable to respond. Write a note? Why? Devi wondered. It wasn't like she'd lost the ability to use her vocal cords, she just didn't have anything to say. How would a note change that? Would writing a note somehow give her the words it would take to tell the truth?

Devi shook her head, frustration welling in her eyes.

"So, you don't want to write a note?" Dr. Berkley asked again and when Devi shook her head again, she nodded. "And that's all right. You don't have to if you don't want to."

Her tone, her expression, took away some of the pressure Devi felt was being put on her.

"I understand if you don't want to say anything to me, but I strongly suggest that you keep a journal from now on. Maybe that will help you sort through your feelings," the doctor recommended with a broad smile.

Devi nodded and then shook her head and then shrugged. Keeping a journal sounded too hokey and she didn't want to sort through her feelings, she just wanted to close her eyes and go to sleep.

"We have prescribed you an antidepressant, Celexa. It's new in the market, but very effective. It should take effect within the week and make you feel better." Dr. Berkley spoke softly. "In rare cases there is nausea in the first couple weeks of use, are you having any?"

Devi shook her head again. She couldn't believe she was on some Prozac-type drug. An antidepressant! Good God, she shouldn't have to go through this, and she wouldn't if she had been able to stick to the plan and died. Anger bubbled within her again and she wanted to scream, she could feel the scream, the threads of it wind against her vocal cords demanding release. But she ground her teeth together, smothered the scream. For now, she didn't think she could stand to hear her own voice.

"Your parents want to take you home," Dr. Berkley continued. "Do you want to go home with them?"

Now, that was a tough question. On one hand Devi didn't want to deal with her family; on the other, she had nowhere else to go. The town house seemed too bleak right now, and she was too ashamed to turn to any of her friends.

Because she couldn't truthfully answer Dr. Berkley's question, she shrugged, but it came out more as a nod.

"Are you still depressed?"

Devi bit her lower lip and then shook her head. There was anger within her, loads and loads of it, disappointment and resentment at being alive, but she when she looked within she didn't feel the same bone-numbing and soul-tearing sadness she'd felt just two days ago. It was unsettling for her to realize that a weight had been lifted.

She felt lighter than before and beneath the anger at being alive was also some relief that she wasn't dealing with death and whatever lay waiting beyond it.

"Do you still want to end your life?"

Devi stared at the doctor as the question sank in. She had no idea if she still wanted to die. She was coming to terms with living, how was she to deal with the idea of failing at death?

She shook her head.

"So, you want to live?"

Devi stared at the doctor again. The questions she was asking seemed reasonable but each one evoked a sense of helplessness within her, because there were no clear answers to these simple, reasonable questions. It should be easy for her to say, *Yes*, when someone asked her if she wanted to live, but something had happened, something terrible. She'd tried to kill herself and after that, the question of life was a difficult one to deal with.

"Do you?" the doctor prodded.

Devi nodded, unsure as to why she thought she wanted to live when all she wanted was to go back in time so she could lie in the bathtub again feeling the life seep out of her.

Dr. Berkley smiled.

"We'll meet tomorrow morning to discuss your discharge. The nurse will explain your charge plan to you. We can't release you on your own recognizance. That means you have to be with your parents. They will be responsible for you. I need to see you next week, so we will make that appointment as well. Do you agree to these conditions?"

Devi felt like she was listening to a judge speak in a courtroom scene of a movie. The words *recognizance* and *conditions* zipped around in her mind and she felt like a prisoner being allowed out on parole, if and only if she agreed to all the rules.

Devi nodded, putting some vigor into her nod. Just like a prisoner who desperately wanted parole, she needed to get out of this white hospital room.

"So, we'll talk next week, okay?" said Dr. Berkley, standing up. "Keep taking the Celexa regularly, and if you ever feel like talking, give me a call." She put her card on the bedside tray and patted Devi's hand where it lay on her stomach.

"Devi, we'll work together to help you stay alive and work through the difficulties that caused you to attempt suicide. You're healthy, there's no permanent damage. I know you felt hopeless to change your life, but through therapy, we can help you find the strength to overcome whatever drove you to this," the doctor said as she stood at the doorway, ready to step out of the white room, Devi's prison.

Devi nodded, though she couldn't imagine how therapy, whatever that meant (they were all quacks anyway, these so-called shrinks) could make it all okay. And what was this about no permanent damage? What about the permanent damage that was already done? Who would, who could, repair that?

When the doctor stepped out, Devi's shoulders slumped and the tension that had been building up in the past few minutes seeped out. She felt as if she'd been through a test and that maybe, just maybe, she passed.

Devi was partially correct. Dr. Mara Berkley was convinced her new patient was not going to attempt suicide again. Not as long as she took the prescribed drugs and met with the doctor regularly.

"She already seems quite alert," she told Avi, Saroj, and Vasu. "Through her communications with me I feel that she's not at risk anymore. But she still needs to be watched, a relative or friend must be with her at all times for the next few days, until she comes to see me again. Make sure she takes the Celexa."

"How long will she need to take the medicine?" Saroj asked, baffled to be speaking with a mental doctor. It was bad enough that Devi dragged them through the emergency room, but this, talking to a shrink, this was just nonsense. Her daughter was fine. All she needed was some homemade food and Hindi movies.

"About six to nine months. This is a process, Missus Veturi. We'll keep checking on her progress and based on how she's responding to therapy and the drugs we'll decide what to do next," the doctor explained.

There was silence in the room and then Dr. Berkley cleared her throat.

"It's not common for a grown woman to stop speaking for days like this. Do you have any idea why she does this?" she asked.

"She does it once in a while," Vasu said, "and it usually does not last more than a few days. She is just . . . difficult at times. Does not want to explain her actions and this one, this one will require a lot of explaining. Maybe that's why she has shut us off."

"You said this started when she was ten years old?" When Avi nodded, the doctor continued, "Did anything happen to her? Anything bad? Was she hospitalized? Was there any previous psychiatric illness?"

"Nothing happened to her and she has never seen your type of doctor before," Saroj cut in sharply and stood up from the purple sofa she was sitting on. "She stole a girl's money and broke that girl's nose. Instead of saying sorry and telling us why she did it, she stopped talking for a week. She is just spoiled and that is our fault, but *nothing* bad happened to her. I didn't drop her on her head as a baby or anything." Anger made Saroj's Indian accent drip through the words, making part of what she said incomprehensible to the doctor.

"Calm down, Saroj," Avi said and sighed. "We are all upset and tired. It has been a long three days."

"Of course," Dr. Berkley said, and then nodded, smiled, and made a gesture with her hand that told them the meeting was over. "So you'll bring her in next Friday at four in the afternoon? I have asked her to try to keep a journal. I think that might help open her up a little."

Avi nodded and then shook hands with her. "Thank you."

"What did you thank her for? She didn't do anything," Saroj snapped at Avi as soon as they were out of Dr. Berkley's office. As he always did, Avi ignored Saroj and then went about getting his daughter out of the hospital.

Shobha grabbed her cell phone on the first ring. She was in an important meeting but as soon as she saw her father's cell number flash, she didn't hesitate. For all her cockiness at the hospital the day before, fear had settled in her belly like heavy mud in water. She couldn't envisage a world without Devi, couldn't imagine a life without her. Even as she went through the motions of the day, in her mind she kept saying to herself that Devi would be okay and soon everything would revert to the way it used to be.

"Daddy?" she questioned automatically.

"The doctor said she's fine and we can take her home tonight. You and Girish should come for dinner."

"You want us to stop by the Dhaba and pick up dinner?" asked Shobha. Girish and she had been bringing dinner over for the past two evenings.

"Your mother is cooking. *Samosas* and whatnot," Avi said. Shobha could hear how tired he was.

"Well then, we'll show up with empty stomachs," Shobha said as she relaxed. Devi was alive and well, she would be home tonight. Everything was already starting to go back to normal. Soon her stomach would stop churning and she wouldn't be able to smell the iron in Devi's blood anymore.

"Girish's car is in for servicing, so I'll pick him up after work and get to your place as soon as possible," Shobha went on, ignoring the questioning looks of her staff, seated around a large half-circle table in a plush conference room.

"Is she well?" Shobha's senior engineer, Vladimir, asked after Shobha hung up.

"Yes," Shobha said. She'd told her staff and her boss that her sister had been in a nasty accident when she'd had to suddenly leave an emergency meeting the Saturday of the "incident." An explanation was necessary when they were in the middle of a major product launch designed to meet financial goals at the end of the quarter.

Damn Devi! She was always inconsiderate. If she had to do one of her fuckups, maybe she should've waited until after the end of the quarter.

Everyone left after the meeting but Vladimir stayed back. "You look tired," he said, sounding concerned.

He was a godlike creature from Ukraine who had shown his interest in Shobha in a hundred different ways since she'd hired him a year ago. Shobha couldn't deny the attraction on her part, either. When Girish ignored her, which was most of the time these days, she would fantasize about giving in to Vladimir. What if he took her right here, on the conference table?

Shobha clenched her thighs together under her sleek black skirt and smiled politely. "It has been a long week," she said.

"You work too hard," Vladimir said, stretching out. His jean-clad legs were long, and his polo shirt fit across his chest nicely. He was off the cover of one of those novels you walked past in the super-market paperback book aisle.

Shobha sighed. God, she had sex on her mind. What would people think if they knew that prim and proper Shobha Veturi was lust-ing after an ex-Soviet macho man while her sister's wrists were still bloody?

"Maybe we can go to Le Papillon for lunch?" Vladimir said, look-ing at his watch. "Maybe you can have a glass of wine? Relax a little?"

Shobha was tempted. A cozy French restaurant, an interested Ukrainian, things could be worse. But she was no fool. Vladimir worked for her. Wine at lunch would be fine on an occasional Friday afternoon, but Vladimir was suggesting more. Maybe a brief wine-inspired interlude on the way back from the restaurant? Oh, but that was tempting.

"I can't. I have to leave early today *and* there is so much to do. I'll just pick up a sandwich from the cafeteria. But rain check, okay?" she said with a smile and left the conference room and the object of her lascivious thoughts behind.

This spurt of lust was new. It was a fresh feeling and something she dwelled on for considerably long periods of time. She never felt this way about Girish. Maybe a long time ago, in the beginning of their marriage, there was curiosity, the need to discover what lay behind the man in the suit, the stern glasses and the professorial face. Now the curiosity was satisfied and she was disappointed. She was thirty-two years old, stuck in a marriage to a boring professor, and bogged down by a strict moral code she forced upon herself. She was frustrated and dissatisfied with her life, her marriage, and her husband.

Oh, she could have an extramarital affair or two, what would Girish know and frankly speaking, Shobha didn't think he'd even care. Their relationship was now beyond repair. There had been hope, but after her uterine surgery, things, as they say, went to pot. Now there was nothing left to salvage. If they were not Indian, they would've gotten a divorce, but they were Indian and they were brainwashed. Shobha didn't believe in divorce or in extramarital affairs.

She didn't want to be like her grandmother. Vasu was a wonderful, kind, loving person, but Shobha knew that in Vasu's family and social circles she was looked down upon for being a divorcée and the kind of woman who had an affair with a married man. Granted, the married man she had an affair with couldn't leave his wife because of societal pressure. Granted that the "affair" had been going on for more than thirty years before he passed away. But the stigma, the bad reputation, no, Shobha thought, as she violently shook her head to remove Vladimir's image from her mind's eye, that just wouldn't do.

She was a respectable woman. Everyone knew that Shobha Veturi could do no wrong. She was an example of the perfect Indian woman living in the United States. She'd heard how other mothers talked about her.

"That Shobha Veturi, smart girl, *nahi*. Had an arranged marriage, but still kept her last name. *Pukka* mix of East and West. And she's doing so well in her career. Making her parents proud."

And when one sister was praised, the other was disgraced.

"Oh and that Devi, no *sharam* that girl has, no shame. Did you hear? Kissing some *kallu*, some black man, in front of Pasand, *chee-chee*. Poor Avi and Saroj, how embarrassing for them, *nahi*. Why can't she be more like her older sister?"

Shobha was not going to topple her image of perfection because she wanted to spend a sweaty afternoon with an accented Ukrainian.

Temptation remained, though, like the aftertaste of a good wine.

She knew jealousy prompted her to ridicule Devi's lifestyle. Devi slept around, partied hard, and had a lousy career. There was no pressure on Devi to be anyone but herself. She didn't have to fit into any mold of perfection. Even Girish liked her, and that tormented Shobha some more.

"She fucks everything that moves, Girish, is that something that appeals to you?" Shobha asked him after a not-so-joyous family dinner at her parents' house. Girish and she were fighting again, about what neither could remember, but the discussion somehow ended with Girish defending Devi and Shobha baring her claws.

"At least she's passionate enough to do that, unlike you," Girish retorted in a low voice. He never yelled at Shobha, never lost his control. He would say hateful, hurtful things quietly and slowly so that you couldn't even blame his hot temper for what he was saying. It was cold and calculated and he hit his mark every time.

"Maybe you'd like to sleep with my little sister?" Shobha asked, blind with anger.

"Don't be disgusting," Girish said dismissively and ended the discussion/fight by walking out of the house and not coming back until the next evening.

They'd been married five years and Shobha couldn't remember a single time when they were truly happy. Usually, with bad marriages, there was something holding it together, maybe just memories of good times. With them there was nothing. A child, she always thought as her heart broke again, a child would've made them closer, brought them love.

The longest night in her life was after the day she found out that there would be no child, that there simply couldn't be. Surgery would leave no ovaries or fallopian tubes, which were eaten away by endometriosis.

That night Shobha wanted to die. She'd sat under a beating shower for over an hour, even past the point when the hot water ran out. There were no tears as she contemplated a future where she'd never know what it would be like to be a mother.

Every day she would know that she would never feel her belly swell, never complain about morning sickness or compare notes on how long the labor was and how difficult. There would be no children coming for the holidays, for dinner, no grandchildren to spoil. The finality of it was akin to death. What was the point if there could be no life beyond hers? And that night she'd wondered how easy it all would be if she were dead. How easy it would be to end her life and not go through the next day and the next day knowing what she knew.

Girish and she had never managed to get close, but after her surgery they drifted farther apart and even stopped pretending that there was anything left to salvage.

Vasu once told Shobha when she complained about her lifeless marriage, "There is nothing deader than a dead relationship. Cut your losses, you have only one life."

"G'ma? You're not saying I should divorce Girish, are you?" Shobha was stupefied.

"Why make his and your life miserable. Get out and find someone who can make you happy," Vasu advised.

Shobha never complained to Vasu again.

She could in some way understand why Devi tried to end her life. Sometimes Shobha could feel the pressure from within to finish it, to get away and not deal with deadlines, Girish, her ditzy mother, life. But she didn't have the raw guts. Even in this, Shobha admitted, she was envious that Devi could do something about her useless life, while Shobha could only pretend that hers was perfect, which made her life worse because it was dishonest.

There Is Absolutely
No Place Like Home

Once, a long time ago, when Devi was eleven years old, she ran away from home. No one noticed and no one found out. And since no one knew, it shouldn't have mattered, but to Devi it did, because she knew, both that she ran away and that no one noticed.

It was a few days after she kissed a boy for the first time.

Dylan (and now she couldn't even remember his last name) lived in the neighborhood and they played football together in the park across the street from their house in Sunnyvale. Joggers pounded on the beaten cement path while people with dogs hung around with plastic bags waiting for their pets to poop. There was a small pond shaped like a drop of water and a fountain at its base that spurted water at regular intervals. A few ducks pranced in the pond, while little children played in the sandbox as their parents watched them with delight and apprehension, enjoying the antics of the ungainly little ones even as they waited for the inevitable fall.

Devi and Dylan had been wrestling for the football for weeks. The first few times Devi hadn't felt anything, but lately she could feel a tingle as his hand brushed against hers. She was just eleven years old and the mysteries of the world lay bare in front of her. All she wanted was to investigate and find out what lay beyond the tingling feeling brought by his hand against hers.

It wasn't that she was unaware of the birds and the bees. She knew the basics, had known because Vasu, against Saroj's wishes, had shown and explained the facts of life to both her granddaughters with diagrams and images. But knowing the basics and "feeling" the basics were a million light-years apart.

She knew it was wrong. She knew she was too young, but growing up was such a delight. Devi didn't even stop to look back at innocence, at lying against a boy, unaware of any sexuality, trying to pry a football from his hands.

Then one day, while they lay sweaty on the grass, the other kids gone, twilight streaking in, coloring the California summer sky, Dylan put his hand on Devi's, firmly, not playfully. Saroj's daughter wanted to run home, but Vasu's granddaughter wanted to stay.

Devi turned her head and awkwardly their lips met. She knew by instinct that she need only to open her mouth and the kiss would bloom, like it did in the movies, so she did and their tongues touched. Disgusted and excited by the intimacy of that first kiss and touching of tongues, Devi and Dylan didn't look at each other again for almost three days.

But they soon found themselves on the edge of the slippery slope again. This time however, Dylan was less enthusiastic than Devi.

When Devi leaned over boldly, even shyly, ready to slip into the delights of the forbidden, Dylan pulled away.

"Father Thomas told me that it was wrong to kiss you," he said solemnly, even though Devi could see that he was just trying to be mean. His lips were twisted, his stance arrogant. He had tempted her into reliving their previous kiss and had then jerked away with righteous fervor.

"Who's Father Thomas?"

"He's our father at our church and I told him that I kissed you and he said I should never ever do it again and . . . that you are a . . ." Dylan shrugged and looked away.

"And I am a what?" Devi demanded, standing up now, her hands fisted, resting against her waist in offense.

"A brownie slut," Dylan said loudly and then ran away.

For a second Devi wondered what chocolate had to do with slut and then realization sank in. She was embarrassed that she wanted to kiss again while Dylan did not. And she was furious that this Father Thomas called her a brownie slut.

Devi never really noticed her skin color compared to those around her. She knew (and how could you not with Saroj talking about it all the time) that she was dark, not pale like the white girls and boys she played with and went to school with. She knew all that but it wasn't something she paid attention to. She didn't go to school every day thinking they were white while she was brown.

But being told so crassly, so accusingly that she was different and not worthy of being kissed tore open the color blinders she'd been wearing. Devi would learn as she grew older to not notice the color of a person, but from that day in her heart she always knew she was brown.

Her legs were shaking as she found her way across the street to go home. Her body felt like it was burning. She could feel her heart pounding against her ears and her bruised pride twitching helplessly, painfully.

"What's wrong, *beta*?" Vasu, who was visiting for the summer, asked when Devi reached home, hot tears streaking down her cheeks.

First there were just sobs, hiccups. And then slowly, tearfully, Devi told Vasu that Dylan called her a brownie slut.

"How dare he?" Vasu said wiping Devi's tears with the *pallu* of her sari.

"Oh, G'ma," Devi screeched, warming up to the sympathy, and she spilled all the beans. Saroj who was bustling around the house only heard the "I wanted to kiss Dylan again and he called me a brownie slut" part and came charging like a bull on the loose.

"What did you expect when you behave like one?" she demanded angrily and didn't wait for Devi to respond.

The first slap rocked Devi almost off the floor. The second was warded off by Vasu.

"Saroj," Vasu warned rising above Devi like Durga Ma, ready to protect her granddaughter from such abuse.

"This is your doing, Mummy," Saroj bit back. "You keep saying it's okay this and it's okay that. And then you tell them both about sex. Of course they want to experiment. She is eleven years old and she wants to kiss some boy. All this garbage you put in her head."

"I put the same garbage in your head and you seemed to have gotten by just fine," Vasu countered.

"Fine? What fine, I had to raise myself," Saroj retorted.

Soon they both forgot about Devi and her tears. And that was when she decided to run away. No one loved her, that was evident, and she wanted to get away, never see Dylan again, at the park or anywhere else. She was even more afraid to bump into this Father Thomas. She imagined a white man with a large beard who looked like Jesus Christ and wore black with a white collar. She could see his stern face and his wagging finger as he told her that it was wrong for a brownie like her to go around kissing white boys.

She didn't know where she would go, but she had three dollars and fifty-two cents, which she carefully put inside the pockets of her shorts. She looked around at her room and felt the itch to stay, forget about Dylan and the whole nightmare. But the word *slut* still rang in her ears and she started packing fretfully. She wanted to take everything, but finally settled for Mr. Turtle; her blue teddy bear; her favorite book, *The Enchanted Wood,* which Vasu gave her for her ninth birthday; her favorite red T-shirt; a pair of socks; two pairs of underwear; and an empty notebook that had a pencil attached to it.

She zipped her backpack, hauled it onto one shoulder, and said a silent good-bye to her room before starting her unknown journey.

Vasu and Saroj were still yelling at each other in the kitchen about some party Saroj had not been allowed to go to when she was fifteen. Neither noticed Devi's departure.

The bus stop was just a few hundred steps away and Devi sat down on a bench, trying to figure out where she could go. Maybe Los Angeles, she thought, and then shook her head, almost sure that three dollars and fifty-two cents wouldn't get her there. Maybe she could go to San Francisco and then work at some restaurant as a waiter, make enough money and go to LA? Yes, she thought that would be a good idea. Once in LA, well, once she was there, someone would want her to be in all those ads about milk and juice. Everyone kept telling Saroj that she should take Devi to an audition for advertisements because she was so cute.

"Better than that Welch's girl, they will just grab her, cent percent guarantee," Megha Auntie said all the time.

A bus stopped.

Devi sat rooted to her seat, unable to get on, unsure how to ask if the bus went all the way to San Francisco.

The bus left and Devi promised herself that with the next one, she would ask the driver where the bus went. She then noticed a man in black come and sit next to her at the bus stop and knew she had to be careful. Saroj had told her, showing the face of a little girl in the back of the milk carton, "Don't talk to strangers. If you do, your picture will show up here and we won't know where you are."

"Did the bus for San Jose leave?" the man asked politely, and Devi shrugged. She didn't have an answer to his question and she didn't want to talk to him.

"Where are you going, young lady?" the man asked.

Devi wondered if she should tell him and then decided against it. If she told him, he might follow her and then what? She didn't want her face to show up on the back of a milk carton for everyone to see.

"Do your parents know where you're off to?" the man asked, and this time Devi all but bolted.

"They know," she said a in a low voice, looking at her sneaker-clad feet.

"I'm Father Velázquez, what's your name?" he asked.

Devi bit her lip hard, contemplating whether to tell him who she was or not. She looked up at him and he had a kind face. His skin was almost as brown as hers and he wore thick glasses. His black coat and white collar didn't look threatening the way she imagined Father Thomas's would look.

"Shobha," she lied after a while.

"Shobha," Father Velázquez said and nodded. "So, Shobha, where are you going?"

"Away," Devi confessed finally.

"Where?"

"I don't know," she told him and then licked her dry lips. "Are you a father from a church?"

"Yes," he said. "Do you go to church?"

"No," Devi said, shaking her head. "Mama says that only Christians go to church. We go to the temple. We're Hindus and Mama does *puja* at home."

"Do you like going to the temple?" he asked then.

Devi shrugged and after a pause asked the question burning on her tongue. "Do you know Father Thomas?"

Father Velázquez screwed his eyes and waited for her to continue.

"Dylan told me that Father Thomas called me a brownie slut . . ." she stopped speaking because her lips were quivering. She could feel the bubble of humiliation rise inside her and spill out of her eyes.

"Shobha," the reverent priest began, "it's a very bad thing to lie. You know that, don't you?"

"Yes," she sniffled.

"Then Dylan did a very bad thing," Father Velázquez told her. "Father Thomas would never call anyone that ugly word."

"Really?" Devi could hardly believe the man.

"Really. I know him very well and he would never ever say anything like that," he assured her. "Is that why you're running away from home?"

Since he knew that Father Thomas hadn't called her a brownie slut, Devi didn't see anything wrong in telling him how Saroj slapped her and then starting fighting with Vasu as they often did.

"Your mother was just worried and anyway, you're too young to kiss boys," Father Velázquez said. "Now, tell me where you live and I'll walk you home."

Devi shook her head tightly. She was horrified of what Saroj would do, what Vasu would say, what her father would say when they found out that she ran away from home.

"They love you, Shobha. No one will be angry," Father Velázquez promised her.

Hand in hand, they went home. Once they got there, Father Velázquez told her to go in and if there was a problem, he'd be waiting right here and would talk to her parents if necessary.

When Devi went back inside, Vasu and Saroj were still bickering in the kitchen. When they saw her, they ignored her and went back to arguing, this time about Devi's grandfather who committed suicide.

She dropped her bag in her room and tried again to be noticed, but her mother and grandmother were too busy dissecting the past. Devi waved to Father Velázquez from her doorstep, not wanting to go out and tell him that even though she came back home, no one seemed to be happy to see her.

All day Devi waited for someone to say anything about her brief runaway episode, but no one did. It was business as usual in the Veturi household.

She never saw Father Velázquez after that and neither did she run away again. The next time Devi kissed a boy, she was almost fourteen and when the boy tried to kiss her a second time she told him that Father Velázquez, from *her* church, told her that it was wrong to kiss boys, especially whities. She did it because she thought it would be cool, smart, even humorous, but when the boy looked at her with disgust, she couldn't remember why it had seemed like the right thing to do when she'd rehearsed it in her head time and again for the past three years.

There was a good reason why she took so long to open her eyes, Devi thought as she looked out of her mother's car at the blank zipping lines of the freeway beneath. Vasu still held her hand, sitting beside her in the leather seat. Her father was completely silent in the passenger's seat in the front, while Saroj, as always, chirped on about the neighbors and gossip.

I just tried to kill myself, Devi wanted to scream, *and I don't care who did what in their garden. Let them sunbathe completely nude and have a swastika tattooed on their butt, how would it make a zit of a difference to me?*

"I have hot-hot *samosas,*" Saroj said as she stopped at a red light. "And I made your favorite *pudhina* chutney."

Chutney? Did her mother really think that she was interested in chutney at this point in her life? And of all the things to cook when your suicidal daughter comes home—the same old mint chutney? Nothing new, nothing different? Nothing to say, *The world has changed. The food in our house definitely has. You can live now?*

It was difficult, however, to take too much offense in the face of such blatant goodness. Saroj was on her best behavior and even though the veneer slipped sometimes, she was trying to make Devi feel welcome.

Her father welcomed her back as well, and he assured her that he was taking care of all the practicalities. He told her, when Saroj wasn't around, that he knew about the unpaid bills and that he was taking care of them. He was pulling her out of her lease on the town house and was in the process of putting most of her things away in storage. She could stay with her parents for as long as she wanted and when she was ready, they'd all go and look for a nice place for her.

It was just like her father had always promised.

When they were little, Saroj never read bedtime stories to Devi or Shobha, Avi did. When Shobha and Devi used to share a bedroom, Avi would tuck them both in bed and pull out two books to read, one for Shobha and one for Devi. Shobha's favorite used to be *Ali Baba and the Forty Thieves,* while Devi insisted on listening to *Oh, the Places You'll Go!* again and again.

"Daddy, you really think I'll be left in a lurch someday?" Devi would ask the same question each time because she loved to say *lurch.* And each time Avi would say that if she got caught in a lurch, all she had to do was say the magic words.

"What are the magic words?" Devi would ask with a giggle because she already knew what they were.

"Daddy, come get me," Avi would say and give her a big kiss on the cheek. "And Daddy will come and get you."

"Really? Even if you're in a meeting?" She'd ask this question differently each time.

"Even if I'm in a meeting with the president," Avi would say, hugging her to him tightly. "That's what daddies are for, to rescue their little girls."

But this time Devi didn't call out to her father, didn't want anyone to see her hanging, left in a lurch. She didn't need help, she just needed to die.

She resented what the situation looked like, as if she ran home to Daddy and his money when she was in trouble. But the resentment was wrapped in a layer of apathy, just as almost everything else was. Her problems seemed to be enveloped in a haze and she couldn't get past the mist to touch them, feel them, and mend them.

Also, to stop her father from taking charge of her life, she would have to speak and she wasn't ready yet. Her voice seemed to be stored in a box and her emotions latched the box shut. She was alive, despite her wishes, but she didn't have to join the human race right away. She could wait.

Since she could remember, Devi had found solace in silence. When they accused her of stealing in the fourth grade, she maintained silence rather than defend herself. What would the point be? And if she protested too much, they'd blame her for lying on top of stealing. But she hadn't been stealing, just borrowing.

And she didn't hit Lilly without provocation. Lilly started it by calling her a thief and a "brown-skinned refugee." Name-calling added to the fact that Lilly was as pretty as Barbie and just as popular—it had been a simple decision. Now, Devi hadn't intended for Lilly's nose to break, that turned out to be a special bonus.

It took a week for her to speak again and even then, she never explained why. She didn't think anyone was interested. What her parents wanted was for such an incident not to be repeated and Devi ensured that. Beyond that she didn't feel she owed them any explanations.

After that Devi went into silence mode for a few days now and again, whenever she got upset or whenever she didn't want to say anything to anyone. It hadn't happened in seven years. Well, let's face it, it hadn't happened since she left her mother's house.

Devi glanced surreptitiously at the white bandages peeking out from under her full-sleeved black pullover. She should've worn white, she thought as nausea built up inside her, then the bandages wouldn't stick out quite as much. She glanced toward Vasu, who was looking at the bandages as well, tightened lines of pain etched on her face. Vasu averted her gaze when she noticed Devi was looking at her and looked blindly out of the window at the cars racing past them.

Devi knew her grandmother was shattered. There was sorrow in her eyes, more sorrow even than there had been when Shekhar Uncle died. That's what they called G'ma's boyfriend. He had been in Vasu's life since Devi had known her. Even though Shobha always kicked up a fuss when they came for a visit and shared a bedroom, Devi never thought it strange.

"They're madly in love," Devi said once when Shobha announced that it was immoral to allow such an illicit affair to be perpetrated in their home.

"He has a wife in India, Devi. How do you think she feels?"

Devi sighed. "She doesn't want a divorce. This is the only solution they have. What? They should live unhappy lives without each other because society in India is screwed up?"

Shobha glared at Devi. "I'm sure G'ma's disreputable ways appeal to you. I find this behavior disgusting."

Vasu was never fazed. Devi couldn't remember one time when she'd seen Vasu this hurt. It must hurt, she realized, to find that the granddaughter you were most close to had secrets. Tears welled in her eyes and streamed down her cheeks.

She wiped them with the back of her hands, feeling the thick bandage against her face. The futility of it all, the tears, her life, came screaming back and the tears dried up.

Damn Mama, Devi thought angrily. She would've been dead by now. Gone. Happily moved on. Instead she was sitting here, having to deal with Vasu's pain, Daddy's pain, and even her mother's confused love. She looked forward to seeing Shobha, something she didn't often do. Shobha was a straight shooter. Even if Shobha was feeling any trauma caused by the attempted suicide, Devi could trust her sister to tell it like it was. Her caustic remarks would be better than this silent remonstration, whispered accusations, show of support, and question-mark faces.

Mama had yelled once, but Vasu and Daddy probably silenced her and that was why she was chirping on about hot-hot *samosas*. As if Devi gave a damn!

"We've put you in your old room," Avi told her as he led her inside the house of her childhood by her hand, like she was a patient ridden with a life-threatening disease, or an old woman who needed physical support. She despised the tone of her father's touch, even as she took comfort in it.

"G'ma and Mama arranged all your things inside, just the way it used to be before you left." He spoke slowly, leaned over, and kissed her on her forehead.

He was talking to her as if she were mentally retarded, unable to comprehend what he was saying if he spoke faster, at his usual pace. She didn't wanted to be here but the only way out of the hospital was through her parents' home. You attempt suicide once and all your adult privileges are taken away. She didn't even have her purse with her, she had no money, no credit cards, no driver's license, nothing.

"Your purse and mail are inside the drawer," Avi said, pointing with his prosthetic arm to the old solid-oak antique desk.

Saroj hoarded antiques and knickknacks. She put them everywhere, to the extent that after Devi left home her desk became the landing ground for various bronze birds that Saroj bought at some estate sale.

"We can remove, move, change, do anything you want," Avi said carefully, unsure probably because she hadn't set foot inside the room but stood at the threshold. "But . . . we were advised to keep your credit cards and driver's license with us. This doesn't mean we don't trust you, just as a precaution."

Devi didn't want to think about what that meant. She wasn't sure but maybe at the back of her mind she wondered if she could run away again. Without a driver's license and her plastic, though, it would be impossible. She wasn't a little girl anymore who thought that the world embraced runaways and gave them lucrative jobs as models for milk and juice products.

"We want you to stay with us, until you feel better," Avi said and Devi, to her horror, caught the glint of tears in his eyes. He hugged her close, his prosthetic arm and his real arm enfolding her, holding her tight.

"Everything's going to be all right, okay?" Avi said and Devi nodded, wanting to comfort him as he was comforting her. But it was futile because even though he didn't know it, she knew that nothing was going to be okay, ever again.

Devi sat down on the bed shakily after Avi left. Saroj had put a white sheet with lavender-colored flowers on the bed. It was all so feminine, so girl-like that tears came to Devi and she didn't know why. She'd been so innocent when this room used to be hers.

Saroj had filled the antique bookshelf Devi emptied when she left home. There were old books, R. K. Narayan, Anita Desai, Khushwant Singh, Kamala Markandaya (which Saroj probably never read), and new ones with fresh, crisp paper. One of the four shelves was filled with cookbooks. From fusion cuisine to authentic south Indian recipes, the books looked untouched, and they would be. These were probably given by well-meaning friends who thought the cookbooks perfect gifts for always-cooking Saroj. But Saroj didn't believe in cookbooks. "What do they know?" she'd say. She knew how much and what from experience. That was the only way to make good food, experience and trial and error.

Devi knew her mother's life revolved around cooking. Always chopping, dicing, and/or planning. It was such an uncomplicated life, it made Devi envious. Maybe Saroj had gotten it right: marry well and cook and take care of family. It all seemed so easy compared to what she'd wanted to do: start her own company, be as successful as Daddy (no, more successful), get Shobha's respect, find a good man to love and marry, have a houseful of children, and still have the stellar career. When she would talk about her plans to friends they would say that if she wanted a career she would have to put the family on hold. That was how it was done.

Now as she stood gazing at the colored spines of the cookbooks on her old bookshelf, she realized that she had neither a career, nor a family. So where the hell did that leave her?

The spine of the book was blank, made with cloth, and it attracted Devi's attention. It was a long book and when she pulled it out she saw that it was covered with batik cloth. The art was in yellow and orange and red, with splashes of green and blue. It was bright, lively, like the colors of Holi blending on the cover of the book.

It was a notebook, empty mostly, except for the second page. It had the feel of an old book; the paper wasn't sharp and firm to the touch, it was soft, aged. There was a smell to it, that of turmeric and cloves, as if the book belonged in a kitchen.

When she read the only entry, she found out that the book had been meant for the kitchen. It was one of Saroj's old notebooks, from the days when she probably used cookbooks. When she didn't believe she knew it all but needed to learn.

On the second page of the book, in Saroj's neat handwriting, was the first and only recipe. Devi recognized it immediately as Saroj's "famous" goat curry. Saroj ordered goat special from the butcher and made the curry, but she'd never revealed that the recipe belonged to some woman called Girija and that Saroj had acquired the recipe in 1970 in Jorhat.

Jorhat, April 15, 1970
GIRIJA'S GOAT SABZI

Get good goat and clean it well. Chop out some of the thick fat but let the rest stay, it doesn't hurt and the fat content will give the sabzi *more taste. Cut some onions and fry in oil. Add onions to oil only after the oil starts sizzling. Once the onions become a little brown, quickly add chopped green chili, garlic, and ginger. Make sure you remove all the stringy parts of the ginger; they don't harm, but still, why have that to get stuck in between the teeth. Fry nicely on medium heat for a while. Don't hurry otherwise the* sabzi *won't turn out right.*

After a while, add some ground jeera, dhaniya, *and* elaichi. *You can also add a little* dal chini *and* lavang. *Fry for a little while longer, until the* dal chini *and* lavang *become soft. Add tomatoes and cook until the tomato is completely squishy and the oil is leaving the sides. Then add the cut goat and nicely coat with the spices, tomato, and onion mixture. Let the goat brown a little and then you can add the chopped potatoes. The potatoes should be big in size, not little, because you want to taste them.*

Fry for a little while longer, add water to cover the goat, and then put the pressure-cooker lid on top. Cook for two whistles and then remove. Sprinkle with chopped dhaniya *on top before serving.*

INDIA	U.S.
Jeera	Cumin
Dhaniya	Coriander
Dal chini	Cinnamon
Lavang	Have to ask Avi.

Devi flipped through the empty pages with a small smile. Saroj probably started this book before she and Avi moved to the United States. How hard it must've been for Saroj, Devi thought, not even sure what the spices she was so familiar with were called in the U.S.

She stroked the soft pages and sighed. *What a beautiful notebook,* she thought as she sat down on her old study table, pushing the bronze birds aside. She looked at the ornate pencil holder on her table and considered the two blue Pilot pens and one pencil carefully. Then she picked up the pencil, opened the page right after the goat curry recipe, and started writing.

The long sleeves of her black pullover slipped up as she wrote, revealing the bandages beneath, but she didn't notice as the red pencil with black stripes flew over the white ruled page.

~⁀

LETTER FROM AVI TO DEVI

Dear Devi,

This is my fourth letter to you in your lifetime.

After I lost my arm and was trying to drink myself to death, the army head doctor told me that I should write letters. As many as I felt like to my friends who died in the war, to my parents, to that ex-girlfriend who was now happily married to some guy who hadn't lost his arm. I didn't have to mail those letters. They were for me, even though I wrote them for others. Then, I ignored his advice, but when you came into my world I started writing.

The first letter was a long time ago. You were nine days old and were crying your heart out. The doctor said, "Nothing is wrong, just colic. Deal with it. It'll be gone by the time she's three months old." The thought of having to hear you and watch you cry for three more months was absolutely terrifying. I couldn't accept that nothing was wrong. Something had to be wrong, babies didn't cry just for the heck of it. But they did and you did.

Saroj was exhausted, so I asked her to sleep while I walked with you. It soothed you and you'd stop crying, but the minute I tried to sit down or put you down, the wail machine would be charged again. So I walked with you that night, all night, and somewhere in between midnight and sunrise, and walking and nursing, you fell asleep in my arms. My arms hurt, my legs hurt, every part of my body ached, but I was afraid to put you in your crib, so I put you on a pillow in my lap and sat down at my desk. I thought I'd get some work done, but all of a sudden I was writing my first letter to you.

The second letter was when you stole money and broke that girl's nose. I was shocked at the violence you exhibited and I have to say, just a little proud that you actually broke someone's nose. I never told Saroj how I felt. She'd have had a heart attack if she knew I actually took pride in your actions.

The third letter I wrote because I was proud. You started working at your first start-up and I was so giddy that you'd be the next Veturi to be part of a new venture that would become a success. I imagined your face on the cover of Fortune and Time. I was thrilled.

In the past years I have written Saroj numerous letters, just two to Shobha, and you three, excluding this one. And now as I sit to write this fourth letter, I realize that all the reasons for all those previous letters are now trivial compared to the reason why I'm writing this one.

When Saroj called to tell me to come to the ER my legs started to shake as what had happened sank in. Even now I can feel the tremors in my hands, my legs, my heart. You are home now, and I'm still shaking. I'm still scared shitless and I can't breathe without feeling the fear rise in my throat.

I look at you and I see that nine-day-old baby who wouldn't stop crying and I think that maybe if I carried you again, you'd stop crying and go to sleep.

I can't imagine what we did, what Saroj and I did that drove you to *this weakness. I know, I know, you'll say that you're an independent woman and you make your own choices. But as a father, I'm not allowed that luxury. I can't ever say that I'm done with you, because a parent's job is never finished, never over, never completed. Even after I'm dead, I'll want to look over you and make sure you're eating right, sleeping well, sleeping alone.*

I wonder if it was me who drove you here. If it was my success that compelled you to attempt suicide. I wonder if maybe we'd stayed in India, like Saroj wanted, this wouldn't have happened. I wonder and wonder and wonder, and as I wonder, I see you in that bathtub, bleeding, and my hands start to shake again and there's a tremor that runs through me. I feel like I have malaria again, like I did when we lived in Jorhat, sick, shaking, unbearably tired, and feeling that something inside me is dying, draining, falling apart.

Is there anything more terrible than seeing your child trapped in such a horror that she wants to die? Could there be anything more painful, more torturous than this? I would happily give away my only arm if I could save you, help you, hold you. But you seem distant, it seems as if a cocoon has enveloped you and we are all walking around like shadows, making a small impression but not enough to wake you up from your nightmare.

Life is so much fun, Devi. I wish you could have some fun, so much fun that you will never, ever think about dying again. We should be afraid of death because that affirms our faith in life. When we embrace death, we give ourselves to the wasteland of hopelessness.

I will hold your hand through this. I will grab your hand and hang on until this is over. I will tie you up, imprison you, until I make you realize that your life is worth living, that your life is brilliant, that you are an amazing girl, and you're the one who makes the sun shine brighter for me.

I love you, Devi, live for me!
Daddy

There Is a Mute in the Kitchen

Devi never cooked. It wasn't that she was a terrible cook; she just didn't cook very often. Saroj had tried to teach her children to cook without having them actually cook in her kitchen, messing it up, and she'd failed.

"Some girls are just not domestic," she would complain, ignoring Devi when she pointed out that all her attempts at learning were thwarted because Saroj couldn't stand even the idea of anyone else but her cooking in her kitchen. Saroj lived in fear that Devi, Shobha, or even Vasu would put things away in the wrong place or ruin her perfectly managed kitchen. That was unacceptable and to avoid any kitchen mishaps, Saroj banned everyone from using her kitchen. She never said it out loud, but everyone knew anyway.

"How dirty can she make it?" Vasu interfered once when Devi pleaded that she be allowed to try a chocolate cake recipe a friend of hers had made all by herself.

But when it came to the kitchen, Saroj ruled supreme and no one could make cake or anything else there.

So after a childhood of only watching the cooking process in the kitchen, it gave Devi immense pleasure to walk into her mother's kitchen and start cooking. She knew no one would argue, make a scene, or ask her to leave. She was a suicidal mute, who would want to take a chance and tip her scales off again?

The idea of eating Saroj's regular, everyday, garden-variety mint chutney didn't sit well with Devi. She wanted to eat something else, make something new, start fresh.

And she liked the idea of cooking, being in a kitchen, an uncomplicated world of spices, produce, lentils, meat, poultry, and rice. There were no arguments here. This was sacred land. Her mind could wander on all sorts of possibilities here and she wouldn't have to worry about where she ended up. Anything was possible and everything was acceptable, as long as she kept her mind confined to food and cooking.

Devi found the dry apricots in the pantry. They weren't exactly old, but they weren't bought yesterday, either. She couldn't imagine why Saroj would've bought them, but was glad she had because they were perfect for what she had in mind. Devi soaked the apricots in sugar water while Saroj watched, her nose crinkled.

"The *samosas* will get cold, Devi," she said. "Why don't we eat these now and you can tell me what you want and I will make it for you later."

Devi didn't even bother to acknowledge Saroj or the questioning glances of her family. She knew they were staring at her, trying to figure out what she was up to. Saroj was hovering inside the kitchen while Avi, Girish, Vasu, and Shobha stood by the counter that separated the large kitchen from the spacious dining area. The house had been built to Saroj's specifications when Avi's company started making money, and the kitchen was the crowning glory. Everyone knew that and maybe that was why Devi took great pleasure in spilling a spoonful of sugar on the marbled floor.

Saroj was ready to run with a hand vacuum and wet cloth when Avi pulled her out of the kitchen.

"Let her be," he said firmly. "And I'll clean the kitchen if it gets too dirty."

Saroj's chin jutted out and she removed Avi's hand from her arm. "I was only trying to help her," she said tightly.

"Don't help her, just let her figure out whatever it is she's trying to figure out," Avi replied just as tightly.

"Why are we standing here watching her?" asked Shobha as she smothered a yawn. "It makes me very uncomfortable to look at her as if she's some lab rat."

"Do you have to go back to work?" Girish asked Shobha, who shook her head. "Then just shut up and watch," he added with a smile.

"Mama, did she hit her head on the bathtub or something?" Shobha turned to her mother, ignoring her husband. "I mean, she never seemed all that interested in cooking before."

"I don't know," Saroj said and winced when Devi indelicately plucked mint leaves from her precious herb pot on the kitchen windowsill.

"What is she making?" Vasu asked.

"I don't know," Saroj repeated, sighing as Devi indelicately opened a closed Ziplock bag of ginger and the three big pieces fell on the kitchen floor. "I think she's making a chutney for the *samosas*. I am not sure."

Devi picked up the pieces of ginger and left them on the counter. She took one piece and started peeling it.

"Ginger-and-apricot chutney?" Girish wondered aloud.

"Let's all not forget the mint," Shobha reminded.

Saroj grimaced, looking at her herb pot, which now had lost its symmetrical look. She was so careful with it and Devi had just demolished all that work. The neat freak inside Saroj wanted to rage: the mother kept her quiet.

Devi made a ginger, apricot, and mint chutney, along with a good amount of chipotle chili peppers found in a bottle, hidden deep down in Saroj's everything-is-in-there pantry. The end result was a fiery, smoky, tangy concoction that beat the pants off of Saroj's mint chutney.

Devi told herself that she knew the difference between "afraid of suicidal person" praise and real praise. This was the real thing. Her chutney was a success. Pride swelled inside her and for the first time in a very long time she felt a small measure of confidence. But then she thought of all the coming days and panic filled her. She couldn't just make chutney every day and get a sense of accomplishment. Oh God, what was she going to do?

After the last *samosa* was eaten without anyone saying anything to Saroj about how good *they* tasted, Girish opened the conversation up to more serious matters, beyond food.

"You gave us quite a fright," Girish said tenderly, his gaze holding Devi's. "We're very happy you're home."

Devi nodded and slid a forefinger on her plate, scooped up some chutney, and licked her finger, daring Saroj to tell her she was eating like a *junglee*.

"Why? What happened? You couldn't tell us?" Saroj asked as Devi sucked noisily on her forefinger. She scooped up some more chutney and shrugged.

"What do you mean by that? You have to talk . . . you can't just . . ." Saroj became silent when Avi glared at her. "We don't want to put any pressure on you," Saroj said on a long-suffering sigh.

"But you are putting pressure on her all the same," Vasu snapped at Saroj, flustered, and then looked at Devi, forcing herself to be calm. "How about a walk? Some fresh air?"

Devi picked up her plate and ran her tongue on it. She set the plate down, perversely pleased that she'd been able to do what she just did without Saroj yelling the place down. As a child it was a treat to lick a plate smeared with remains of delicious goodies and she used to have to do it stealthily, but now, now she was a basket case, she could do anything she wanted to do.

Devi nodded to Vasu. On her way out, she realized that for the first time in her mother's house, she'd not picked up her plate, rinsed it, and put it inside the dishwasher. She'd also left the kitchen in a small mess. It made her happy.

Of all the places she'd been to in the United States, Vasu loved California the most. Partly because all her family lived here, and partly because the weather was always pleasant and nature was within touching distance.

"I feel that nature balances herself in California," Vasu began. "It never gets oppressively hot as it does in Hyderabad. There, sweat patches everywhere, underarms, on the back, everywhere. That is what summer is all about, sweat patches and thighs sticking to plastic chairs. It is so embarrassing to get up in a crowd and hear that plopping sound when your thighs separate from the chair."

Devi tugged at the sleeves of her shirt without thinking about it. She wasn't sure if she was supposed to participate in this conversation. Knowing her grandmother, she was probably supposed to hang around, listen, and then learn. With G'ma there was always a lesson to be learned from stories. All stories had morals and everything was an education. Unlike other grandmas who probably told stories about fairies and princes on white horses, G'ma told stories about tough women, wading their way through the morass of societal rules to only sometimes win.

The all-time favorite story of Vasu's to tell when Shobha and Devi were younger was that of the *Rani* of Jhansi. Vasu probably associated herself with the Queen of Jhansi, the queen of a small province in central India.

"Her father was a Brahmin and her mother was a beautiful, cultured woman," she would start the story every time, referring to the *Rani*'s parents.

"What does *cultured woman* mean?" Shobha would ask before the story could move on, which was her ploy once she was a teenager to try to not let the story continue. "Is this one of those euphemisms for doormat?"

Vasu, unlike Saroj, was not easy to bait, and despite Shobha's best efforts, the oft-told story would continue its course.

"She married *Raja* Gangadhar Rao and became the *Rani* of Jhansi. Her given name was Mannikarnika, but after marriage she was called Lakshmi Bai." Vasu would enjoy telling this part, twisting her tongue around the difficult Hindu names.

"Okay, in the rest of the world women change their last names, God knows why, but here they changed the poor girl's entire name. What about her identity?" Shobha wouldn't be able to help herself from getting on the feminism soapbox.

Devi usually listened quietly to the story without interrupting G'ma too much. That way the story ended soon and they could quickly get done with the moral of the story and the lesson of life

G'ma was trying to impart. In trying to stop the stubborn Vasu from continuing with her story, Shobha was only making her more determined and was also extending the time it took to tell the damn story.

"They had a child, but the boy died when he was only four months old. Stricken with grief, Gangadhar Rao adopted another child, Damodar Rao. But after Gangadhar Rao's death, the British refused to acknowledge the adopted son as legal heir and tried to annex Jhansi. They offered the *Rani* a pension and asked her to leave Jhansi. But the *Rani* refused and fought in the battlefield to save her country from the British. She started the first war of independence." Vasu's voice would climb up with pride as she told this part. "She tied her son up on her back and went on a horse to fight the British. That is courage and love for one's country."

"But she died, right?" Shobha would be bored by this time.

"Yes, but she died a warrior's death," Vasu would say emotionally. "She was a brave woman who never gave up her integrity, no matter how bad things got. You should remember that, both of you. You should fight till the end, not give up in the middle and lose the battle."

"Why fight on if you're going to lose the battle anyway?" Devi wanted to know. "I'd have taken the money the British offered and taken care of my son."

"Yeah, and what happened to that poor kid anyway, the one she strapped on her back? Talk about improper child care, someone should've called social services," Shobha would put in.

"The story isn't about the boy, it is about *Rani* Lakshmi Bai and how she stood by her integrity and her . . ."

By then Devi and Shobha would start demolishing the story and never concede that the *Rani* of Jhansi was a brave woman who fought a losing battle because it was a fight worth fighting.

It wasn't like either Devi or Shobha had anything against patriotism or the Queen of Jhansi; it was part of their dealings with Vasu. She would always tell them how wonderful India, her country, was, and they would always fight back that the United States, their country, was better.

But now as Devi walked with Vasu in the park near her parents' house, she remembered the Queen of Jhansi and wondered if she had failed after all to learn the moral of that story. Hadn't she given up, midway, not wanting to make it to the end? Among all of G'ma's tough-woman stories, not one ended with the heroine committing suicide or even attempting it. Did G'ma now look at her and see a coward? Devi wondered with dread as she tugged again at the sleeves of her shirt.

"Of all the people I know, you were the last person I thought would commit suicide," Vasu said, speaking about the "incident" for the first time.

Vasu stopped walking, put her hands on Devi's arms, and shook her lightly. "You were supposed to come through winning. What happened?"

Right there, she looked like Saroj, Devi thought. Maybe this was where Mama got it, that nagging bad temper.

Vasu dropped her hands and sighed. "You cannot hide forever. Just because you won't talk about it, doesn't mean it didn't happen."

Devi nodded then. She knew, the memory of the "incident" would be with her forever, but for now it could stay some other place. She wasn't ready to think about it.

"I wouldn't have been able to handle it, Devi, if I had to stand over a dead grandchild," Vasu told her bluntly. "I simply wouldn't."

Devi put a hand on Vasu's cheek and smiled. She wanted to tell her that they couldn't choose what they would and wouldn't face in life.

"Life is precious," Vasu said, "and your life is golden. I want you to think about living, about going on, about moving on. I want you to tell me why you wanted to die and then I want you to tell me how you are not going to let this despair take over you again."

Devi shook her head and dragged her hands over her face. Her bandages peeked out from under her sleeves.

Why couldn't they just leave her alone to lick her wounds?

Not wanting to continue the conversation, Devi gave Vasu a tight nod and left the park to go back to her parents' house.

There were so many questions! Everyone had questions, a thousand questions. Everywhere Devi looked she felt that there were questions. Why? Why? Why? She didn't know why, all she knew was that her life didn't resemble the life she envisioned, not even remotely. She was twenty-seven years old, she was relying financially on her father, she'd moved back in with her parents, and now it looked like she had inherited the suicide gene from her crazy grandfather.

Devi sat down on one of Saroj's cushioned metal chairs in the patio. She didn't want to go in and deal with everyone, especially Saroj. G'ma, she could handle, G'ma, she had no trouble with, but Saroj, ah, that was a different story.

Even now, the memory, part real, part surmised, of her mother seeing her in the bloody bathtub gave her the shivers. It was supposed to be the perfect plan, but it was foiled. Now what?

How long was she going to take to recover? Did she want to recover? What did it mean to recover? Was she supposed to be happy that she was alive? Or was she supposed to try again?

She saw her mother's face peek out of the window once and then again.

"Devi, I am going to make your favorite tomato *pappu* and fried potato *sabzi*," Saroj said, bright-eyed and bushy-tailed.

She hadn't planned to, but Devi found herself walking into the kitchen yet again and rummaging through the fridge to find something else, something she hadn't eaten before. Damn her mother, always cooking the same old food. First she saves her life, and then she cooks boring food. Unexplained anger bubbled through Devi as she let her hands fly over spices and vegetables while Saroj watched, in wide-eyed horror, as her fridge and spice cabinet went from neat and tidy to something completely the opposite.

It really started with that dinner, though the chutney would be considered the first original recipe. Soon enough Saroj found herself completely kicked out of her kitchen as Devi cooked outrageous meals every day. When she was angry, the food was spicy, when she seemed happy, there was dessert, and when she looked bored, the food tasted bland.

DEVI'S RECIPE
THE ANTI-SAROJ CHUTNEY
Day 1 after coming home from the hospital

The classic chutneys are coriander, mint, and chili. Everyone makes those chutneys, and oh yes, let's not forget the tamarind chutney that every Indian restaurant will serve in watery portions. But I don't want to make or eat classic chutneys.

I was lucky Mama had dried apricot in that pantry of hers. My God, but she has stuff in there. She even has a small bottle of red caviar. Mama would never eat caviar ("Raw fish eggs? Why would anyone want to eat that?"), but it's there nevertheless along with the now indispensable bottle of chipotle chili peppers.

Soaking the apricots in water seemed a good way to make them mushy but soaking them in sugar water seemed like an even better idea. It would make the chutney sweet. Surveying the fridge, my eye caught the ginger. Mama buys big chunks of ginger. Lots of garlic and ginger in her food. Maybe not garlic in the chutney, but definitely ginger. Lots of ginger for a sharp tangy taste.

What else? I saw the mint. Mama's prized little herb pot. Tearing away the mint, ah, now that was a special treat. Anything else? Of course, the chipotle chili peppers to give the chutney a smoky flavor.

Take the apricot, ginger, garlic, peppers, and salt (I added the apricot syrup in small quantities as well, depending upon how liquid I wanted the chutney to be, not too liquid) and blend it to a pulp.

The chutney is best savored when licked from a plate!

The One-Armed Man

Avi lost his right arm in the 1965 Indo-Pak battle. When Saroj found him, and she told this story to anyone who'd listen, he was living in a pigsty. He was on sick leave and had been for the past month. He spent his days in his room at the officers' mess, drinking and smoking all day and eating very little. No one was allowed inside the room, and when Saroj barged her way in, she was appalled.

First, there was the stench. The room smelled of stale beer, whiskey, rum, and wet cigarette ash. Clothes were everywhere, some dirty, some not so dirty. There was not a spot in the room where one could sit without encountering dirt of some nature. The previous night's untouched dinner plate and the morning's breakfast plate lay by the grimy feet of a man who looked as if he were living on the street. A piece of toast dangled in the man's limp left hand and a cigarette hung in his mouth.

Saroj had never met Avi before, never had any reason to. He was older than she and he was in the Infantry Corps, while Vasu was a gynecologist in the Army Medical Corps. There was no reason for Vasu's path and therefore Saroj's to cross Avi's.

Avi's mother lived in Sikkim with her retired army officer husband. When Avi refused to go to his parent's home after he was released from the hospital and didn't reply to their letters or return their calls, his mother called Saroj's friend Rashmi, who lived in Dehradun, and asked her if she knew anyone who lived in Udhampur and could check up on her son.

Vasu was posted to Udhampur then, fifty kilometers above Jammu and a couple of hundred kilometers below Srinagar. The war had sent many of the wounded to the Udhampur Military Hospital, and since Avi had been posted to Udhampur before he'd lost his arm, he was back, taking some time off, struggling to accept that he was one of the few in his battalion to survive and that life had been bestowed upon him at a price.

When Rashmi called Saroj, it seemed like a mission of mercy, to check up on a wounded soldier, a war hero who'd lost his arm in battle. She was barely nineteen and fell headlong in love with the disreputable Captain Avinash Veturi. It didn't happen at first sight, but it didn't take too long for Cupid to strike the fatal blow.

"How the hell did you get in?" were Avi's first words to Saroj.

"The door was open," she replied. "My God, it stinks in here."

"Then get the fuck out," Avi said, throwing the piece of toast on the floor, spitting out the now dead cigarette, and picking up a bottle of army grade XXX rum. He took a long swig and wiped his mouth with the back of his hand. And at that moment Saroj romantically thought he looked like Devdas, the bitter and melancholy legendary lover pining after his lost love, his Paro.

"Get the fuck out," he repeated and she all but left. Who wanted to deal with an ornery wounded type, even if he was wounded saving her country? Then she caught sight of his stump and something in her heart slipped. How hard it must be for an independent and proud man to come back with less than he had gone into battle with.

"Thank you," Saroj said softly.

Avi looked at her then, for the first time. "What?"

"Thank you," Saroj said again. "You went out there and fought for our country, so thank you."

"What the fuck do you know about anything?" Avi said, but his voice was not so bitter.

"I know that you need a bath," Saroj said, tapping her temple with a forefinger. "And a shave . . . after that . . . oh, we will need lots of time to talk about what else I know."

Saroj expected that he would get up and take a bath and shave and become Mr. Perfect, but instead he told her to "get the fuck out and never come back again."

Saroj did get out but promptly went back the next day and the next. After a week she took a tape of Ustad Amjad Ali Khan and played it to him. She brought along a copy of *Malgudi Days* and read it out loud to him.

He took a bath, but didn't shave, didn't give up alcohol.

One day Saroj made some *pulao* with her famous potato *raita* for him and he had three servings. They started building a tenuous friendship.

Besides Avi, Saroj also got close to Avi's mother, whom she called every other day to give a report on how her son was doing. Mrs. Veturi was delighted that someone was taking care of her son and later on, when Avi told his parents he was marrying Saroj, Mrs. Veturi had been overjoyed and believed that it was because of her that Avi had ended up with such a wonderful wife.

"Your mother said you should quit smoking," Saroj told him one day.

"You are not my wife and my mother can go hang herself," Avi responded, but two weeks after Saroj had asked him to quit, he did. He went cold turkey and to his own amazement didn't turn into a monster as he went into nicotine withdrawal.

"You shouldn't drink until after eight in the evening," Saroj announced after he quit smoking.

"And why should I wait that long? I am on leave."

"Because I need you to take me here and there. It's a beautiful summer," Saroj replied.

Avi had been defenseless. She was the sweetest woman he ever met. She smiled when he barked at her, she coaxed him and cajoled him. She was his miracle. He lost his arm, but he found her, and somehow the trade seemed even to him, then.

The first time he kissed her, it had been innocent, a thank-you, and that was when it struck him that he wanted to marry Saroj. But she was so young, just nineteen. He couldn't expect her to spend her life with a twenty-nine-year-old one-armed man.

They were at a *tambola* party the Saturday they decided to marry. Avi was nursing a scotch while she was drinking a glass of water. After several weeks of rumination, Avi had decided that it was time to tell Saroj it was over. This could hardly go on. People were already talking and Saroj's reputation was going down the gutter each time she was seen with him. He was ruining her chances of finding a suitable husband, as everyone was assuming they both were an item, which they were definitely not.

The arrival of his posting orders to Jorhat from Udhampur seemed to be a sign from a higher power. He was going to move; this was the best time to end their undefined relationship.

"They posted me out," he told Saroj calmly, "Jorhat. I leave next week."

"Jorhat? In Assam? Oh, all those mosquitoes," Saroj said and then sighed deeply. "Well, I guess we'll have to get married right away. I was thinking of doing it in Hyderabad, that's where we're from, but now there's no time. We could get married at the army temple. We can have a reception right here, at the mess. What do you think?"

Avi was stunned. He downed his entire scotch and then looked at her suspiciously. "Maybe I've been drinking too much, but did you say you want to get married to me?"

Saroj tittered nervously. "Yes, dummy. I've been waiting and waiting and now you're talking about leaving. I can't just come with you. As open-minded as she is, Mummy will kill me if I go to Jorhat without a *mangalsutra*."

"Saro, I only have one arm," Avi said, holding up his stump. "This is it. I can't ask you to tie yourself down to a cripple."

"No, Avi, you're not a cripple. If, say, I didn't have an arm, would you love me less?"

He had never told her he loved her or made any kind of promise, but she had assumed and her innocence drew him in some more. She was naive, unaware of the trust she gave and generated.

"No, I wouldn't," Avi said. "I'll talk to your mother . . . ah . . ."

"She's right there, talking to Major Jaggi. You could talk to her now," Saroj coaxed and the last of his reserves melted.

Vasu raised her eyebrows all the way to her hairline. "You're almost ten years older than her," she told Avi as they sat in some privacy in the army mess's garden.

"I know, I know all that. But Major Rao, she is my miracle, and I don't want to let her go," Avi said sincerely.

"This is your decision, yours and hers. I don't believe in interfering in Saroj's life. But she is very young, used to too much, and when things get hard, I don't know, I just don't know," Vasu cautioned.

"Things are already hard," he said, looking at his lost arm. "She pulled me out. I am hopelessly in love. I don't want to go to Jorhat or anywhere else without her."

Vasu smiled and put her hand on his. "Then by all means, take her. But make sure she finishes her degree. She has one more year to go, I am sure she can transfer to a college in Jorhat."

"Thanks, Major Rao."

"Call me Vasu, we are family now."

And so Sarojini Rao became Sarojini Veturi. She never finished her bachelor's in sciences and ignored her mother's advice that she get a job and stand on her own feet. Saroj wanted to be a wife and mother, she didn't want a career, and Avi said that he didn't care if Saroj worked or not. And in those days it hadn't been an issue. In those days, it was Vasu who was the strange one, working for a living instead of being ensconced in a house taking care of her husband and children.

But now, when Saroj saw her family going off to work, having lives of their own, businesses they were part of, a world beyond the confines of their homes, she felt stifled within the boundaries she'd set for herself. A career would have allowed her access to the outside world, would have given her something else beyond the barren existence of unwanted wife and unneeded mother.

But twenty-twenty hindsight is always so clear. Then, she had been in a great hurry to get married and have children. She didn't want the sorry excuse of her mother's life; in love with a man who was married to another woman, working for a living in a man's world, and not even having the comfort of a close relationship with her only child.

That wasn't going to happen to her, Saroj vowed to herself when she got pregnant, just a few months after she married Avi. They were both ecstatic about her pregnancy and when they had a girl, they were overjoyed. Saroj was positive that this new person in her life would be her friend, they would be as close as mothers and daughters could be.

Avi wanted to name their first daughter Shobhana, after his favorite grandmother, who'd passed away when he was a teenager. And in her happiness, Saroj didn't object. She happily ignored the various other names she wanted for her daughter, modern names, with class, but because it mattered to Avi, she embraced the name Shobhana. She shortened it to a more contemporary-sounding Shobha immediately.

Those were the happiest days of Saroj's life, and in all the years that followed, Saroj found she couldn't surpass the joy she'd felt then.

Avi was posted to Jorhat and Saroj relentlessly complained about the mosquito-infested backwater stuck in the easternmost part of India, but later on, after moving to the United States, she would've happily lived in a swamp in Jorhat for the rest of her life.

The army accommodations in Jorhat were meager, but sufficient for Saroj's small family. Across the street from the army houses was a tea plantation. Saroj and Avi would take little Shobha for a walk in her pink pram bought by Vasu under Saroj's eagle eye.

"Pink? How much of a stereotype is that?" Vasu had asked when they stood in a baby store in Jorhat city. There were five prams to choose from—blue, green, checkered black and red, white with pale yellow flowers, and pink. Saroj picked the pink one with pink lace.

"*My* baby," she said patting her large belly. "And I want *that.*"

"What if it's a boy?" Vasu cautioned.

"It'll be a girl," Saroj said with confidence. There was no doubt in her mind. It would be a girl. Avi wanted a girl.

"Just like you," he would say, stroking her belly.

Oh, it had been such a honeymoon, and even now Saroj was convinced that if they had stayed in India instead of moving to America, they would still be happy.

After Shobha was born, Avi became restless. He got a letter from an old and close friend. Vikram had attended Avi and Saroj's wedding and Saroj had liked him. He was so much fun, easygoing, still single, flirting with everyone, including Vasu. But after that letter, Saroj started to resent Vikram.

"He mentioned something when he came for the wedding," Avi said when Saroj told him that this was all very sudden.

"So he came all the way from San Francisco to ask you to ... what? Leave the army and join his company?" Saroj was speechless. This was the life she wanted. She was an army officer's wife. She was still in the same circles she had grown up in, she had a baby, and her mother was posted in Baroda, at the other end of the country. It was perfect!

"What the hell am I doing here?" Avi raged, moving his stump. "This is all I am left with. The army gave me this and what else? No medal, no nothing. Just some extra money in my paycheck, as if that will take care of ... No, Saro, I want to do this. Vikram thinks I am the right person to help him run the company. I need this and I need your support because I can't do this without you."

If he had said that he expected her support or had ordered her to do his bidding, Saroj would probably have protested, but he said that he needed her, that he couldn't make it without her, and Saroj's resolve weakened.

Shobha was barely a year old when Saroj packed her family bags and moved to the United States. Her resentment toward the country started during the long interminable flight. It seemed like it would never end. They flew from New Delhi to London and then from London to New York and then from New York to San Francisco.

Avi was staring at the tall buildings in San Francisco with stars in his eyes. Saroj was not impressed. She wanted to go home where she could chat with the milkman in the morning and buy vegetables in her front yard from the vendors. She didn't want to learn to drive a car on the other side of the road and didn't understand the concept of supermarkets. When she turned on the radio, Kishore Kumar and Lata Mangeshkar were not singing. It was all so damn hard.

As if that wasn't bad enough, Avi was gone most of the day and came home late in the night. Saroj was left alone with Shobha and no one to talk to. It was not like how it is now with a hundred Indian restaurants all over the Bay Area and an Indian grocery store within sneezing distance. There was nothing in those days.

The loneliness bit into her. She made a few friends, wives of other Indian men, but it wasn't the same, it wasn't enough. When she stepped out of her house there was nothing familiar, no vegetable vendor selling coriander and mint, no coconut vendor selling coconut water. It was a bland place they'd moved to, this country with no *masala*. And then there were the looks. Oh, how everyone stared at her, at her saris and her *salwar-kameez*. She heard snickers and comments, she was constantly afraid of foreigners, but they were there everywhere. And technically she was the foreigner; the white people belonged to this country. Saroj hated it.

"This isn't working," she burst out in tears one day, yelling at Avi. "I'm here all day, stuck in the house, and you're gone, having fun."

"Fun? Saroj, I'm working all the time. I'm trying to make something out of my company . . . our company. This is yours, too, Saroj," Avi said, trying to placate.

Things were going from bad to worse and then they became terrible when Saroj got pregnant again.

"I want to go home," she announced. "I want to have this baby in India."

"Where in India?" Avi asked. "With Vasu?"

The idea of being with Vasu while she was pregnant didn't have much appeal but Saroj persisted that it was Avi who wasn't letting her go home. She maintained that fiction for a long time, even though she knew that there was nothing to go back to. But India was still home. The United States never became home. It was a foreign land, and even though Shobha and Devi said they were American, Saroj tried to instill Indian values in them. In Shobha she succeeded to a point, but with Devi . . . well the proof was in the *payasam*. Hadn't she just tried to kill herself? If only they had stayed in India, things would have been different, better, Saroj was sure of it.

. . .

A whole week passed and the "incident" seemed unreal now, even though in the back of her mind there was a constant struggle. One Devi wanted to stay home and enjoy cooking and not talking, while the other Devi wanted action, wanted to get into that bathtub again and end it once more.

She had her first meeting with Dr. Mara Berkley, who seemed unhappy about Devi's silence, but took it in stride and asked Devi yes-or-no questions. She was pleased about the cooking.

"You know, those who think about death, don't cook," Dr. Berkley told her sympathetically. "Inside you there's something that wants to live and taste and explore."

Devi didn't know how to explain to the good doctor that it was to avoid looking inside her that she started cooking. It was her only escape from the silence outside, and the chaos within. It was the only way to not think about the answers to the questions everyone in her family was always asking, even if they didn't open their mouths.

"Have you started a journal?" the doctor asked and seemed very excited when Devi nodded.

Could she really call Saroj's old notebook a journal? Or was it a recipe book? Or was it Saroj's little secret unraveled? All those recipes she called her own were maybe not; at least one of them wasn't. One of the recipes actually belonged to a person called Girija.

While Dr. Berkley spoke with Avi, who had brought her to the doctor's office, Devi waited in Avi's Jeep, wondering if it would really be a crime if she started the car and drove away. She didn't have her credit cards or her driver's license, but so many people didn't and they got along just fine. Before she could tempt herself any further, Avi came back, a smile adorning his face.

"Do you want to drive, *beta*?" he asked, and when Devi raised an eyebrow suspiciously, he pulled out his wallet and handed Devi her driver's license.

It had taken Devi five tries at the DMV ten years ago to get her license, yet it was now that it made her most happy to hold it in her hands. This was freedom, she could go away if she wanted to, anywhere.

She felt like celebrating her newly found liberty.

Growing up, Devi's memories of hot-hot *biriyani* were associated with special occasions. On Saroj and Avi's wedding anniversaries, Saroj would make *biriyani;* on birthdays, she would make *biriyani.* It was her standard "happy news" dish. Shobha's marriage has been arranged, let's make *biriyani.*

Entering the kitchen, her driver's license ensconced safely in the front pocket of her Levi's, Devi felt an itch for *biriyani.* She put her hand inside her pocket and ran her fingers over the plastic texture of the license and smiled. Did this mean she was all right and that she could move back into her own place? She knew her father had canceled her lease and wanted her to stay with them while she recuperated. He had told her not to worry about anything but getting better. But all Devi really wanted to do was get away from the stifling presence of her entire family.

And what the hell was wrong with Girish and Shobha? Earlier it would take mammoth planning sessions between Saroj and Shobha before they'd come over for dinner or lunch, together. Now, for the past week, they'd come every night, together or around the same time.

As if it wasn't bad enough having Vasu, Mama, and Daddy hovering, now she had to also deal with Shobha's not-so-sharp remarks and Girish's overwhelming concern. Yes, she was going to run away. Drive down Highway 1, sit on a vista point, and see the ocean slam into the rocks below. Go to Sausalito and look back at San Francisco. Do anything to get away from this house and the people in it.

"Do you want me to cook tonight?" Saroj asked her standard question. She tried every day to take the kitchen away from Devi's grasp, and every day Devi shook her head and got to work.

Devi pulled out a sticky notepad that Saroj kept inside a drawer for making her shopping lists and started writing on it. When she was done, she handed it to Saroj, who quirked an eyebrow.

"I don't think your father is very fond of prawns, Devi," she said, not quite sure what Devi was planning to concoct this night.

Devi just turned her back to Saroj and started attacking the herb pot's coriander section.

. . .

If Devi didn't feel so suicidal already, now would be a good time to start feeling that way. Everyone, even Shobha, was being nice and kind. It was cloying, as if she'd eaten too many sticky-sweet jalebis.

Worst of course was Saroj. The woman couldn't leave her alone in the kitchen to do as she pleased. In the days after the "incident," Devi completely took over cooking and had no clue why. Food was an essential; thinking about what to cook for lunch during breakfast, and what to cook for dinner during lunch, kept her mind busy. And during dinner, well, during dinner she thought about what to cook the next day.

If she couldn't use her tongue for talking, she felt she had to use it for something else and her taste buds, since the "incident," had come alive. Food, which had been merely meals before, objects of sustenance, had become objects of art.

"If you keep cooking like this, I'm going to bloat up completely," Avi said, grinning from ear to ear. He was very proud that Devi was working her way out of a postsuicidal slump through cooking. And then there was the food: it was as if almost dying had rearranged her genes and given her an instinctive insight into cuisine. She knew, she just seemed to know what to add to what to make the food taste just right.

"This is excellent *biriyani* . . . the spices, Devi . . . just wonderful," Vasu said, smacking her lips in satisfaction during dinner.

Devi was pleased the Cajun prawn *biriyani* was receiving so much praise. She stroked the plastic flatness of her driver's license again and wondered if this would be the last meal she made at home.

She picked up a prawn and carefully removed the shell and then bit into the lush pink flesh. Would this be the last meal she ate? She wiped her hands on a napkin and decided to stop eating. As good as the *biriyani* tasted, it also made her nauseous.

Saroj seemed to be enjoying the food, and that surprised as well as pleased Devi. Mama never ate anything but Indian food. Once in a while she'd try Thai, but her heart was with good old-fashioned south Indian food. Growing up, Saroj served only Indian food in the house. There were no two ways about it with her.

"You can eat all the nonsense you like outside this house. In here, I will only make *good* Indian food," Saroj told her family.

At least she didn't insist they become vegetarian like a lot of Indians abroad did. Devi couldn't imagine how her life would be if she couldn't eat salmon mousse or *rogan josh*.

"If we were in India, this would've never happened," Saroj told Avi while they were clearing up the dishes after dinner. "Girls don't commit suicide like this in India, not those from good families at least."

Avi always helped with cleaning up. Even though he was a hand short, he did what he could. Saroj couldn't fault him on that, but that didn't stop her from complaining about how slow he was, or how he put the dishes in the wrong place. There were serious problems in their marriage, but she didn't want to talk about those problems. Fussing about small household matters was easier than delving into the deeper, darker aspects of her relationship with Avi.

"No matter where we were, Devi would still be Devi," Avi pointed out as he placed a casserole with Devi's shrimp *biriyani* on the kitchen counter. "Save some for lunch tomorrow."

"Okay," Saroj said, tasting some of the *biriyani* and sighing in pleasure. She hated to admit it, but Devi was cooking like a veteran chef. It had been a week since she'd been released from the hospital and now everyone was afraid that they were putting on weight. Girish and Shobha were coming for dinner every night, the family was sticking together, ensuring that the "mute in the kitchen"—as Shobha called Devi—would have all the support she needed.

"What did she do with this *biriyani*? It tastes so good. I never would've thought prawns in this would work, but *she* knows. I can't understand it," Saroj said as she ate some more of the *biriyani* before putting it inside Tupperware and sealing it shut.

Avi shrugged.

"She never cooked before, but now she wants to cook all the

time, like my food is not good enough. What do you think?" Saroj was babbling and didn't really expect any answer.

"And she won't talk. It has been a week since she came back home and still, she says nothing. This is your doing. You spoiled her so," Saroj continued as she stacked dirty dishes in the dishwasher.

"And maybe if you were a little more compassionate, Devi would have come to us, not found a knife to hack through her problems," Avi retorted angrily and then calmed visibly. "Damn it, Saroj, this is no one's fault. It just happened. Deal with it."

"Deal with it?" Tears sprang into her eyes. "My baby . . . just . . ." She was sobbing now, and Avi flung the hand towel he was holding on the counter.

"I can't stand with this constant *rona-dhona*. You need to get a grip and stop crying at the drop of a—" Avi stopped speaking, raised his hands in defeat, and walked out into the living room in frustration while Saroj stared out the kitchen window, bewildered and hurt by his tone of voice and his words.

A long time ago when she cried, Avi would put his arm around her and cajole her into a good mood. But sometime in the past three decades that changed. It used to be he couldn't stand it when she cried; now he couldn't stand her when she cried.

In the living room her family sat without speaking to each other. Her mother was sitting next to Devi who was watching the news on CNN, while Shobha stood on the stairs with her cell phone glued to her ear. Girish was reading the newspaper, and Avi was lighting his pipe. He had given up cigarettes but in the past three years, since he'd retired, he smoked the pipe occasionally. Saroj tried to stop him, but gave up after the first few arguments.

Is this what she wanted?

She had done it all perfectly. Married a financially viable man, had two beautiful children, and had seen one of them married, while the other . . . well, she saved her younger daughter's life.

Yes, she was where she wanted to be, but this was not how she'd expected to feel when she watched her family. She hadn't thought that seeing them all succeed would make her feel like a failure.

"Damn it, I have to go to work," Shobha said, flinging her cell phone on the leather couch next to Vasu. "Sorry, G'ma, it's just . . . those fucking idiots. I have to go."

"It's late, *beta,* can't it wait until tomorrow morning?" Saroj asked.

"No, Mama, it can't," Shobha muttered, not even looking at Saroj.

"Shobha, I know, but . . ."

Shobha looked up at Saroj in exasperation. "I'm a VP of a company. I have responsibilities. Since you know nothing about working in the real world maybe you should keep out of it."

"Fine, leave," Girish said lightly, as if Shobha hadn't been speaking in a loud voice, as if everything was business as usual, which unfortunately it was.

"How will you get home?" Shobha asked Girish as she opened the front door.

"I'll get home," Girish said and went back to his newspaper.

Shobha said her good-byes hastily and left, slamming the large mahogany front door on her way out.

Saroj's heart sank. She had stood by her man while he worked insane hours to set up a company. He hadn't done it on his own. She'd helped, hadn't she? She'd kept his home life happy, kept him content, kept his children out of trouble. She knew what having a career was all about and she knew that sometimes work slid into the nighttime. She understood Shobha had to leave, she'd just hoped . . . She shook her head as the tears sprang up again. There was no point in crying. No one in her family respected her. She didn't have a job, had never worked, and they always reminded her of that.

She went back into the kitchen to finish cleaning up.

"I'm sorry about Shobha," Girish said, following her in. He pulled out a glass from a cabinet and filled it with water from the fridge.

"You don't have to apologize," Saroj said with a half smile. He'd never bothered to be so polite before. This was a first.

"I know . . . but she'll never apologize," Girish said and shrugged. "She's busy. It's the end of the quarter . . . oh, what the hell, she's always busy and always rude and always angry. I guess you're right, I shouldn't apologize for her because if I did, I'd have to quit my job and take up apologizing full time."

Saroj bit her lip. She didn't know what to say. He was saying something bad about *her* daughter and a part of her wanted to jump to Shobha's defense. On the other hand, Girish was Shobha's husband and Saroj felt that a husband of all people had the right to badmouth his own wife.

"I'm planning to ask Devi to give me a ride home. The doctor thought it wouldn't hurt for her to spend a little time on her own. So Avi and I thought it wouldn't be a bad idea," he told Saroj. "Maybe that'll . . . I don't know . . ."

"Is that okay, you think?" Saroj asked, concerned and nervous. "She hasn't driven since or been alone. It should . . . nothing will happen, will it?"

"No, no," Girish said. "She seems to be pretty much back to normal, except for the talking and the cooking. And the doctor did say that those who cook are not very inclined to commit suicide."

"Did she?" Saroj smiled. "Devi does cook so well. Thanks, Girish, for everything."

"Good . . . well . . . I'll see what I can do," Girish said and sauntered out of the kitchen with his glass of water.

Saroj went back to her cleaning, her heart feeling just a little light. Someone had noticed her, someone had paid attention, and for today, that was enough.

~∘

DEVI'S RECIPE
CAJUN PRAWN *BIRIYANI*
Day 8 after coming home from the hospital

The classic recipes are goat, lamb, vegetable, and/or chicken biriyani. But when I was in New Orleans, at this restaurant, they served Louisiana barbecue shrimp, which was simply delicious. When I asked the waiter what was in the shrimp sauce, he rattled off a number of spices (rosemary, thyme, basil, oregano, et cetera) and so, I went with memory.

I marinated the raw prawns in mashed garlic, rosemary, basil, oregano, thyme, sage, paprika, black pepper, white pepper, cayenne, and onion powder, along with a dash of Worcestershire sauce.

I decided to cook the rice in the pressure cooker, always quick and easy. I heated some ghee in the pressure cooker, added crushed cloves, cardamom, and cinnamon, and a bay leaf for a minute or so. Then I added some onions and fried until the onions became golden brown. Then went in the rice, and enough water, and I closed the pressure cooker. The rice was ready in ten minutes. In a separate pan, I sautéed the marinated prawns in butter, along with extra chopped garlic and the marinade, and added them to the cooked rice. I garnished it with chopped fresh coriander and voilà, Cajun prawn biriyani. I served it with some regular cucumber raita.

Mama had been so sure that Daddy would hate prawns but I saw him clean out each one on his plate and even get a second helping. Sometimes we forget why we don't like some things and then when we try them again, we realize that we had been wrong.

Giving Serious Thought to Adultery

Girish was a classical music buff and in the beginning of their marriage, Shobha joined him for a few musical events and lectures. Once he dragged her to a basic violin seminar in the hope that she would start appreciating the string instrument (his favorite) as he did.

It had been six months after they returned from their honeymoon in Hawaii, where they spent most of their time separately. Girish went scuba diving and hiking around the Na Pali Coast, while Shobha drank colored drinks with umbrellas in them and read a good book about advanced databases and a bad one about a schizophrenic woman, a paperback she picked up at the hotel's gift shop.

"Music is life, Shobha. There is music in everything. Don't you agree?" Girish asked on their way to the seminar at Stanford. Shobha gave him a smile and nodded, trying to infuse as much enthusiasm into her demeanor as she could. After all, technically, they were still newlyweds.

The man giving the seminar was a frail old gentleman with a deep London accent who kept waving his hands as he spoke. His brown pants hung loosely on his hips and Shobha was sure that one more vigorous gesticulation with his hands and the pants would drop. Needless to say, she didn't pay much attention to the lecture. But something did catch her wandering mind. Apparently a violin has four strings designed for the notes: A, D, E, G. You can get other notes, too, by using fingers to shorten the effective length of these strings.

The old man in his accented voice told the audience, "To get the F out, you will need to actively finger the G-string."

First, Shobha just stared at the man and then looked around to see how everyone was reacting; everyone seemed serious and intent on what the man would say next, some were even taking notes. But when the old man repeated how one could get the F out, Shobha started to laugh softly.

"What the hell is so funny?" Girish asked in a tight whisper.

"Didn't you hear him?" Shobha asked, tears brimming in her eyes as she tried to stop laughter from spilling out of her.

"What?" Girish demanded impatiently.

"You have to finger the G to get the F out," Shobha whispered loudly, cracking up yet again.

Girish didn't get it, but then again he never got it. The joke remained as elusive to Girish as did Shobha's G-spot.

As Shobha drove the Audi on 101 to get to her office in Cupertino, her mind whizzed with the possibilities. It was almost ten at night. At the office, it was just going to be Vladimir, Pavan, who was the product manager, and herself. There was some problem with the product that was to be released soon and Shobha wanted to brief herself on how long it would take to fix the bug so that she could present the case in front of the executive committee the next day.

She hoped the product launch would not be delayed; if it was, this would be the second time in two quarters, and Shobha knew that she'd need to start looking for a new job and soon.

Success was not as firmly lodged in her pocket as everyone assumed. She'd climbed to the position of vice president, but she still managed to fuck things up. She should've been worried about her job, about the product launch, about the end of the quarter, but all Shobha could think of was Vladimir's callused hands and thick fingers. Oh, he'd be able to find her G-spot. She was sure of that.

To die . . . to die without ever having an orgasm during sex, damn it, she wanted more out of life. Devi, now, Devi probably had had several thousand orgasms thanks to her hundreds of disreputable boyfriends. If Shobha killed herself today, there would be nothing to say. *She never had an O-moment,* that's what they would say. Worse, they'd think that she'd lived the perfect, happy life and now . . . ah, she was dead, what a waste.

She parked in the outside parking lot, scared of going into the basement at this hour of the night. A heady feeling inundated her as she raced up the stairs and slipped her key card into the designated slot. There was a bleeping sound and the security light next to the door changed from red to green.

Vladimir and Pavan were sitting in the server room, their faces glued to a computer screen.

"Okay, what's the problem?" Shobha asked without preamble as she stepped inside the room and the glass door squeaked shut behind her.

"Looks like we might have found it . . . ," Pavan began sheepishly in his heavy south Indian accent and then shrugged. "Still, it will take at least a week."

"Right," Shobha said, breathless. Vladimir was smiling at her. His cotton shirt was unbuttoned almost to midchest and the jeans were still as snug as ever.

"Okay, one of you give me the rundown and let's see what we can do," Shobha said and sat down at a desk. She opened the drawer at the desk, pulled out a writing pad, and rummaged for a pen in her purse.

"All right, let's start." She was scribbling on the writing pad even before Vladimir opened his mouth to tell her what was wrong and how they were planning to fix it.

It was almost eleven by the time they were done. They had come up with a plan of action and how to present the scenario to the executive committee the next day.

"I could eat a pizza and have a cold beer," Pavan said with a sigh. "But I have to go home and eat *dal* and *sabzi*."

Pavan had gone to India three months ago and like many of his Indian friends had come back to the United States with a wife. The marriage was arranged by his parents; he only saw his wife's picture and spoke with her on the phone before the wedding.

"Well, then maybe you and I can go and get a beer," Vladimir suggested to Shobha after Pavan left. "I don't have a little wife waiting for me at home."

"No, I should go home," Shobha said, her reluctance obvious.

"Come with me," Vladimir said playfully. It could be just a friendly gesture, not a come-on. Shobha wasn't sure.

An O-moment was not worth a professional nightmare, Shobha thought, and shook her head. And then there was the chance that Vladimir was a real duffer in bed and that accent was just a pickup line and nothing more.

"My husband is waiting for me," Shobha lied easily. "I'll see you tomorrow."

She didn't start hyperventilating until she got inside the car. What the fuck was going on? Shobha thought angrily. It was Devi who'd tried to kill herself, so why the hell did she feel she had to make up for lost time?

Shobha had never thought she'd have an arranged marriage. She'd assumed, like everyone else, that one day she would meet the right man, fall in love, marry him, and have a couple of kids. She'd never doubted her ability to find a husband or have children. Devi and she usually complained about arranged marriage, said that it was for people who were incapable of finding their life partners, losers who were looking for other losers.

Saroj would first try to convince them that arranged marriage was the best way to marry and then would plead that they only fall in love with good boys from the right caste and from good Indian families. Neither Devi nor Shobha thought she'd end up with an Indian in the first place so the matter of caste and family was moot.

Shobha had been at Cal, going through the grind of Berkeley undergrad, when she met him. He was doing his MBA and they met through a friend of a friend. He was not Indian, not from a good family (his mother had two ex-husbands, his father had four ex-wives, and someone, a brother or an uncle, had spent some time in prison for armed robbery), and definitely not what Saroj wanted. He was working for Intel and doing his MBA part time. He was an engineer on the management fast track.

His name was Dave Anderson. He was white, as white as they came, with blond hair, and very blue eyes. He was different from the men Shobha had previously been interested in.

No one at home knew about him. Shobha was living in the dorm and didn't think it was anyone's business that she was seriously dating an American. She'd dated before, had had boyfriends, but that had been innocuous, almost platonic really.

Dave was the first man she had sex with and Shobha admitted that the earth didn't rock and the bells didn't ring. After Dave came Girish, and that didn't turn out to be much of an improvement. But at least she'd been madly in love with Dave.

Dave unfortunately was interested only in sleeping with Shobha and after the first pathetic night of sex, Dave was gone. All of a sudden there were no messages on the answering machine, no phone calls, no nothing. Shobha, at the age of twenty-two, experienced firsthand what it meant to be dumped. She could hardly believe it. Other people got themselves into situations like this, not Shobha Veturi. She mourned for a while and then swore she would never ever get into this relationship business again. Dave made her feel cheap and used and thanks to him Shobha developed a healthy, if racist, attitude toward the alleged loose morals of the American white male.

When Saroj started talking about arranged marriage a few years later, Shobha said, "Yes, go find me a boy and I'll marry him."

Her father tried to dissuade her.

"You're so young, Shobha, you'll meet someone. What's the rush?" Avi said, but Shobha wouldn't budge. It was time to be married (after all, she was twenty-seven and by all Indian standards past ready for marriage) and since falling in love was out of the question, there was only one alternative left: arranged marriage.

Girish was also not the type to walk into an arranged marriage and his parents weren't the type to force the matter, but it happened all the same. Girish's paternal grandmother was adamant that the girl be a Telugu Brahmin and that the marriage be arranged. The woman was dying of cancer and Girish, who'd never had more than a few short-term relationships with women, thought there would be no harm in getting married the arranged way. After all, they had been doing it for years in India, and it seemed to be working well for all parties involved.

Saroj met Girish's grandmother at the *seemantham* of the pregnant daughter of a common friend. Between piling fruit in the lap of the girl in her seventh month of pregnancy and eating sweet *payasam,* Saroj and Maha Lakshmi got talking about their respective daughters and grandsons. Shobha and Girish seemed like a pair made in heaven, and when their horoscopes were matched discreetly, both Maha Lakshmi and Saroj were convinced that as matches went, this one was near perfect.

For two independent, well-educated, non-Indian-raised people, Shobha and Girish walked into arranged marriage with blind-eyed optimism. It could've worked, Shobha was sure, if only they had children.

Sex, which had never been the cornerstone of their marriage, was now a rare event that occurred only when they felt that they had to do something about their marriage. Sometimes it was Shobha who felt guilty and instigated their insipid physical relationship. Sometimes, it was Girish. In neither case were the unions satisfying for either of them.

They never talked about their current situation or discussed if it could be remedied. They both let things slide into normalcy and soon neither was upset or worried that they had no marriage and no real future together.

Then one day the unthinkable entered Shobha's mind, and it wouldn't leave. It started as a cliché: how many times had she seen a movie where the wife found an earring in her husband's car/coat/office/person that belonged to the *other woman?*

It wasn't like she ever got into Girish's car alone. She didn't have reason to when he wasn't there, but that day had been different all around. Shobha drove out of the driveway only to be hit by a kid in a beat-up Toyota (what impertinence). Though no one was hurt, Shobha's Audi looked like it had been in a small brawl and needed AAA assistance. Shobha was in a rush, and Girish didn't have to be at the university until later in the afternoon.

"I'll call the garage, you take my car," he suggested, dangling his car keys in front of her. "I can always walk to work or get a cab."

Shobha didn't have to be asked twice. She dumped her laptop and leather bag behind the driver's seat and drove away after saying a hasty thank-you to Girish. Nothing happened all day. She got through her meetings, did her work, everything was normal. Normal until she went back home.

Papers from a file she'd brought from work spilled out from the passenger's seat. Shobha bent down to grab them from under the seat and that was when she saw it.

A small, round, pearl earring encased in gold.

It belonged to an Indian, no doubt about that. The gold encasing the pearl was twenty-two karat, not fourteen or eighteen, and only an Indian would go around wearing twenty-two-karat extra-shiny gold. She didn't even think that the earring could be a colleague's, a friend's, a stranger's whom Girish gave a ride to. She simply knew that it belonged to the *other woman,* the one who was having the good sex with her husband.

As soon as she saw Girish, who was in the kitchen, immersed in a book, sipping coffee, she asked him, point blank, accusation rippling through her words, "Whose earring is this?"

Girish looked up and shrugged vaguely. "Should I know whose it is?"

"This was in *your* car," Shobha informed him, wagging the earring in front of his face.

Girish shrugged again, just as vaguely as he did before. "So what?" he asked, going back to his book.

"So whose is this? Someone special?" Shobha asked, incredulous that he was unmoved, anger making her voice quiver.

Of all the reactions she'd imagined, this was the wrong one.

Girish burst out laughing. "Good God, Shobha, do we have to be part of a bad Hindi movie where you come and ask me if I have a . . . what do they call it in Telugu, *chinna illu*, small house, where I keep my mistress?"

When he put it that way it did sound ridiculous.

"Well, you're right of course, who'd want to be *your* mistress?" Shobha said, hiding her doubts behind suddenly developed nonchalance. With the same affected casualness, she put her sensible black-shoe-clad foot on the trash-can lever and tossed the earring on top of a blackened banana peel before closing the can.

And almost instantly she regretted throwing the earring away and not keeping it as evidence. Because once sown, those doubts wouldn't die. She was convinced, or a part of her was convinced, that Girish was having an affair, and with an Indian woman. Another part of her was convinced that Girish was not having an affair with anyone and Shobha just wanted him to, so that her irresponsible thoughts about her newly hired Ukrainian engineer would seem less irresponsible.

"I think he's doing it with someone else, G'ma," Shobha told Vasu when she was visiting.

"Shush, Shobha. You're imagining things. Girish is a decent man," Saroj admonished, immediately taking the son-in-law's side.

They were in the kitchen. Saroj was making her famous (all of Saroj's dishes were somehow her famous this or that) *rajma,* which she made with dried kidney beans, not the tasteless ones you got in a can that the lazy Indians in the United States used.

Vasu, who was sipping a hot cup of Darjeeling tea—Saroj kept it stocked just for her visits—didn't skip a beat at Shobha's declaration.

"Why would you think that?" Vasu asked calmly.

"I just know," Shobha said, uncomfortable talking about the pearl earring she'd found in Girish's car. It was too cheesy, too much of a soap opera, and she was embarrassed that it was something as silly as an earring that had triggered this line of thought.

"Is it because you don't do *it* with him often enough that you think someone else is?" Vasu asked, looking Shobha right in the eye.

Oh, that was a little too much on target.

"G'ma, whose side are you on?" she demanded.

"On yours," Vasu said without hesitation. "And that's why I think you should ask yourself why such an idea is even lurking in your mind. Saroj, you've been married more than three decades; have you *ever* thought that Avi was cheating on you?"

"Absolutely not," Saroj replied instantly.

"There," Vasu told Shobha. "See, that is trust. They may not have the perfect marriage, but there is trust."

After that the conversation went to hell in the proverbial hand-basket because Saroj wanted to know what Vasu meant by *they may not have the perfect marriage* and Shobha did not bring up the topic of Girish's alleged infidelity ever again.

But the doubts lingered. Was it a student? A friend of hers? A friend of his? A married woman? A single woman? A call girl? (Did they have Indian call girls in the United States who wore twenty-two-karat gold when they met their clients?)

And because she wondered if Girish was slipping it inside some woman at a Motel 6, Shobha felt no (or only very little) guilt when she imagined Vladimir's hands on her body. The sensations she was sure would be exquisite. Sex, the word had meant nothing to her for all these years, but now that she was deprived and there was a red-blooded male who wanted to take her in every which way *she* could imagine, sex had started to mean the world.

Shobha used her key to go inside the house, which was dark except for the small night lamp glittering green against the white walls of the living room.

It was almost midnight and Girish was still not home. Shobha wondered if she should call his cell phone and check on him, make sure he had a ride back from her parents' house, and then decided against it. If he didn't have a ride back and she called, he'd expect her to come and pick him up and she didn't feel like doing that.

She changed quickly into the T-shirt she slept in and then, when she still didn't hear any Girish sounds, snuck into her husband's study. She had been going there often since the "pearl earring" discovery, rifling through his papers, checking his e-mail (his password was always just GIRISH—what a nightmare for his IT department), and sometimes even reading his research papers. She was convinced that somewhere here was evidence of Girish's adultery, of his imperfectness.

Everyone always told her that Girish was wonderful, a perfect gentleman, and therefore a perfect husband. Even Shobha's closest friend, Jaya, remarked how perfect Girish was.

Jaya once visited with her husband, Akhil, from New Jersey, and Girish had been a wonderful host, as he always was. After that, whenever Shobha complained about Girish, Jaya would remind her that Girish unlike Akhil didn't have a bad temper causing him to throw things and yell the place down. Akhil hadn't hit her—and by God, let him try, she would have his balls in a blender—but still, Jaya said she would trade husbands any day.

"So bloody what if he can't find your G-spot? Buy a vibrator. I did and it keeps me happy and happy and happy," Jaya instructed.

Shobha gave the vibrator serious consideration, but the idea was simply too classless for her liking.

There was another reason why adultery seemed to be the next imminent event in her life, and that was curiosity. Would Girish care? Would he find out? What would he do if he found out?

She wondered if there would be a *The Grass Is Greener* moment where Cary Grant and Robert Mitchum duel it out for Deborah Kerr. Would Girish turn from stodgy man to loving husband, like Cary Grant? Would there be a Robert Mitchum? Would she stay with Grant or go with Mitchum or find a third man to have another affair with?

She wanted to cheat on Girish. That was a fact. She really, really wanted to, but she felt her vagina closing off every time she thought about it. Years of programming, Saroj's brainwashing, stayed with her. Good Indian girls didn't cheat on their husbands: That was also a fact.

But she was neither good nor truly Indian. Unfortunately, all this deliberation, she knew was for nothing, as the only candidate

for an extracurricular fuck seemed to be Vladimir and he was un-
available for professional reasons. The last thing she needed was a
sexual harassment lawsuit. Since her marriage was pathetic, the
only thing that Shobha truly cared about was her career and she was
definitely not going to fuck with that.

Killing with Kindness

After Shobha stormed out of the house to go back to work, Avi suggested that maybe Devi could drive Girish home. It would be a break for her and she could drive back *alone*. He seemed nervous as he made the offer, and once again Devi felt the mixture of panic and peace she'd experienced while lying in the bathtub a week ago, contemplating how deep to make the cut and where.

"But you'll have to come back right away," Avi warned her, and Devi nodded, carefully, slowly. She didn't want anyone to think she was too eager. But she was, oh, how she was.

She was not the claustrophobic kind. She didn't mind being stuck in an elevator full of people or walking into a crowded room. Things like that didn't bother her, but this, this constant incursion into her privacy, was stifling. Someone was always there, constantly looking, wondering. Did they think she'd try the bathtub again? Didn't they realize that it would never be the bathtub again? Just looking at a bathtub gave her goose bumps. She wasn't sure if she saw a bathtub as an opportunity lost or a slim escape from death.

Death, which had been her mantra for a while now, was still ticking like an unstoppable alarm clock in her head. But along with the ticking were new sounds, the sounds of her father, her mother, G'ma, even Shobha. They were all there, tightly surrounding her, and even though it was suffocating, it was also rewarding. Someone gave a damn and when someone gave a damn, it was harder to kill yourself.

"So, you plan to stay silent . . . for how long?" Girish asked as Devi drove him home.

Devi knew he'd been trying to get her alone to talk to her. She'd heard him whisper with Avi as they both debated whether her driving back alone from Palo Alto to Sunnyvale could be dangerous. She was relieved when she heard her father say that he didn't think there was anything to worry about. Devi seemed normal, almost happy, and he felt that it wouldn't hurt for her to be alone for just a little while. A drive would probably do her good.

Devi couldn't agree more. It was a relief to get away. She looked forward to the drive back, the solitude, the ability to relax and to not worry about what was expected of her. And the opportunity to decide once again in the quiet corners of her mind, without any witnesses or watchers.

"I heard this joke," Girish said watching her carefully. "It's a good one. Want to hear it?"

When Girish didn't get a response from Devi, he leaned back in the seat. "You know, it's not healthy to keep it all bottled in. So, do you want to hear my joke?"

No response.

"Well, I'm going to interpret your silence as a yes," he said, his tone light and casual. He was putting it on, Devi knew.

"So, Dopey, Sleepy, and Grumpy went to a bar with the Pope. They talk about the weather and how the Lakers are doing and then after a couple of beers, Sleepy asks the Pope, 'Pope, Pope, do nuns dress in black and white?' The Pope says, 'Yes.' Then Grumpy asks, 'Pope, Pope, do nuns have beaks?' The Pope shakes his head. 'Pope, Pope, do nuns have webbed feet?' The Pope shakes his head again, looking very confused.

"Sleepy and Grumpy turn to look at Dopey, who is looking really uncomfortable, and start saying, 'Dopey screwed a penguin, Dopey screwed a . . .' Is this not funny?"

It wasn't the joke that was funny; it was the fact that this was the only joke Girish knew and the only one he told. But today Devi wasn't inclined to laugh, because today neither the joke nor the time and place of it seemed appropriate to her.

"I thought it was funny," Girish said and sighed. "If you won't talk, this is going to be one long drive."

They drove silently for maybe forty-five seconds when Girish blew air out. "You now, my wife thinks all my humor is sarcastic and now you won't laugh at my jokes. Things are not going all that well for me. Maybe I should climb into a bathtub and then fall silent. What do you think?"

Devi had half a mind to tell him that if he was planning to get into a bathtub, he should secure the deadbolt on the front door, just in case Saroj did a walk-in.

She kept silent, concentrating on the dark road ahead.

"How would you feel if I tried to kill myself and then turned around and never said a word?"

Oh, trying to make her guilty based on a hypothetical would work. Sure!

"My heart all but stopped when Saroj called," Girish said; all humor had left his voice. "And it still hasn't started beating again. I'm scared. I'm scared to know why you tried to commit suicide. I'm scared of not knowing . . . actually, I'm just plain old scared . . . of you, of what you're doing to yourself and those around you."

Devi gave him no response. Not even a shrug or a nod or a shake of the head. Nothing.

"If things were so bad, why the hell couldn't you just ask for help?"

Devi turned left into the street where Girish and Shobha's house was.

"We're all very worried. *I'm* very worried."

Devi parked the car in their driveway.

"Damn it, Devi . . . you just don't give an inch." His words were delivered irritably. There was anger, sprinkled with concern and helplessness. Devi wanted to say something then, because Girish rarely spurted out emotion like this, but her throat was closed, allowing no words to get by.

Girish didn't even say good night as he got out of the car and slammed the Jeep's passenger door shut behind him. Devi didn't wait to see him open the front door before hastily backing out of the driveway.

She started driving aimlessly on 280. It was pitch dark, but there were still cars, white lights and red lights, sparse, but companions in the dead of the night.

Devi had promised Avi with a nod of her head that she'd drive straight home after dropping Girish off. But even as she'd made the promise she'd known she would need more time alone. She knew her father had been tempted, despite his faith in her, to come along, just to make sure she wouldn't wander away. But Devi knew that he wanted to let go as well. How long could he keep his daughter, suicidal or otherwise, constantly in front of his eyes? Sooner or later he'd have to let go and this was the first step at showing her that he trusted her to live, to accept life and not slide away into despair again.

Devi took the Half Moon Bay exit and then got on Highway 1. She rolled down the windows and let the air run through her hair, making knots and coils that she would have to untangle later, if there was a later. She could smell the Pacific and she could, if she just closed her eyes for a second, hear the waves slamming against the rocks down below.

When Shobha first told Devi about Girish, she'd burst out laughing. It was preposterous. Shobha was not the arranged marriage kind. Actually, Devi wasn't even sure if Shobha was the marrying kind.

"So what's the catch?" Devi asked. Shobha shrugged and said, "It's time. I'm ready and this guy sounds right."

"The guy sounds right?" Devi couldn't believe this was the same Shobha who had stood with her and voiced to Saroj (in an angry and loud voice) their low opinion regarding arranged marriage.

"Look, I'm twenty-seven years old *and* I don't have to give you an explanation," Shobha said caustically.

Devi had been visiting Saroj and Avi and was not surprised to see Shobha's car in the driveway, but was surprised to see a car taking her own spot in the driveway. That car belonged to Girish. He was visiting, along with his parents and grandparents, to finalize the wedding date and make the engagement official with a small informal ceremony. Shobha had insisted Saroj not say anything to Devi until she did.

"How come I get to find out about this now?" Devi demanded as she peered from the kitchen into the living room to see her brother-in-law-to-be.

"It just worked out that way," Shobha said as she set out a tray with Saroj's prized white-with-pink-flowers kettle and tea set.

"You didn't want me to know because you're embarrassed," Devi said smugly. "My big sister is walking into an arranged marriage with . . . and what does the suitable boy do?"

"He's a quantum mechanics professor at Stanford," Shobha said, this with some pride.

"So you're marrying a simple *buddhu* professor?"

"He isn't a dumb professor. He plays squash," Shobha said defensively.

"He plays squash?" Devi smirked. "Is that what you talked about when you spent . . . ah, what? Half an hour talking and figuring out if you'd make the right kind of couple? And what did you say about yourself when he said he plays squash?"

"I told him I ran," Shobha said and then sighed. "Can you not be such a bitch about this?"

"Bitch? Come on, Shobha, you've got to—"

"This is what I want, can you respect that? I don't make comments or pass judgment over your innumerable loser boyfriends, now, do I?" Shobha turned to offense for results.

"I sleep with these losers, I don't marry them," Devi pointed out.

"Regardless, that's your choice and this is mine," Shobha said as she picked up the tray and then set it down. "Can you bring the tea? I'll feel like some country bumpkin if I carry it in."

Devi picked up the tray. "Are you sure?"

"Yeah," Shobha said. "We went out on a few dates and he seems nice. A little stiff but I think we'll get along."

"Why?" Devi wanted to know as she looked once again at the man who would soon be part of her family.

He didn't look anything special. He had a decent face but it wasn't a traffic stopper or anything. He seemed reasonably tall, wore elegant glasses (not geeky ones). But what caught Devi's eyes was the stillness he wore on his face. He seemed calm, like a person who'd made his peace with the universe. He didn't seem to have the ability to have passionate outbursts the way Shobha did. He seemed stable, while Shobha had always been a little volatile.

"We're so different, I think we'll balance each other out," Shobha responded. "He'll stay calm through an earthquake and I can lose it in paradise, so we should fit and work out."

"But what if you don't?" Devi asked.

Shobha quirked an eyebrow and lifted her shoulders lightly before letting them drop. "I'll cross that bridge when I get there."

That night, after Girish and his family left, Shobha and Devi found themselves emptying a bowl of homemade *kulfi* from the freezer while Avi and Saroj slept.

"What about you?" Shobha asked. "Do you think about marriage and children?"

"All the time," Devi said, digging her spoon in to scoop out some *kulfi*. "But it seems like such a risk. You fall in love, you fall out, or worse, he falls out and you're still in. And then you bring children into the equation. I feel it's just too damned risky."

"That's a fatalistic view of relationships," Shobha commented, licking a big chunk of *kulfi* stuck to her spoon.

"Yes it is," Devi agreed. "But I'd like to be a mother. I'd like a son, no daughters for me."

"Well, gee, didn't think you were so old-fashioned. Want a son only? Want to propagate the world with more male specimens and the Veturi last name, huh?"

Devi grinned. "Not that way. Daughters just seem to be more trouble than sons. Look at how we relate with Mama and how she relates with G'ma. Disaster! I want a son, less chance of fuckups."

"I'm afraid my children will grow up to be serial killers," Shobha said, and Devi looked up from her *kulfi*, puzzled.

"Why?" she asked and then swallowed a big lump of ice cream.

"I don't know. I'm scared I'll be a terrible mother," Shobha said, laughing a little.

"What's all this noise?" They didn't even notice Saroj until she was in the kitchen in a pink nightgown with little light blue roses. "Why are you both still up?"

"Oh, I'm going home," Devi said, standing up. "How about you?"

Shobha nodded as well. "Yeah, me, too."

"No, sit," Saroj insisted. "I'm here. I'm awake. You ate all the *kulfi?*"

"It was very good," Devi said.

Immediately Saroj smiled and said, "Yes, it was. Avi's favorite. Before we got married I made it for him all the time."

"Trapped him with *kulfi?*" Shobha asked as she got up and started to look for her purse.

Saroj laughed. "What were you both talking about?"

"Children," Devi said.

"Oh yes, I would love grandchildren. Shobha, don't wait too long, *hanh?* Have those children soon. Devi will probably never have children."

"Why won't I?" Devi demanded and then the conversation became playful and loud, so loud that Avi came to investigate what was wrong.

Despite the various strains in their relationships, there were times and topics of conversation that brought them closer.

If she hadn't lost the baby, Devi wondered how it would've been. If by some stroke of luck, she'd been allowed to keep the baby and she'd touched the wrinkled face, held the little body, felt the small fingers. Would Saroj have accepted a grandchild regardless of its illegitimacy? And what about Shobha, how would she have felt?

Devi now knew what Shobha went through every day of her life. She'd only lost a baby. She knew that if she ever found a man worth being with again, she could have another baby. But Shobha knew, every morning, every night, all day that there would be no baby. Whose grief was bigger? Whose sorrow larger?

At least Shobha had some semblance of a good life. She had a career and maybe she could still repair her marriage. Devi had nothing. No career, no baby, no life. Shobha had prospects, Devi had none. She couldn't see anything bright and shiny in her tomorrow. She couldn't even see a tomorrow.

If only she could've kept the baby, all her tomorrows would've been alive, enriched by that little life. But she couldn't and no matter how many times her doctor told her that it wasn't her fault, that sometimes nature just decided to let a baby slip away, Devi couldn't help but blame herself. Like dominoes, one after the other, her world started to collapse.

The futility of it, the loss of it, frustrated Devi. She slammed on the brakes of the Jeep, then pressed on the accelerator again and took the first exit from the freeway.

She parked her father's car at a vista point where a big sign specifically said that cars couldn't be parked there after sunset.

She stepped outside and wrapped her arms around herself as the chill in the air penetrated her long-sleeved white shirt and jeans.

She pushed her sleeves up her arms and looked at her bandaged wrists. The bandages had become smaller. She went to see her regular physician every other day to have the wounds dressed. The cuts were deep, but they were healing. Her doctor had suggested reconstructive surgery for her scars but Devi shied away. If she lived she wanted to be reminded of the "incident," and if she didn't, how would it matter?

She unwrapped the bandage on her left wrist first and felt the cool air slide against her rough wounds. She stuffed the bandage inside her jeans pocket and unwrapped the bandage on her right wrist. The cuts were angry, sore, and raw. They were healing, but slowly. There would always be scars, if she lived. And even if the scars on her wrists became less visible in time, she'd still know they were there.

She could see the Pacific roll onto the tiny patch of sand far below her and slam onto the rocks. The waves were white foamlike creatures dancing in the night down below. Back and forth they went, created and dismantled by the force of the water.

It would be so easy, she thought as her heart hammered against her ribs. So very easy. All she had to do was let go. Just walk to the end of the world and fly. Her feet seemed impatient to get to the edge. There was an itch in her arms. They wanted to rise up and seek the skies.

So she closed her eyes, spread her arms, and took a step forward.

· · ·

Avi called Girish five times and on the last call they contemplated whether they should telephone the police and let them know that a suicidal mute was on the loose in a green Jeep Cherokee. After a heated discussion, they decided to wait another half an hour before doing anything.

It had been ninety minutes since Devi dropped Girish off, and for the past hour panic had sunk into her family.

"Did you have a fight with her?" Shobha demanded as she paced the living room, her feet clammy against the hardwood floors. Tension was making her back stiffen, and her heart was pounding.

"No," Girish said and then sighed. "Well, I got a little frustrated with her."

"So you had a fight with her?" Shobha accused.

"It wasn't a fight," Girish said, sounding just a little guilty. "She's probably just driving down Highway One, soaking in the sea air."

Shobha glared at him. "She's suicidal, not some rational fun-loving person who thinks how great the sea air is. What if she isn't soaking in the sea air? What if she's thinking about jumping off a cliff?"

"She's not going to jump off a cliff," Girish said, but Shobha could hear the fear in his voice.

He was afraid. Would he be this afraid if it was her thinking about jumping off a cliff? Would anyone in her family worry about her this way if she was late getting somewhere?

"I should've come and picked you up," Shobha said as she sat down on the floor. "What were you all thinking? Letting her drive like this? Are you fucking nuts?"

Girish rose from the rocking chair next to the telephone rashly, and the chair creaked against the floor. "Her doctor thinks that she isn't suicidal anymore. She thought it'd be okay for her to spend a little time alone."

"What the fuck does her doctor know?" Shobha demanded and winced because it sounded so much like her mother. Saroj never believed in doctors, never trusted them, maybe because G'ma was one.

"Now you sound like Saroj," Girish pointed out and then shook his head. "Nothing is going to happen to her. People who cook don't kill themselves and that's a direct quote from the shrink."

"I can't believe this," Shobha muttered. "Devi was always nuts, a little flaky, but this? How can she? What the fuck happened?"

Girish shrugged.

"Have you ever thought about it?" Shobha asked suddenly, as the question crossed her mind.

"Thought about what?"

"About killing yourself?"

Girish went completely still for a moment. "No. How about you?"

"Never," Shobha lied even though she could clearly remember wanting to end her life when the doctors told her she could never create one.

"Do you think something terrible happened to Devi?" Shobha went on wonderingly. "Do you think she got raped?" The idea was horrifying, but it was a possibility.

"Raped? Why?" Girish seemed flustered. "Where do you get such screwed-up ideas? Why would she kill herself if she got raped?"

"Because some women are not able to handle something that horrible," Shobha explained. "Are you sure she's not standing on one of those cliffs waiting to jump?"

"I'm sure," Girish said, not sounding sure at all.

Devi stood at the very edge of the cliff, her heart pounding, the cold sea air biting at her sore wrists.

She could hear the winds down below, the waves, and . . . giggling? She stood still and looked around to see who was there. For a moment she was scared; what if it were a ghost? An evil spirit?

Having always been afraid of the monster under her bed, even as an adult, her imagination ricocheted against the improbable until she inhaled the distinct smell of marijuana.

In her zest and focus to end her life she'd somehow missed the silhouette of a motorcycle resting by a bench, and she could now clearly see little puffs of gray smoke zigzagging upward against the dark canvas of the night.

It seemed incongruous to think about suicide when there were people sitting on the bench, giggling and enjoying a joint or maybe two.

"Give that to me," Devi heard a female voice say. "Not here, you idiot . . . what if the cops come."

"No one will come," a male voice said, and then there was some more giggling. It was a scene out of a cheesy teenage movie and Devi stood rooted, now unable to hear the waves below. She could only hear her oblivious companions kiss and shift on the bench. She could hear them moan and grunt. And above all she could hear them having fun.

When had she stopped having fun? When had she stopped having a good time to the point that suicide started to sound like a great idea?

She remembered the first time she'd smoked pot, all too clearly, as it was also the first time she'd had sex. Saroj would have been mortified to learn that the boy had been an Indian as she was convinced that good Indian boys "don't go sleeping around like those immoral white boys."

Ashish was Gujral Uncle's son and Gujral Uncle and Avi had known each other since before either of them had moved to the United States. Devi had been seventeen, primed to enter the forbidden land, made more attractive because of Saroj's constant vigil on her virginity. Gujral Uncle and Auntie were playing cards with Saroj and Avi at their place when Ashish and Devi snuck into his room. She settled comfortably on his bed while he shut the door and opened all his windows.

"Oh, my God," Devi gasped when she saw him draw out a joint. "Is it . . . is it?" she asked eagerly.

Ashish grinned widely and lit the illegal substance. Devi saw stars that night. Unlike what had been promised to her by all her friends, her first time was actually enjoyable. Ashish and Devi vowed eternal love, heady with the taste of lust. It lasted about six months and Ashish was now happily married to a nice girl his parents found him in India, while Devi was standing at the edge of a cliff, literally.

Almost involuntarily she took a few steps away from the edge. And suddenly she was afraid that she would trip and fall, end up in the waters anyway. The waves below didn't look inviting anymore. They seemed ominous, life-taking.

There was more to life. There simply had to be. She wouldn't accept defeat, wouldn't accept this as the end. She had lost so much, now she had to try to get some of it back. It would never be the way it used to be, but she didn't want it the way it used to be. She didn't want to live that life again, where the wanting and getting didn't have a meeting point.

But I'm scared, she almost cried out. What if it did end up the way it was? What if she once again ended in a bathtub slicing up her wrists?

"Ah," she heard a feminine cry of fulfillment, followed shortly by a heavy grunt from the man.

Devi's thoughts scattered.

"Get off me," she heard the feminine voice say. "You're too heavy."

"Okay, okay." She heard a sturdy, satisfied male laugh.

Devi's lips curved. No, she wasn't ready to die, she decided, and then realized that she wasn't ready to live, either. She was at an impasse, but she knew one thing, she wasn't going back to that edge again.

Her feet found momentum all of a sudden and she raced back to the Jeep and drove off, away from the cliff and toward the bright lights of Highway 280 and her parents' home.

~⌇

DEVI'S RECIPE
LIFE
Day 8 after coming from hospital

Tonight I made Cajun prawn biriyani. Tonight I almost ended it all, once again. Tonight was a long night and I wait for tomorrow when I can put this in the past, where it belongs. No one knows that I stood at the edge of a cliff and thought about taking the plunge into the black Pacific, but I know and that knowledge bends me in so many ways. It makes me feel guilty.

The worry and concern I seem to have caused surprises me, even as I tell myself that I have no reason to be surprised. They love me. I've always known that. They may not love me as I need them to love me, but they do and with their love they tie me to this world. And I want to stay, not just because of them, because of me as well.

I have made a decision and I have to follow through with it. I have decided to live, and now I need to find out how to make it happen.

A pinch of hope, with a dollop of family-inspired guilt, plus a tablespoon of sense should get me there, hopefully. I will work on myself. I will make the wrongs of my past right. I will not find myself again at the edge of a cliff contemplating how long the fall, how deep the crevice.

In the Business of Living

The news arrived in a blue envelope with several Mahatma Gandhi stamps pasted on the front above Vasu's name.

"But you've only been here three weeks," Shobha protested over dinner, her nose dripping slightly as the chili in the chicken curry burned her mouth.

"Geeta is my closest friend," Vasu said sadly. "She needs my help."

Devi was angry as well, an emotion that always struck her when it was time for Vasu to leave. Even as a child she would throw a tantrum with the hope that it would make Vasu stay longer. She wasn't speaking yet, but her anger was obvious. Her chicken with blueberry curry sauce, served with fragrant cardamom rice, was peeling off the first layer of everyone's stomach lining.

When she served Vasu she was extra forceful, and blueberry sauce from the curry splattered on Vasu's pale yellow cotton sari.

"Devi, you know Geeta Auntie," Vasu tried to explain.

"Your friends have always been more important to you than your family," Saroj declared saucily. "Devi needs you here, but you have to run along to hold Geeta Auntie's hand. So she had a small heart attack. It is a *small* heart attack. She will be fine and it's not like she doesn't have her own children who will take care of her."

"She is almost eighty years old," Vasu said angrily. "You have no compassion."

"If she's eighty she already has a foot in the—" Shobha was cut off by Vasu's glare. "Why can't you just call her and send some flowers?"

"Because I want to be with her," Vasu said in a no-further-discussion tone.

"More than you want to be with us?" Avi asked as he reached for the water. He usually never drank water while he ate but lately with Devi's moods seesawing from bland to spicy, it had sometimes become a necessity.

"You are all trying to emotionally blackmail me," Vasu said with a sigh. "Okay, why doesn't Devi come along with me to India? It will give her a—"

"My daughter will not run along with you to India where you will abandon her to hold Geeta Auntie's or some other poor old friend's hand," Saroj said loudly and angrily. "She needs her family and she will stay with us. You should stay here and support her. But if Geeta Auntie is more important—we have nothing more to say to each other."

Saroj rose from the table and walked out into the patio without finishing her meal.

Her friends always came first. It had the power to anger Saroj even now, when she was an adult with grown children. How many times had Vasu left Saroj with a neighbor for a week or two to rescue some friend or the other? How many vacation days had Vasu's friends eaten away so that Vasu could never take Saroj anywhere on holiday?

And now, when it was obvious Devi needed her, she was already getting ready to go take care of some old hag who'd had a heart attack. Wasn't Devi important? Wasn't Saroj?

Vasu made her so angry. She lived her life on her own terms, sacrificing everyone else on the way. She came across as this righteous, free-minded person, but Saroj had paid for Vasu's free-mindedness. As a child she had listened to other children in school whisper about her dead father and about Shekhar Uncle. She had faced that man at breakfast in their house, knowing that he spent the night with her mother.

Vasu hadn't made the transition from being a widow to a mistress easy for Saroj. She simply told her impressionable seven-year-old daughter about Shekhar Uncle.

"No, he isn't your new father," Vasu explained when Saroj wanted to know. "He's *my* friend. I am allowed to have friends just like you are."

It seemed logical to Saroj then and she accepted Shekhar Uncle as her mother's friend. But she wasn't stupid or blind. She knew that none of her friends' mothers had men friends, and even if they did, none of those friends stayed the night.

When she told Vasu that her friends were calling Vasu bad names because of her relationship with Shekhar Uncle, Vasu calmly told Saroj that she didn't care. She couldn't understand why Saroj would.

Now Saroj wondered if it would have been so difficult for Vasu to have conducted her affair with a married man with some discretion. Would it have killed her to not let the entire world know? But that was not how Vasu lived. She clearly told anyone who would listen that she didn't hide herself and her feelings. She was brave, open, and just a little stupid, Saroj thought. It was stupid to let the world know that she was a widow with a married lover. It was stupid to tell a young child about an illicit affair and drag her into a contemptuous world she wasn't ready for.

Vasu turned a blind eye to all the criticism and societal pressure. She didn't hear the whispers, or see the condemnation. But Saroj did.

Devi came outside with Saroj's half-full dinner plate and turned on the outdoor lights. She had reheated the food in the microwave, and Saroj was touched by her concern.

Devi put the plate on the patio table in front of Saroj and sat down beside her.

"It is very spicy," Saroj commented as she pierced a piece of chicken on the fork. "I am angry, too," she said as she chewed on the meat.

Devi sighed and leaned back into the chair.

Shobha joined them and sat on a chair across from Saroj. She put her feet up on the table and then dropped them onto the tiled floor when Saroj groaned, pointing to her food.

"You can be so Indian, Mama," Shobha said. "Never point feet at a person and all that."

"I don't know where your shoes have been and why would you put them next to my food?" Saroj said angrily. "And, madam, I *am* Indian. So are you."

"Nah," Shobha said.

"What do you mean, *nah?*" Saroj said on a mouthful of rice.

"I was born in India, but, Mama, I'm not Indian," she said.

"Yes, you are," Saroj said, and then Devi and she grinned, looking at each other as if they were sharing a private joke.

"What, the mute and you are best pals now?" Shobha demanded sarcastically.

Saroj shook her head, a big smile on her face. "You had an arranged marriage. I fell in love and got married."

"And that makes me more Indian than you?"

"No, maybe just as Indian," Saroj said, a laugh escaping her.

"Next you'll say Devi is also Indian," Shobha muttered.

Saroj raised her hands in defeat and laughed softly.

Her daughters! Her wonderful daughters! Sure they had problems and they didn't listen to her, because if they did their lives wouldn't be such messes, but they were still hers.

"Okay, I have decided to stay another two weeks, but then I have to go," Vasu said as she came outside. "Now is everyone happy?"

Devi all but jumped out of her chair and hugged Vasu. Shobha gave her grandmother a big smile.

Saroj sat sullenly, resenting Vasu for interrupting her good moment with her daughters.

⁓

DEVI'S RECIPE
ANGRY AT VASU GRILLED CHICKEN
IN BLUEBERRY CURRIED SAUCE
Day 15 after coming from hospital

It is a shame that Mama doesn't use the hundreds of other fruits and vegetables and spices available from around the world. If it isn't Indian, according to her, it isn't good. I think she stared so long at the blueberries that they shriveled.

The butcher gave me three whole breasts of fresh free-range chicken. All of a sudden I have become very particular about ecological vegetables and free-range chickens. If they've petted the chicken and played with it before cutting it open for my eating pleasure, I'll be happy to purchase its body parts. Even if I have a tough time understanding this ecological nonsense, I feel better for buying carrots that were grown without chemicals, and I can't come up with a good reason to deny myself that happiness.

I marinated the chicken breasts in white wine and salt and pepper for a while and then grilled them on the barbecue outside. The blueberry sauce was ridiculously simple. Fry some onions in butter, add the regular green chili, ginger, garlic, and fry a while longer. Add just a touch of tomato paste along with white wine vinegar. In the end add the blueberries. Cook until everything becomes soft. Blend in a blender. Put it in a saucepan and heat it until it bubbles.

In the end because G'ma wouldn't shut up about going back right away, I added, in anger and therefore in too much quantity: cayenne pepper. I felt the sauce needed a little bite . . . but I think I bit off more than the others could swallow.

I took the grilled chicken, cut the breasts in long slices, and poured the sauce over them. I made some regular basmati with fried cardamoms and some regular tomato and onion raita. I put too much green chili in the raita as well.

Let the Past Go Fast

It was a lazy Sunday morning. Cars were being driven slower than usual and the California sun beamed down on the brown hills surrounding Silicon Valley.

Devi stood outside the New India Bazaar and felt her hands grow clammy. Saroj's neighbors' car was parked outside and so was Vikram Uncle's. Vikram Uncle and Megha Auntie had come to see her the first week she stayed with her parents. They came for just half an hour and left, looking sad and unhappy.

Most of her parents' friends had either visited or called and each time they'd stayed for a very short period of time, distraught that Devi had attempted suicide and confused that she refused to speak. Devi found the visits trying and the one-sided conversations immensely patronizing and condescending.

"You have to go in sometime," Saroj said and took Devi's elbow in a firm grasp. "So what if everyone knows? So you made a mistake. You don't have to hang your head in shame all your life."

Devi wrenched her elbow free and took a deep breath. She didn't want to face these people. Family was different, but to these people she was gossip. They probably had already talked to their friends and their friends' friends about her.

"You know Saroj and Avi Veturi's girl . . . no, no, not the smart one married to that Stanford professor, the younger one. She committed suicide. *Nahi*, she's not dead. Saroj apparently found her bleeding in her bathtub. These girls today, they watch too much television and try to imitate soap operas."

She didn't want to go in, but for once Saroj was right. How long would she hang her head in shame?

They were in the frozen food section and Saroj was piling the shopping cart with *paneer* when Megha Auntie spotted them. She wasn't alone. Her daughter, Anita, who lived in New York with her investment banker husband, was with her. Anita was seven months' pregnant and chewing on a Mars bar.

"*Hai*, Devi, Saroj." Megha Auntie patted Devi's shoulder. "So, *beta*, how are you doing?"

Devi nodded and then smiled at Anita.

"Still not talking?" Megha Auntie asked, speaking in a low saccharine-sweet voice as if Devi were five years old and had lost her favorite Barbie.

"She is doing well, very happy," Saroj intervened smoothly. "So, Anita, how are you feeling? You shouldn't be eating sweets, *nahi*? Megha told me you have gestational diabetes."

"Oh, Auntie, once in a while is okay," Anita said and shared a *we-are-being-tortured-by-each-other's-mothers* look with Devi.

Devi didn't know Anita or her younger brother Purohit very well. Even though Avi and Megha Auntie's husband, Vikram, had been in business together for years, their families were not close. Saroj and Megha were too busy competing with each other to form any kind of stable friendship.

"*Arrey*, Saroj, Devi." Raina Kashyap, Saroj's neighbor, came along with her overflowing shopping cart. "Have you seen the *karela*, limp and dry, and they're charging four dollars a pound. *Kya zamana hai*, everyone is trying to swindle us."

"The tomatoes are very cheap. Cheaper than in Safeway," Megha Auntie said and then wriggled her eyes at Raina, inclining her head toward Devi. "Have you seen our Devi . . . she's looking bright and happy, no?"

"Oh yes, yes," Raina said immediately, contrite that she hadn't already mentioned something to soothe the suicidal girl's obvious insecurity.

Oh Lord, were these women really worried that if they didn't say something nice to her she'd do herself in again? How long would this go on? How long would it take for everyone else, besides her, to let go of her attempted suicide?

"How was the meeting with the psychiatrist?" Raina asked and Devi nodded.

"Not talking still, *beta?*" Raina asked and smiled as if Devi had lost a few screws. "You just let your mummy and daddy take care of you and everything will be all right. Okay?"

Devi nodded again, calmly, when all she wanted to do was throw the bag of spinach she was holding at the women.

"Okay then, we should go," Saroj said as if sensing the anger in Devi.

By the time they got home, Devi was seething with rage and had a sick feeling that this anger would never end. Even if she let go of the past, others would remember and they'd never forget. This would go on and on.

"She locked herself in her room," Saroj said, concern lacing her voice. "They wanted to ask her how she was doing and—"

"Why did you have to take her with you?" Avi demanded angrily. "Does the entire Indian population of the Bay Area have to interrogate her?"

"Avi," Saroj protested, "she has to get out of the house sometime. How many days will you keep her locked in?"

Vasu was relieved that she decided to stay for another few weeks. As crude as she was, Shobha was right. Geeta was eighty years old, so close to death anyway. Devi was young, vibrant, depressed, needy.

She left her daughter and her husband to bicker in the living room, knocked gently on Devi's door, and then tried to open it. The door swung open easily and Vasu's heart clenched when she heard Devi's sobs muffled against the pillow, her body racked with a combination of despair and fury.

She sat down beside Devi and stroked her hair. "Come here, *beta*," she said and Devi shifted to lie on Vasu's lap. Tears were still flowing but the sobs had quieted.

"People will not forget it for a long time," Vasu said when the last of Devi's tears had seeped into her yellow cotton sari. "They will wonder. They will be fascinated."

Devi shook her head and then more tears rolled down her cheeks.

"What you did is very juicy, Devi," Vasu reminded her. "Gossip-wise, it is so interesting. If I were a lesser woman, I would want to call India and tell all my friends about it and hear them go, *No, really.*"

Devi let out a watery laugh and a fresh sob went through her and fresh tears blossomed and fell on Vasu's sari.

"Oh, *beta*, it is okay," Vasu said and rocked Devi to and fro. "Life never turns out as we plan. People will talk, they always do, but you have to ignore that and live your life.

"That is what I had to do. You think if I cared I would have had those beautiful twenty-five years with Shekhar? And then when he died, I was no one to him, not even his widow. That was hard, so difficult. I gave him so much, took a lot in return, too, but in the end, he was someone else's husband. I was aware of it. The people around me were very aware of it.

"Every station I got posted to, there would be whispers and talk. When Shekhar would come for a visit, they would all gossip and make rude comments. I lived with it because I knew this was the price I had to pay for Shekhar."

Devi looked up at her grandmother and for an instant Vasu thought that Devi would speak. She would talk, open up, the mystery of her attempted suicide would cease to be an enigma.

"Yes, *beta*?" Vasu asked hopefully, but Devi just shrugged and closed her eyes.

"You will be fine," she said softly. "People will eventually forget, but until they do, you have to be strong and overlook them and their opinions. You are alive now, and that is all that matters."

Death had become a friend to Vasu in the past few years. So many of her friends had passed away. Shekhar had left her, too, and now she was looking forward to dying. She was needed by Devi and that made her feel jubilant, but she also knew she was ready. Since Shekhar had gone she had been counting the days, waiting to leave as well.

Without him the world didn't make much sense. She wished Devi had someone the way she'd had Shekhar. He had been her anchor, her life. If only Devi had an anchor, someone who would keep her rooted, this would never have happened.

Maybe it was time to look for a suitable boy for Devi. It could be done differently. It didn't have to be a conventional arranged marriage. Vasu could just introduce Devi to the boy and then let them find out if they wanted to be together. Isn't that how a lot of young Indians were getting married in the States?

As Devi lay on her lap, Vasu started to make a list of people she could call in India who would know of a suitable boy in the United States.

Vasu always liked Avi. He was a good man, an ambitious man who had come so far in his life despite losing an arm.

As she sat across from him waiting for him to make a move on the chessboard she looked at the large pictures resting on the mantel on top of the never-used fireplace. Saroj had set off the pictures in brass antique frames, which she polished regularly.

There were four pictures, four events that Saroj probably considered important ones. One was of Avi and her on their wedding day. They had married in a registrar's office without the usual fanfare. Saroj had been disappointed, there was no doubt about that, but Avi had been so averse to marrying in the conventional way that Saroj had given in. Now when Vasu looked at the past she realized that Saroj seemed to have always been giving in to Avi.

Saroj looked bright and beautiful in the picture, nothing like the dried-up bitter woman she had become. She wore a red-and-white silk sari with flowers in her hair and a ruby necklace wrapped around her neck. But her eyes shone the most. They held bright expectation of the future. Avi looked disreputable in a gray suit. He hadn't shaved that day and there was a laconic look in his eyes. But he was smiling, and looking at that picture no one would doubt how much this couple loved each other. Now when Vasu looked at Saroj and Avi she wasn't sure if there was any love left.

Her heart constricted at that thought. No, her daughter deserved a happy marriage. After all that she had done and sacrificed to ensure a happy union, God wouldn't be so unfair as to mess up her marriage, would he?

The second picture was of Shobha and Girish's wedding. Saroj had pulled out all the stops for this one. This wedding had been the one she had wanted.

Shobha was dripping with jewelry in the picture, and it looked as if she were getting ready for third-degree Chinese torture instead of a happy future with her new husband. Girish looked uncomfortable in his south Indian wedding attire. The *panchi* was askew, his *kurta* completely wrinkled, and the red *tilakam* on his forehead seemed to be in his eyes. They both were smiling, but their eyes and smiles were empty.

Vasu remembered Shobha saying, "Thank God the ordeal is over," when the wedding celebrations ended and she was ripping off her sari to wear something more comfortable.

How could it be that all three generations—grandmother, mother, and daughter—had been in unhappy marriages? How had fate twisted their lives to bring about this triple tragedy?

"Your move," Avi said, leaning back and putting his pipe in his mouth.

"Hmm," Vasu replied as she rested her chin on her hands, leaning forward toward the chessboard.

"She looks better," Avi said with a broad smile when they both heard Devi's small laugh from the television area of the living room.

Saroj had divided the living room into three parts. There was an antique table with two chairs near the French windows where Vasu and Avi played chess. Sofas were ensconced around a large-screen television, music system, VCR, and DVD player in a separate area.

A third section, next to the kitchen and dining area, held another sofa set where the family entertained formally. It was only used rarely.

"What is she watching?" Vasu asked, looking over to see her

granddaughter dip her hands into a bowl of popcorn as her eyes glinted with humor.

"Some movie," Avi said and smiled contently. "She'll start speaking soon."

"Is that why you're always at home?" Vasu asked as she moved her rook so that in the next three steps she could threaten Avi's queen.

"Hmm," Avi said, wrinkling his nose and then looking at Vasu. "What do you mean?"

"No golf, no lunches, nothing. When I first got here your social calendar was too full, now you are always at home," Vasu explained, and when Avi shrugged she put her hand on his. "She is not going to slip away if you get back to your life. You don't have to watch her all the time."

"The last time I stopped she almost died," Avi said, shaking his head. "Golf can wait, and why should I eat out when I have a master chef at home?"

The girls had always been important to Saroj and Avi. Sometimes Vasu felt that they had given up their lives for their children. She saw it all the time back home where couples forgot to be couples because they were busy being parents. Is that what happened to Avi and Saroj?

The third picture on the mantel was of the four of them, Avi, Saroj, a fifteen-year-old Shobha, and an eleven year-old Devi. Saroj wore a heavy brown-and-ivory-colored silk sari, Avi was in a dark suit, Shobha wore a classic green-and-red half sari, while Devi wore a maroon blouse with puff sleeves and a silk skirt in maroon and gold. They looked like a typical south Indian family. The picture was taken in India at a friend's wedding in Madras. In the background of the picture was the yet-to-be-used marriage *mandap*, decorated, ready for the bride and groom to sit in and be married.

This was the family Saroj always hoped for. Her daughters dressed traditionally, with white jasmine in their hair, a handsome husband by her side, and India in the background.

The happiness that was so evident in Saroj's wedding picture was not there in this one, though. The picture showed a contrived family. The happiness on their faces seemed fake.

The fourth picture was of Saroj, Vasu, and Ramakant. It was a black-and-white picture. Whenever Vasu looked at the picture she felt a pinch inside her. Is that what Ramakant used to look like? He was ordinary looking, just as Vasu was. They held hands while a three-year-old Saroj stood in between them, leaning slightly on her father. Vasu remembered how Saroj had hunted for that photograph when she was packing up to leave for the United States the first time all those years ago.

"I want it." Saroj had been adamant.

"I don't know where it is. I don't even know which one you are talking about," Vasu had said.

"I want it. That's the only picture with all of us," Saroj had said, tears brimming in her eyes. And then she found it, hidden in a book along with other black-and-white pictures of Ramakant and his parents and family. She didn't take the rest, just that one where she leaned on her father's leg and her parents were holding hands.

Saroj was a pretty little girl. Her hair used to curl up when she was young. Now it was wavy. Vasu had always thought she had the brightest eyes and the prettiest smile.

How the days had flown by, Vasu thought fondly and sadly. Her little girl had her own little girls.

Devi laughed again, and Vasu felt some relief from the past. Even though she had never been able to have a sound relationship with her daughter, she had one with her granddaughter.

"Check, Vasu," Avi said triumphantly and drew his opponent's attention back to the board.

"Not so fast, mister," Vasu said and got to work on saving her king.

The Good Mother

Devi was a closet feminist.

Shobha was not in the closet. She wished things were different and accused feminists for screwing up her lot in life. "Some bitch burns her bra and now all of a sudden I have to work for a living *and* keep house. If it were the good old days I could happily sit at home doing nothing while Girish brought home the money."

When Devi pointed out that Shobha could still do that if she wanted to, Shobha flared up. "But they already burned the bra and I'm already a different woman because of it. I can't go back and change how I feel about women who sit at home and don't work."

That Devi concurred with. Because Saroj never worked, both her daughters had developed a healthy disrespect for homemakers. Devi didn't voice her opinion as loudly as Shobha did, but she didn't appreciate women who gave up lives outside their homes to be wives and/or mothers. It was women like that, she believed, who made it hard for career women like herself to break the glass ceiling. No matter what, every man who hired a woman thought about the woman going away on maternity leave and then not coming back to work because she didn't want to leave her child in day care.

Devi had seen it many times. And each time she saw someone do it, she was furious. Everyone has to have a role in society, and in her book of definitions a homemaker was defined as a lazy woman who sat home pretending to have a full-time job.

So it seemed ironic to Devi that she was spending most of her time in the kitchen, chopping and baking and stirring. She, who had never cooked, never been part of the kitchen militia, was a general now. She loved it. And she realized that she owed her culinary epiphany to her mother.

Even now as Devi started to pick out the spices to splutter into the hot oil for the *masala* lima beans, her fingers automatically went through the ingredients she had seen her mother pick up. Some black mustard, a little *jeera*, a little coriander, a little red *gram dal*, and she immediately started to stir, in exactly the same way as Saroj always did, to ensure that none of the spices got burned.

Her food tasted different from her mother's but she had learned to cook from Saroj and that made Devi feel closer to Saroj in a way she never had before. Silence and the kitchen had brought them together, and it was a time and place that Devi had started to relish.

Since Devi wasn't talking, Saroj followed suit and just asked nod-or-shake questions whenever needed.

"Is this some kind of *masala dal* variation?" Saroj asked as Devi put a bunch of coriander leaves in front of her. "Chopped small?" Saroj asked Devi, who nodded.

"I still don't know why you won't just talk," Saroj said as she cut the coriander with a sharp knife. "It is okay that you made a mistake. You can talk . . . why are you adding Tabasco? Why can't you add *apna* homemade chili powder?"

When Devi just shrugged, Saroj sighed. "I should keep my mouth shut, I know. You are cooking as if you have been cooking since you were a little girl. God knows I didn't teach you, so where did you learn?"

Devi smiled and pointed to Saroj.

"From me?" Saroj asked, surprised. "Really?"

Devi nodded with a smile and Saroj smiled back, her pride shining in her eyes.

Life had fallen into a pattern for Devi, for whom patterns had never been relevant. She enjoyed waking up at the same time every day, cooking lunch, then dinner. She went grocery shopping after lunch to buy ingredients for dinner and the next lunch. There was comfort in monotony.

Vasu accompanied her to the supermarket, and Saroj helped her cook. Shobha and Girish showed up every evening for dinner. She knew her family was rallying around her and she knew why. Devi wanted to thank them but the words had disappeared. How could she just say *thank you* for what they were doing? How could that ever be enough? Since she couldn't think of a way to show her gratitude, to explain what she realized was the biggest mistake of her life, she decided to continue her silence.

It helped that Dr. Mara Berkley, whom she had visited three times since the "incident," didn't find her not talking strange or insane.

"It's okay, you don't have to talk," she had said in their first session, and after that had not pestered her to speak. She simply asked questions that could be answered with a nod or a shake.

"You'll speak when you're ready," Dr. Berkley assured her. "But until then you still have to try to tell me how to help you. Your father tells me that you're cooking up a storm."

Devi smiled shyly.

"Have you always enjoyed cooking?"

Devi shook her head.

"So, this is a new thing?"

Devi nodded.

"How did you learn to cook?"

And as she thought of the answer she realized that she had learned to cook from Saroj. She had watched her mother mix spices, grind ingredients, splatter oil, and burn dishes. She had seen her mother serve simple Indian food that tasted fabulous. Was she creating her own identity by cooking her own kind of food? She didn't know.

No matter how much she resented her mother's interference in her life, now she was starting to realize that every part of her life was touched in some way or the other by Saroj.

Pesky, annoying Saroj, who was always such a nuisance. A

woman with no career and no self-respect, a doormat, had given her so much. She birthed her twice, once after thirty-five hours of labor and again in that bathtub when Devi slit her wrists.

Talking, or rather listening to Dr. Berkley forced Devi to assess her life, past and present, and she had come to the conclusion that her mother had always tried her best, given all that she could. And slowly, but steadily, Devi stopped resenting Saroj. If only Saroj could see this as well and if she did, maybe she would stop being angry with her own mother. It was obvious to Devi that Vasu had shaped Saroj's life; influenced her in countless ways. A mother always touched her children's lives no matter what the children thought. In good ways or bad, the influence would remain.

And then Devi wondered if she would have made a good mother. If her baby, if she hadn't lost it, would have loved her or hated her. It had become easier to think about the baby now, to remember it with some joy and some sorrow instead of feeling like an utter failure each time she thought of little flailing hands and feet.

She had told Dr. Berkley about the baby. She hadn't meant to but she slipped up and her secret had spilled out. Dr. Berkley gave her a lump of Play-Doh in their second session together, so that Devi could start communicating using shapes and images. Devi hadn't thought she could conjure up anything with her fingers, but when Dr. Berkley asked her what she felt she had lost the most, the clay shaped itself into a baby.

"Was it a miscarriage?" Dr. Berkley asked.

Devi nodded, tears streaming down her cheeks.

"Is that why you wanted to die?"

Devi nodded again and then shook her head and then nodded again. That was one of the reasons, but there were so many other reasons, one tangled up in another.

"Are you scared of telling your family about the baby?"

Devi nodded. It was not just simple fear, it was a mountains-big fear.

"Was the father of the baby an old boyfriend?"

Was he ever her boyfriend? No, he wasn't, so Devi shook her head. And then because she didn't want to talk about this anymore, she dropped the clay she was holding into the sparkling glass ashtray in front of her. And as she realized that she had dropped her clay baby into an ashtray, her eyes filled again and she started to cry.

When she came home after that session, she felt some peace, and felt clean for the first time since she'd almost died. Something inside her told her that it would all work out and that she would eventually heal. She would soon start finding the words again, the right words that she needed to tell her family about the baby, its father, and the "incident."

Just Looking for Happiness

Usually Saroj enjoyed the afternoon rummy parties she and her friends had been having for the past twenty years. But not this afternoon. Everyone knew what Devi had done, and they were talking ceaselessly about suicide and how many people they knew who had attempted or committed suicide.

Usually Renuka Chopra and Saroj got along like rice and pickle, but this day Saroj wanted to strangle her with the *pallu* of her blue-and-yellow sari.

"My brother's best friend in college hung himself from the ceiling fan in his hostel room." Renuka offered her suicide story dramatically. "His tongue was sticking out, not nice and clean like they show in the movies. It was horrible. Poor Brijesh, he didn't sleep properly for years after that. So, Saroj, I know what you are going through. But remember, she is alive."

Did she look like she needed consoling? Saroj wondered as she smiled unconvincingly.

"Why don't we start the game?" she suggested before someone else could start telling her suicide story.

"Ah, can we wait another five minutes?" Meera Reddy, their hostess, asked and then grinned. "I thought I would surprise all of you. We are having a special guest today. Guess who?"

"Madhuri Dixit," Karuna Rao offered immediately.

"Just because she married some guy in LA doesn't mean she shows up in the Bay Area to play cards with us," Kala Shetty muttered. "So, Meera, *kaun aa raha hai?*"

Meera smiled smugly. "Not Madhuri, but someone closer to our times. Amrita Saxena."

"Of *Kala Gulab* and *Love in London?*" Renuka asked, her eyes shining brightly.

"The same," Meera said gleefully. "She married husband number three five years ago. He's some Gujrati business fellow, and he knows Sri. We met them at a party last week. They just moved to Atherton and I asked her if she had time for a rummy game. She jumped at the idea. Bored it seems. They were in New Jersey and she had lots of friends there, so she's looking for new friends. I thought we could help her."

All the women agreed that it was fabulous even though they were jealous that they had never invited someone as posh as Indian movie star Amrita Saxena to their house for a rummy game.

Saroj couldn't help but feel excited. She had seen Amrita Saxena dance around trees with her favorite movie actors before she left India. Amrita Saxena was part of her teenage years, part of the life she'd left behind in her homeland.

"*Arrey,* we should ask her how it was to act with Vikram Anand," Karuna said brightly.

"And Shashi Kapoor," Saroj piped in.

"And Raj Kumar," Renuka said dreamily. "He would talk in that deep voice and I would start getting goose bumps in the most unlikely places."

"*Chee,* Renuka," Meera said with an embarrassed smile. "How you talk."

"What? You don't have a big thing for *apna* Amitabh?" Kala teased. "Honestly, are there any real men in the business besides Amitabh?"

"Oh, I like Aamir Khan," Saroj said in defense of the new generation of stars, and the conversation went from suicide to Bollywood in no time.

Meera and Karuna were new to the group, but Saroj had known Renuka and Kala for more than two decades now. They had followed their husbands and their husbands' dreams to the United States. Kala's and Renuka's husbands had opened a software company together. They'd sold the company during the software boom in the early 1990s and had recently started a business in India.

Saroj was immediately envious. She'd insisted Avi join Kala's and Renuka's husbands but he'd refused, saying that he simply didn't have the energy to start yet another business.

"But we could move to India then," Saroj had said in despair.

"But I don't want to move to India and I know nothing about semiconductors, Saroj. I'm not interested in what they're doing," Avi told her.

Saroj was further baffled when Renuka and Kala refused to move full time to India.

"*Arrey,* visiting is okay, but I can't live there. My mother-in-law will drive me crazy," Kala said to Saroj. "You haven't been to India for a long time or you wouldn't want to move back there, either. I like to visit, but California is home."

In the beginning Kala and Renuka had joined her in bitching and moaning about how hard their husbands worked and how difficult it was to raise their children alone in a strange country. They got together at least once a week and brought a piece of India into their lives. They would order Hindi movies on video from India and have marathon movie sessions.

Saroj realized that Kala and Renuka were the women she was closest to, yet she couldn't tell them anything about how things were with Avi, how Devi's silence was gnawing at her, and how she was worried about Shobha and Girish, who didn't seem to be happy at all.

"I met your Girish the other day," Kala said as if on cue. "We were at the Stanford shopping mall and he was there, too, buying some chicken or something at the butcher. Didn't remember me and when I told him who I was, he just smiled, was very polite and then left. I don't think he remembered me. Total absentminded professor, your son-in-law."

Saroj laughed. In the beginning they envied Saroj for snagging such a catch for Shobha but now they sympathized with her for having such an unfriendly son-in-law.

Kala's daughter, Puja, had married an American man. Kala hadn't minded at all, though Saroj couldn't understand why. Nice Indian girls didn't go around marrying American men. It just wasn't right. Mark was a lot friendlier to Kala than Girish was to her. Her daughter had an arranged marriage to a nice Indian boy and they both were at each other's throats all the time, while Kala's daughter married some white boy and . . . well, everyone had their own *karma* to contend with.

"How about Devi?" Meera asked. "Are you going to start looking for a boy now?"

Saroj shrugged and said, "Maybe."

Everyone was too polite to point out that looking for a boy for Devi would be a futile attempt. No decent family would be interested in an arrangement now that Devi's latest escapade had hit the gossip charts of the Bay Area Indian community.

"Why don't we just start playing?" Karuna suggested, trying to break the awkward silence that filled the room.

And then as the first set of cards was being dealt, Amrita Saxena showed up.

"I got lost," she said sheepishly. "Everything is so different from New Jersey, a lot of adjusting for me."

Amrita Saxena spoke with a polished semi-American accent. It was not *aDjusTing* the way Indians said it, it was *adjusting* where the *t* and *d* came out with American flourish. Saroj had lived in the United States for more than three decades now and still spoke with a *pukka* Indian accent.

Saroj disliked Amrita Saxena instantly.

Karuna, Meera, and Renuka seemed unperturbed by the accent and were starstruck, as if they had just met a goddess but Saroj knew that Kala would agree with her that Amrita Saxena was a fraud.

"And Shashi Kapoor, what was he like?" Meera asked with excitement.

The card game as such was not really being played.

"He's such a doll," Amrita replied, and Kala rolled her eyes. "An amazing man, very devoted to Jennifer when she was alive, never strayed even though there was a lot of temptation."

The other three were so enthralled with Amrita and her stories of the Hindi film industry that Kala and Saroj had to nudge everyone to drop a card or pick one up.

"Really?" Karuna said. "You mean . . . women threw themselves on him?"

"It happened all the time, but he's a gentleman," Amrita said. "When I made *Hum Tum Sath Sath* with him, I was going through such a bad period. I was divorcing Rakesh—"

"Rakesh Bajaj?" Renuka asked to confirm.

"Yes." Amrita sighed. "He was my first true love, but . . . a girl learns everything is not written in stone."

"Marriage is not written in stone?" Kala asked impertinently.

"Rakesh used to slap me around," Amrita explained, a small tremor in her voice. But then she was an accomplished actress and knew how to deliver her lines, Saroj thought without feeling any compassion.

"It was a long time ago but I can still remember the fear and pain." She sighed dramatically and Saroj wanted to stomp her feet on the ground. She had read the gossip magazines and many of the reporters thought the reason for the divorce was not Rakesh Bajaj's abusive ways but Amrita Saxena's affair with the director of her hit film *Jamuna*, Pradeep Shankar. And the journalists were probably right: Amrita Saxena married Pradeep Shankar just a few months after her divorce from Rakesh.

These movie stars lived such debauched lives, Saroj thought in disgust as the excitement of meeting a live actress faded swiftly under Amrita's false accent and melodramatic tales.

"And then why did you divorce Pradeep Shankar?" Saroj asked and saw Meera shake her head and mouth a *hush*.

Amrita looked straight at Saroj and smiled sadly. "When we got married we loved each other so much. It didn't matter to me that he had that limp. Polio. He was always ashamed about it. But for me, he was my god. And I loved him, but I couldn't compete with the passion he had for his work. I even quit acting for two years after we were married, but he was never there, always working, always gone. Can you imagine what that was like?"

For an instant Saroj wondered if Amrita knew the truth about Avi's bad working hours and the emptiness of her marriage. Was Amrita baiting her?

Amrita licked her lips and set the cards she was holding down on the table. "He was in love with the camera more than he was with any woman, definitely not me. I couldn't compete and how long was I supposed to play the extra in the movie of his life?" She paused after delivering that electric line and then rose from her chair. "Excuse me," she said and then asked Meera directions to a bathroom.

Kala sighed dramatically as soon as Amrita was out of earshot. "*Extra in the movie of his life? Kya* acting. My God, the woman never left the movies."

"And what is all this about *he was my god.* All *bakwas,*" Saroj said.

"Oh come on, Kala, Saroj," Meera said angrily. "What is wrong with the two of you? She's a nice woman."

"Yes," Karuna said, "and imagine being hit by her husband. I feel so sorry for her."

"Hitting, nothing. She was doing it with that director while she was married to her first husband," Saroj retorted.

"And how do you know that?" Renuka asked, annoyed. "Come on, Saroj, she is the genuine article."

Kala and Saroj shrugged and put the cards they were holding on the table.

"No more rummy, *han?*" Saroj asked as she stood up. "I'll go see if the bathroom is available."

The door to Meera's guest bathroom was open and Amrita Saxena was standing in front of the mirror applying lipstick.

"*Ek* minute, okay," Amrita said, her mouth wide in a big O. She tore a piece of toilet paper and put it between her lips. She dropped the paper with shape of her lips in red on them inside the toilet and smiled at Saroj.

"Have to keep up appearances, right?" she said and then her smile folded. "You don't like me, I can see."

Saroj was baffled and had no idea how to respond.

"I can see," Amrita Saxena repeated and sighed. "I know it's hard for Indian women to understand why I divorced two men and am married for the third time. You think I liked divorcing?"

Saroj shook her head. "Look, I don't even know you. I am sorry if I came across—"

"I can see very clearly how you look at me," Amrita Saxena continued as if Saroj hadn't spoken. "I loved Pradeep. He was my savior. After Rakesh, he was the man I wanted to be with, and I was married to him for four years. I stuck it out for as long as I could, you know."

Saroj nodded. "I am sure you had your reasons."

"But he just didn't have any time for me. I quit acting but that didn't change anything and when I started acting again he was so insecure," Amrita Saxena said in frustration.

Saroj wanted to tell her that she wasn't interested in listening to this, that she didn't care one way or the other for her reasons. She would still dislike her. Women who didn't make their marriages work always had good excuses. Her mother most definitely did.

"And he ignored me all the time. When we finally realized that something was wrong, nothing was left in our marriage," Amrita Saxena said angrily. "So I left him because after four years, there was no love, no need, no nothing. Not even sex. And then years later, I met Johar. He's a good man and he waited for me. I didn't want to marry him, I didn't want to marry again, but he wore me down. We were together for almost six years before I agreed to marry him."

Saroj sighed. "Look, I am really sorry that I gave you the impression I didn't like you. I liked your movies a lot when I was in India. I think you are a fabulous actress and a wonderful dancer."

Amrita Saxena laughed shortly. "I'm just too defensive, right?"

Saroj smiled and felt some reluctant sympathy for Amrita Saxena. "I think I would be the same. My mother divorced my father when I was five years old. I never forgave her for that." She hadn't

meant to tell this stranger something so personal but Amrita Saxena had gone out of her way to explain why she divorced two men
and Saroj felt compelled to tell her about her prejudices.

"Why did your parents get divorced?" she asked.

Saroj shrugged and then shook her head. She didn't want to
delve into that subject. Vasu said it was because they never could get
along, that he was abusive, but Saroj couldn't remember anything
anymore. She did remember the fights, the yelling and screaming,
but didn't all couples fight? And did all couples who fought get divorced? And did all divorced women take up with married men?

"Sometimes there is just no other option," Amrita Saxena said
and squeezed Saroj's shoulder in sympathy. "Divorcing Rakesh was
easy, he was abusive, but Pradeep, that was hard. I just had to realize that I couldn't continue to be in a loveless marriage anymore. We
stopped communicating and I just want to be happy. You know?"

Driving home from the failed rummy game, Saroj brooded over
what Amrita Saxena told her. Amrita Saxena said she just wanted to
be happy and she had had to divorce twice to find that happiness.
Saroj wanted to ignore the similarities between Amrita Saxena's
marriage to Pradeep Shankar and her own marriage, but they were
too obvious, almost like a make-believe story written for her benefit.

Was that the only way for her to be happy? Saroj wondered.
Would she have to let go of Avi and her marriage to find happiness?

If Devi hadn't attempted suicide, Shobha would have bitched and
moaned to her parents instead of Girish about going to their house
for dinner *every* night. But it was a tacit understanding among the
members of the Veturi household that everyone was going to be
present for every dinner.

Even Girish managed to switch his classes around and show up.
He also made it a point to come on Saturdays and Sundays in the afternoon for lunch as well, and then stayed until dinner.

"How long do you think we have to do this?" Shobha asked as
Girish drove down 280, cursing the Sunday drivers.

"Go to your parents' place?"

"Hmm."

"We go until we have to go."

Shobha sighed elaborately. "I can't stand going there anymore. I mean, yesterday Mama went on and on about that movie actress she met. Jesus, how long do we have to do this? I don't mind going once in a while but going this often . . ."

"I don't know." Girish honked as a Mazda Miata recklessly changed lanes and caused him to brake. "You son of a bitch, who gave you a driver's license?"

"Why is it that you don't get mad, ever, but if you're driving, you can hardly keep calm?" Shobha asked pointedly. This was not the first time Girish had sacrificed a conversation with her to yell at or honk at an errant driver.

"Hey, it isn't my fault they all drive like they had a lobotomy . . . you idiot . . ." Girish swerved the car to prevent from slamming into a blue Mustang that had come out of nowhere.

"This is the reason we can never have a conversation while you drive," Shobha muttered.

"Conversation? I thought you were just bitching about going to your parents' place," Girish said.

"And you just love visiting your parents, don't you? That's why we see them, oh, once every two years, maybe," Shobha yelled at him. "Forget it, I don't want to talk to you anymore."

"I thought you wanted to have a conversation," Girish said. He was obviously goading her, trying to piss her off, and Shobha didn't want him to succeed.

"Yes, I did, but since you're so busy talking to yourself and yelling at other drivers, who by the way can't hear you, I'm letting it go," Shobha said. "Good God, Girish, you make me so angry."

"Everything makes you angry," Girish pointed out and then started to hum softly as he drove right in front of the blue Mustang that had cut him off a few minutes ago and stepped on the brake.

After the Devi incident, Shobha wanted more than anything else not to end up in her sister's situation. She didn't want to sit in her bathtub and slice her wrists off because there was nothing left to live for. She wanted to fix her marriage, but unlike the software programs she dealt with at work, her marriage required a lot more than lines of code to fix.

In the past few days Girish had become even more distant, if that was possible. They spent no time together. They were always at her parents' house or at work. The worst of it was that Shobha liked it and it looked like so did Girish. It was easy to deal with their marriage when they were never alone with each other. They usually drove separately from their respective jobs to her parents' house on weekdays. On weekends they sometimes drove together; other times Girish got a ride back with Devi or Avi while Shobha left early in her own car.

"Girish," Shobha said as he parked his car in her parents' driveway. "Why don't we take a vacation?"

Girish looked at her as if she had asked him to go to Mars with her.

"Just you and me," Shobha said. "Someplace nice, San Juan or Hawaii. I could use a break and so could you. Once the summer semester is over, you'll have a couple of weeks."

Girish shook his head, disbelief and disgust creeping into his face. "Your sister just tried to kill herself. She's so bloody depressed that she won't even talk and you want to go to some island resort and drink colored drinks with little umbrellas in them?"

It wasn't like that, Shobha almost cried out. She just wanted them to get away so that they could be together and work on their marriage. Save it, somehow.

"God, Shobha, you can be so selfish," Girish said as he got out of the car.

Shobha sat inside the car until her nerves calmed and the tears didn't threaten to fall.

She was always misunderstood. *He* always misunderstood her. Sometimes she wondered if it was deliberate. Did he know he hurt her? Or did he think he couldn't?

She couldn't decide whether it was Girish's words that stabbed through her, robbing her of breath, or if it was the fact that the man uttering those words was Girish, her husband.

When they got engaged, Devi had smirked and asked Shobha if

this was what she'd wanted from life: *an arranged marriage to a simple* buddhu *professor?* she had asked.

Simple? Shobha didn't subscribe to that analysis. Girish was hardly simple. She hadn't met anyone who could complicate situations for her the way he did. She couldn't get through to him because he was so fucking complicated. There wasn't a single simple bone in that man's body.

When she stepped into the living room, she saw Girish laugh at something Vasu was telling Avi. She could see Saroj and Devi in the kitchen puttering around.

They all fit so well together. They were polite to each other, friendly. They helped each other out, while she stood outside watching them.

Girish seemed happy, in his element, cracking jokes, politely making conversation, passing out compliments. There was no sarcasm tainting his tone. The Girish with the sarcastic voice and judgmental demeanor made his appearance exclusively for her.

Who was the real Girish? This man who was so lighthearted and happy, or the man who looked at her with disgust just a few moments ago as he called her selfish?

Who had she married?

And then it struck her, not like a thunderbolt from a wild crackling sky, but like the opening of a box to reveal its secret contents.

My marriage is over.

She blinked as she thought the words and repeated them again inside her mind to taste them, feel their texture, and try to accept them.

It wasn't easy. The at-the-top-of-her-game Shobha had failed at something. She failed miserably at being happily married. She'd finally come face to face with that stark truth, and its intensity was blinding.

What did one do with such information? Just carry on, or walk away?

She wanted to shake Girish from his laughter and inform him that their marriage was over. Or maybe he knew and was pretending he didn't, as she was tempted to do.

"Girish, Devi made your favorite *sooji ladoos*," Saroj said, as she came into the living room with a silver platter on which a small mountain of *ladoos* stood majestically.

"How's her mood? If she's still angry about something, son, I recommend you stay away from these. They're probably full of chili powder," Avi teased.

"Don't worry, only sugar in these, and hazelnuts," Saroj said, holding the plate up. "You wouldn't think that those nuts would add so much taste. I don't know when she learned all this, but these *ladoos* are the best I have ever eaten."

Girish filled his mouth with one and made a *hmm* sound in his throat.

Devi was standing by the kitchen door, looking eagerly at Girish, and when he smiled at her and said, "These are fabulous, Devi," she all but blushed, averting her face from the scrutiny of her family.

Devi's eyes met Shobha's as she turned her head away from Girish, and Shobha felt something shift inside, an understanding blossom. As suddenly as she thought that strange thought, she discarded it. It was insane. No, it couldn't be. It was too fantastic to be true.

But as Shobha stepped into the living room and ate a rather delicious *ladoo,* she wondered if she'd seen fear in Devi's eyes as they clashed against hers, a fear that Devi had gotten caught with her hand in a jar full of *ladoos.*

~

DEVI'S RECIPE
GIRISH'S FAVORITE WITH A TWIST
Two Weeks After

Mama said that it was very nice of Girish to come by every night for dinner. She said that I should make something for him and since he likes sooji ladoos, *maybe I could find the time to make some. She bought the* khoya *from India Bazaar. I didn't because I didn't want to make* ladoos, *but ultimately, I thought the hazelnuts lying in Mama's pantry could be put to good use.*

Mama did most of the real work, while I just rolled the ladoos with a ball of crushed hazelnut and raisins in the center. Mama fried the sooji in ghee and then added the grated khoya. Then went in some water and sugar, along with a spoonful of cardamom powder.

I just crushed the hazelnuts along with the raisins in the food processor and made small balls. Once the sooji mixture was cool, I made a big ball, stuck a hole in it with my finger, and stuffed the hazelnut-and-raisin ball inside. Then I closed the big ball. It was really simple to do, but I didn't want to make the ladoos. I made them only because Mama asked me to. In any case, everyone seemed to like the ladoos.

Friends Come in All Colors

Devi always had more friends than Shobha. When they were teenagers, Devi always had something fun planned for the weekends, while Shobha huddled in her room with two of her friends. Saroj was never sure what they did in there, though they claimed they were studying.

She discreetly went through Shobha's and Devi's rooms when they were young (you had to be careful about drugs and that sort), but never found anything except a Harlequin romance in Devi's room and a translated edition of the Kamasutra in Shobha's.

Even now, Shobha had the same two friends she'd always had. Jaya, who was married to that ugly fellow and lived in New Jersey, and some Chinese girl who now lived in Austin with her husband and two kids. Shobha and Girish as a couple had few friends, though mostly Saroj noticed that Girish had his own circle of cigar-smoking, Oxford-type friends. Shobha seemed to only have colleagues. Always working, that girl. In one way, Saroj admired that about Shobha but in another, she didn't think it was healthy to be such a workaholic.

Devi on the other hand seemed to have too much fun. But she was also diligent, just always working in the wrong direction.

Devi was a lot like Vasu when it came to friends. She always had

too many friends who needed her help. And she gave help end-
lessly. Where were all her friends now? Saroj thought angrily as she
peeled a ripe and sweet pomegranate for Devi.

Avi told Saroj that a few had called to check up on her, and he'd
told them that Devi wasn't ready to talk to people, which was true.
The girl was not speaking. But still, where were these friends when
Devi was so depressed that she tried to kill herself?

"I don't think *anar* goes well with lamb, Devi." Saroj tried once
again to dissuade her daughter from cooking the lamb with pomegranate seeds. Who had ever heard of such a concoction? It simply
wouldn't work.

Devi firmly put a piece of unpeeled pomegranate in Saroj's
hand.

"You know, I can cook," Saroj said. "You don't have to cook
tonight. You have to go see that doctor in a while."

Devi put some flour along with salt, black pepper, and cayenne
in a freezer bag and threw the pieces of cut lamb in it. She shook the
bag until all the pieces were coated with the flour mixture.

"How do you want to serve this?" Saroj asked. "Should I make
rice?"

Devi shook her head and pointed to the bag of pita bread she'd
bought earlier that day from the bakery.

"Should I make *rotis*?" Saroj asked.

Devi shook her head furiously and pointed to the pita bread again.

"What?" Saroj muttered and then sighed. "Why can't you just talk
like all normal people and we won't have to go through this."

Devi threw the bag with the lamb on the counter in frustration
and cut a pita open with a knife and pointed to the lamb, the fresh
lettuce on the counter, and the pomegranate seeds Saroj was working on.

"Oh, you'll put them all inside the pita," Saroj said as understanding dawned, and then she wrinkled her nose. "Why can't we
just make simple lamb *sabzi* and have it with rice? I will make some
masala dal . . ."

Devi blew out her breath loudly and pointed jerkily at the pomegranate.

"You know, this would be easier if you would talk," Saroj repeated and nodded to Vasu, who'd just come into the kitchen. "She is going to put the lamb and the lettuce and the pomegranates in the pita bread."

"That sounds nice," Vasu said noncommittally. She wasn't looking too good to Saroj. Her face was drawn, and she looked older than she had when they'd picked her up at the airport just a few weeks ago.

"Mummy, you need to see a doctor," Saroj announced.

"I am a doctor," Vasu reminded her as she sat down on a dining chair across the kitchen. "How are you doing, Devi?"

Devi waved to Vasu and Saroj made an irritated sound. "You look . . . not well. You should see a doctor. Your travel insurance covers it, Mummy."

"I am on that side of seventy where people don't look that well," Vasu said and leaned back in the chair. "Devi, do you want me to come with you for your appointment this evening?"

Devi nodded.

"How long does she need to see this mental doctor?" Saroj asked.

"As long as it takes to get her better," Vasu said.

"But she is already better," Saroj countered and leaned over to kiss Devi on her forehead. She was just fine, Saroj thought happily. She just needed to open her mouth and start talking, that's all.

Avi picked up the phone when it rang. The caller said he was a friend of Devi's and wanted to speak to her. When Avi explained that Devi wasn't speaking at all, her friend wanted to know if he could then speak with Avi and Devi's mother. Since Devi's friend seemed reluctant to say much on the phone, Avi suggested he come to their home that evening while Devi was meeting with her psychiatrist. Avi didn't know what Devi's friend wanted to tell him and he didn't want to put any unnecessary pressure on Devi.

"Why did you ask him to come when Devi isn't home?" Shobha asked.

"I don't know what he has to tell us, and . . . I just don't want Devi to get upset," Avi explained.

"And you are sure he is a friend of Devi's?" Saroj asked, immediately suspicious. "Is he Indian?"

"I don't know," Avi said. "I spoke to him on the phone."

"What's his name?"

"Jay."

Saroj sighed. "That doesn't tell me if he is Indian or not."

"No," Avi agreed patiently.

"Did he sound Indian?"

"No, but neither does Shobha," Avi pointed out. "Look, he'll be here soon and you can see for yourself."

"What if he just wants to make trouble?" Saroj demanded.

"What trouble could he make?" Avi retorted. "And even if he does, Devi isn't at home."

"Girish? What do you think?" Saroj turned to her son-in-law.

Girish was reading the newspaper but he looked up and nodded. "Sounds fine."

"Now ask him what sounds fine," Shobha quipped as her husband went back to the paper. "Trust me, he won't know. He simply doesn't listen to anything anyone says."

"Did you say something, darling?" Girish asked lightly.

"Very funny," Shobha said and sat down beside her father.

"Contrary to what your mother thinks, I can't imagine this fellow being some crook who wants to take advantage of us," Avi said as he put his arm around Shobha. "I have a little more faith in people than your mama does."

"You trust everyone too easily," Saroj complained.

Avi was saved from answering by the doorbell. Saroj went to the door unhappily, not looking pleased at what she believed to be an intrusion into her family.

She opened the door and Shobha leaned over the arm of the sofa to see Devi's friend.

"Uh-oh," she said with a broad grin. "Mama is going to lose it."

"Who are you?" Saroj questioned the visitor rudely.

Jay looked very confused at the hostility but to his credit didn't run as any lesser man, Shobha believed, would.

"I'm a friend of Devi's," Jay said politely. "I spoke with Mister Veturi . . ."

"Avi," Saroj turned and yelled. "Is this the person you spoke to on the phone?"

Avi went to the door and nodded at Jay. "I couldn't see him through the phone line but I'm pretty sure he's the one," he said, amusement in his eyes. "I'm sorry, my wife is—"

"That's okay," Jay said responding to the humor in Avi's eyes. Devi had probably warned him about Saroj's opinion of the world's black population, Shobha thought.

The introductions were made, and even though Saroj couldn't stand the idea of a black man sitting on her sofa, she went to make tea. After all, a guest was a guest and in her house, no one treated a guest badly. She kept an ear to the living room, though, just in case someone said something important and she missed it.

"Like I said, Devi's meeting with her psychiatrist," Avi said. "Anything you can tell us to help her will be appreciated."

"I found out just yesterday. I went to her condo when I couldn't reach her by phone and her neighbor told me what happened," Jay said. He was obviously uncomfortable talking about Devi behind her back.

"She's better now," Shobha said. "Just doesn't talk, but cooks really awesome food."

"Devi? Cooking?" Jay smiled.

"We think she hit her head on the bathtub," Shobha joked.

Jay laughed as he was meant to, then as if coming to a decision, sat upright. "We dated, a long time ago."

Saroj came into the living room, running, with four cups of tea sitting precariously on a tray because of her speed.

"You dated Devi?" she demanded, accusingly.

"Yes, ma'am," Jay said. "For a few months, three, four years ago. We became friends and I don't know if she told you, but she was in the hospital six months ago."

"What was wrong?" Girish asked before anyone else could.

Jay's Adam's apple bobbed in and out. To Shobha it was a scene out of an Agatha Christie novel, *And the murderer is . . .*

"She was pregnant. She had a miscarriage."

The tray slipped out of Saroj's hand and the cups on it smashed onto the floor. Tea spilled onto the expensive Bokhara rug, on which Saroj didn't even let her children walk with shoes.

"What? When? What?" she asked, stumbling over her words.

Shobha could feel a burning sensation rise through her. From the frozen look her father was wearing it was evident that he was having trouble digesting this piece of information as well.

"You're sure? There's no mistake?" Girish asked. The news jolted him into standing, and the newspaper that was lying on his lap scattered onto the floor.

"No," Jay said and walked up to Saroj. He took her hand in his. "I'm so sorry."

"Was it your baby?" Saroj asked as she pulled away from him.

"No," Jay said immediately. "I was out of town in New York for a few months and she was dating someone else. I don't know who. But she didn't want him to know."

"How do you know about the miscarriage?" Girish asked.

"She called me in the middle of the night. She'd started bleeding and wanted me to take her to the ER," Jay explained. "She miscarried. There was nothing they could do. She was in a lot of pain and there was all that blood. I asked her if we should call her boyfriend but she wouldn't even tell me who it was. I thought we should call you all but she didn't let me do that, either. I had to go back to New York and—"

"How pregnant was she?" Saroj asked, speaking over Jay's words. She was standing very still, unmoving. In any other situation Saroj would've started cleaning up by now, would've rallied the family to make sure that the rug didn't stain.

"Eleven weeks," Jay said. "The doctor said it happens and she seemed okay about it. She kept saying that it was meant to be. I thought she was fine. I know I should've done something. If I'd done something, she wouldn't have—"

"It's okay," Avi said, speaking for the first time. "You came here, talked to us. You were there to hold her hand. We're very grateful."

"I'm so sorry," Jay said, looking and feeling guilty. "I didn't think she'd have told you and I thought that maybe this is why she doesn't want to talk, because she doesn't want to tell you about the baby."

"Good Lord." Shobha stood up shakily, her voice trembling. "Of all the stupid things she could do. Damn it, she could've told us. What the hell was all the secrecy for?"

And for the first time in a long time, Girish put his arm around his wife while she leaned into him.

As soon as she saw his car by the curb, Devi knew. She had felt elated after her session with Dr. Berkley. Vasu and she even stopped to pick up a Hindi movie DVD on their way home, but it looked as if a Hindi movie scene was already playing out inside the house.

Jay had wanted to call Avi the night of the miscarriage. He was very upset that Devi wouldn't call anyone, not even the father of the baby. He held her hand through the worst but he wanted someone to be with her, for her, when he was in New York. He called regularly for a while and Devi knew he was convinced she was doing all right. But she'd deceived him, just as she'd deceived everyone else.

"Are we going to sit in the car all night?" Vasu asked and then peered at the car by the curb. "Do we have a guest or did someone just park there? Come, Devi, let us go inside."

Devi had half a mind to pull a Thelma and Louise. Maybe Vasu wouldn't mind running off to Texas or someplace else. They'd work in diners and hide in trailer parks. It could be done. Devi was prepared to face anything other than the people inside the house who now knew all the reasons, well, most of the reasons anyway.

How would they react? Devi wondered. Her father? He'd be devastated. Her mother? She would probably be very irritated. One, for losing a grandchild, and, two, for having a daughter who got pregnant out of wedlock. Shobha? Definitely angry. And Girish? Oh, he'd wonder and wonder and wonder and wonder.

Was it worth it to go inside and face those people? Wouldn't it be better to just disappear into the night?

Vasu sighed deeply and opened the passenger's door. "Devi? What's wrong?"

Oh, and what about G'ma? She didn't know yet, but if they went inside she would know, too. And how would she react? She would be devastated as well. Devi usually told her everything, always had, but this she hadn't. This and everything else that followed.

G'ma had known when Devi started dating a professor, old enough to be her father, at Cal. Older men were safer, Devi always said. No bouts of passion, but no bouts of violent, irrational behavior, either. G'ma hadn't judged her, though Shobha's eyes bugged out.

"Doctor Menon? You're sleeping with that old fart?" Shobha was incredulous.

"He's very handsome," Devi said, reminding her that every female student who went through Dr. Menon's class wound up having a crush on him.

"He's old enough to be your grandfather," Shobha said, "and if Mama finds out, you're dead. You're beyond dead."

"And how would she find out?" Devi asked, daring Shobha to be a tattletale.

"Gossip, it flows," Shobha told her.

But gossip hadn't flown. Her three-month relationship with Dr. Menon quietly died down when she started dating a bookstore owner on Haight. That Saroj heard of. Everyone heard of that one. Devi Veturi was dating a black hippie with dreadlocks and was seen kissing him outside some Indian restaurant in Fremont.

Saroj was furious. But Vasu stood by Devi, supported her, and told Saroj to mind her own business and not try to control her daughters' lives.

What would Vasu do now? Support Devi or hold up an accusing finger like the others certainly would? As Saroj most certainly would? And who could blame them? She threw their lives into turmoil and then she wouldn't tell them why. And now some black dude was showing up at their doorstep to tell them that six months ago she'd lost a baby.

Maybe he hadn't told them, a hopeful voice within her whispered. Maybe he was just here to see how she was doing, to say hello, to hold her hand through this as he had through so many other crises. But the hopeful voice was crushed by the facts she was privy to. She knew Jay, knew him well enough to know that if he was here and heard that she wasn't talking after the "incident," he would spill the beans. Even after the miscarriage he had tried very hard to convince her to tell her family and/or the father of the baby. He wanted to make sure there was a support system around her to help deal with the trauma of the miscarriage.

Oh, that terrible night was vivid in her mind. All of it was stark, white against the blackness of other memories. She had heard of women losing their babies. It happened, they said, in the first trimester. She had heard that it was traumatic. Now she knew that no matter how many times she got pregnant, there would always be that one baby who hadn't made it. It didn't matter that the baby didn't have a name or a face. It had been her baby, growing inside her and then dying inside her. And there was nothing she could have done to make it live.

Devi wanted to turn and tell Vasu. She wanted to open her mouth and just tell her the truth. But her lips stayed tightly locked. There were other forces within her that kept her silent and she weakly stared at the car by the side of the road in front of her parents' house.

She could leave and never come back, find a way to survive, or not. But she knew she'd already gone down that path of running away from her problems and it had been the path of a coward.

Devi opened the car door and stepped out. She heard G'ma sigh noisily as she got out of the car as well.

"What's going on?" she asked Devi, who caught her lower lip between her teeth to stop herself from crying.

She opened the door and wasn't disappointed. The scene was straight out of a bad Hindi movie. Shattered teacups, tea, and a tray were spilled on Saroj's precious Bokhara. A newspaper was scattered on the floor by the coffee table. Saroj was standing rooted, shocked, tears flowing freely down her face. Shobha was distressed? Girish was holding her? Her father's face was buried in his hands and when he looked up, his eyes were red.

"What happened?" Vasu demanded, looking at everyone, including the black stranger in the room. "Who died?"

Vasu couldn't remember a time when she was more shocked. How many secrets did Devi hide? Were any more left? And how would she find out about them? Did she want to?

When Devi came back after sending Jay off, Saroj was the first to confront her. Vasu's fears that Saroj would start a rant about children out of wedlock were unfounded. Saroj surprised everyone with her reaction.

"How could you not tell us? We lost . . . that baby was my grandchild, too," Saroj said blisteringly, her nose watering and tears streaming down her face. And then without warning she took a step toward Devi and surrounded her in tight arms. "Oh, *beta,* I wish this hadn't happened to you. Oh, I wish I could have protected you from this."

Vasu could see Devi's resolve not to cry weaken as she hugged her mother back. Tears started rolling down Devi's cheeks.

Vasu expected Saroj to say and do a number of things, but this had not been a possibility.

"But don't worry," Saroj said, holding Devi away and facing her bravely. "It will be okay, you will have more babies."

Vasu wondered if Saroj was ignoring the fact that no one knew who the baby's father was. No one seemed to want to ask.

After that there was a lot of hugging and a lot of crying. Girish stood away from everyone by the French windows leading to the patio, while Shobha sat on one of the antique chairs at the chess table.

Devi seemed to say she was sorry as she looked each member of her family in the eye. When Shobha just raised her hand asking her not to do anything, Devi left and went into her bedroom.

Vasu followed her, still unable to figure out what she could say. How could a miscarriage be a good thing? Was there anything good about this that she could bring to light and ease some of the pain?

Devi sat down on her bed cross-legged and put a pillow on her lap. She smiled at Vasu and then shrugged again.

"It was very difficult, wasn't it?"

Devi nodded.

"I lost a baby before Saroj, but I got pregnant again, just two months after that, so it wasn't so bad. But for those two months it was a deep pain and I can only imagine what you are going through. All I can say is that everything happens for the better. And even though I cannot come up with one good thing about you losing your baby, I am sure God has a plan and—"

"Really?" Shobha asked as she stepped inside Devi's room. "Come on, G'ma, we aren't five years old, and so young that you can cook up these godly tales for us."

"Things get better," Vasu said wearily. "They do. You have to believe in that."

Devi put her thumb up in a questioning gesture.

"Yeah, G'ma, how?" Shobha added as she leaned against Devi's old dresser.

"How do they get better?" G'ma shrugged. "God has a plan—"

Devi flung her hands in the air and Shobha groaned dramatically.

"Not the old *he-has-a-plan* nonsense," Shobha said rocking against the dresser. "What about me? What kind of a plan did he have for me? That I should have no children?"

Vasu shook her head.

"And Devi had a miscarriage because this God of yours thought it was a good idea, right? And she was so thrilled about the whole thing, she tried to kill herself, right?" Shobha demanded. "Come on, G'ma, God's dead."

"*Shobha*," Vasu said, stricken instantly. She had always been an atheist, this one, but now she seemed to have lost faith in the universe. For Vasu, losing faith in God was the same as losing faith in the people, the world. Vasu was afraid for Shobha because without any faith, without any hope, the future was dark.

"I don't see God coming out of any walls in this house trying to redeem our lives," Shobha said. "If that hurts your feelings, you need to take it up with *your* God."

Devi put her face in her hands as she shook her head.

"What? Now all of a sudden you believe in this God business?" Shobha asked.

Devi lifted her face from her hands and shook it.

Devi called herself unsure, an agnostic. She didn't know whether this God person existed or not, but she wasn't about to bad-mouth him. Her belief in God was shaky at best; she believed in him only because if he did exist, she didn't want to be on his wrong side.

When they were younger, Devi would tease Shobha that she would have to face God's wrath because she said bad things about him. And even though Devi didn't really believe in this God, because she didn't say anything bad about him, she felt she was on the safe side.

It surprised and disappointed Vasu that neither of her grand-daughters had a healthy respect for Hinduism or God. She dutifully prayed every day, did her *pujas,* and followed the rituals. She felt she showed the world that you could be religious and broad-minded. To Vasu religion was personal and she didn't believe in all the ostentatious ceremonies held in the name of religion. Marriage, thread ceremonies, death ceremonies, pregnancies, maturity, and God knows what not. To her they seemed fraudulent exercises designed for people who didn't really have faith in God and only followed ceremony as a pretense. Vasu had tried to inculcate the same sense of religion in Saroj, but she'd gone her own way. Saroj was a social Hindu who went to *pujas* and the temple because it was a social event. She went to meet with friends and find India in the United States, and show off her heavy gold jewelry.

"Even if you don't believe in God, you have to believe in fate," Vasu said to Shobha, carefully measuring her words. She didn't want to give her false hope, but she wanted her to at least have some hope. "You can't have children, yes, but Devi can and when Devi has another child, you could be part of that child's life. Not like a mother, but like a second mother."

Devi looked up at G'ma and stuck her tongue out comically.

"She's saying she doesn't think so," Shobha muttered. "And I agree. All she'll want me to do is change shit diapers and put up with the baby when it cries."

Devi nodded in agreement.

"See, she doesn't want her kid to have a second mother, just a nanny," Shobha said with a half smile.

Vasu looked from Shobha's sad face to Devi's stricken face and wished there were a more tangible proof of a better tomorrow that she could offer them.

"I don't know what to say," she finally admitted in defeat. "I always tried to . . ." She let her words trail away in frustration.

"Don't worry, G'ma," Shobha said as she fidgeted with Devi's wooden jewelry box on the dresser. "Life goes on."

"Yes, it does." Vasu nodded in agreement and smiled at Devi. "It does, Devi. You will see, things will get better. They already have."

"Remember when G'ma gave this to you, Devi?" Shobha said, stroking the ivory-inlaid design on top of the jewelry box. "I was so jealous. I wanted this box so much."

"I brought you something else," Vasu reminded her.

"Yeah, but I was fifteen and didn't really care for the leather-bound edition of the Mahabharata as much as I did for an authentic Rajasthani hand-carved jewelry box," Shobha said as she flipped open the box in question.

"So you didn't like the book?" Vasu asked playfully. Devi grinned.

"Loved it," Shobha said, sounding distracted as she went through Devi's jewelry. "I have no idea where it is. Probably somewhere here, tucked away with Mama's books. But I . . ." Her fingers stopped moving through the jewelry all of a sudden and Shobha closed the box shut forcefully.

"If I gave you a jewelry box would you have been more careful with it?" Vasu asked, still playful.

Shobha looked as if she were in a trance. She threw a glance at Devi and then blinked her eyes.

"Maybe, G'ma, just maybe," she said. "We should go. Girish looks like death warmed over and I'm so tired, I can hardly stand."

Vasu watched Shobha leave and then turned her attention back to Devi. The poor girl, how hard must it have been to keep this a secret? And how much must she have hurt that she wanted to kill herself?

"Don't you worry, Devi," Vasu said confidently, "you'll have another baby." But Devi was staring at the jewelry box that Shobha had just closed with unswerving eyes.

~)

DEVI'S RECIPE
LAMB CLITORIS
The day everyone found out

Jay once told me that the pomegranate seed is sometimes compared to the clitoris for being pink, succulent, and an aphrodisiac. So I decided to name the recipe Lamb Clitoris in honor of Jay, the clitoris, and of course the day when my wall of secrets fell apart around me.

I put some flour, salt, and spices in a freezer bag and then put the pieces of lamb in and then went shake-shake-shake. The lamb was nicely covered with the flour. I browned the lamb and then put it aside.

Then I fried some onion with cinnamon, cloves, and cardamom, added some tomatoes and then the lamb, and cooked until the lamb was all flaky. I mixed chopped lettuce, pieces of avocado, and pomegranate seeds, along with a little bit of lemon juice.

I cut the pita bread open, put the lamb curry in, and then the lettuce-avocado mixture. All done!

These days whenever I cook, I stop to think that if my baby were alive, what would I be cooking? Where would I be? I think about it a lot. I think about it a lot while I cook and then I imagine that the child was to be and the child was as old as me and I was as old as my mother and everything was different.

Deader Than a Dead Relationship

Saroj made her own spices. It was something she believed in and couldn't imagine why people would buy those ridiculous packets of ready-made spices available in Indian grocery stores.

"It is simple to make," Saroj said when she saw Devi write *rasam* powder on her shopping list. "I just ran out a few weeks ago. But we will make it together. Okay?"

For a moment Saroj thought Devi would refuse. She probably thought that she didn't need her mother's help and Saroj wanted so much to help.

Devi nodded and struck *rasam* powder from the list.

"Should we make it now?" Saroj asked, pleased, and Devi nodded again.

"Good," Saroj said as she rolled up the sleeves of her *kameez*. "Very, very simple."

Saroj brought out her cast-iron pan, the one she'd brought all the way from India when she once went on vacation. "This is the best pan to use because it gets very hot," Saroj said and started going through her spice cabinet.

She heated the pan and started filling it with coriander seeds, black peppercorns, cumin seeds, fenugreek seeds, mustard seeds, a few sticks of cinnamon, fresh curry leaves, and a little asafoetida.

"You have to be careful not to burn the seeds," she told Devi. "The spices come alive when they are roasted like this. Can you smell it?"

The kitchen air thickened with the smell of the spices, their essence spilling out of the hot cast-iron pan. The mustard seeds started to splutter a little and Saroj shook the pan, moving the whole spices around. Right before they turned dark brown (she always knew when that time was) she picked up the pan and, using a wooden spatula, poured the mixture inside the coffee grinder she used especially for spices.

"Don't use Daddy's," Saroj told Devi. "Coffee ruins the taste of the powder."

She then added oil to the hot cast-iron pan, which immediately caused sizzling, broke open three dried red chilies, and dropped them in.

"This makes the flavor of the chili come out," she told Devi as she put the lightly fried chilies into the grinder as well.

She started the grinder, stopping to smell the spices and feel their textures with her fingers at regular intervals. When everything was ground to a fine powder she brought out the medium-sized airtight glass container labeled RASAM POWDER and poured the powder inside it.

"There, wasn't it simple?" Saroj said, flushed with delight. She could teach Devi how to cook as well. No one was born knowing the basics and even though Devi was doing a fabulous job, when it came to Indian food and spices, how could the girl know anything? She needed Saroj's advice.

Devi smiled and then started scribbling on the shopping list again.

Saroj wondered if it had made any difference at all or would Devi have been just as happy if she'd bought the *rasam* powder from the store.

That evening Devi made *rasam,* but she served it with a flaky pastry on top.

"This is really good," Shobha said as she bit into the pastry soaked in *rasam.*

Everyone joined Shobha in complimenting the food, but they were all subdued. Girish was so withdrawn that even Saroj felt sorry for him. She wondered how bad things had gotten between him and Shobha. Just because she didn't acknowledge something was wrong didn't mean she was blind or stupid. She saw what was going on, could feel the tension between them, and was unhappy because of it. But if Shobha didn't talk to her about her problems what could she do? She couldn't help those who didn't ask for help. And even if Shobha came and asked for help to make her marriage better, Saroj wasn't sure what assistance she could offer .

How could she offer any marital advice when her own marriage was in ruins? Just because she didn't acknowledge that, either, didn't mean she didn't know it.

Vasu was sipping the *rasam* from her spoon slowly, her head lolling a little, almost falling into the bowl. The news of the miscarriage really shook her up. Saroj understood. Devi had been closest to her and Vasu was probably wondering why she knew nothing about Devi's life as it had been a few months ago.

If only Devi would start speaking, Saroj thought unhappily. This cooking business was great, but the girl had to talk, tell them what happened, so that the wounds could heal. Losing a baby was never easy and in Devi's case it obviously was a huge tragedy, something so massive that it drove her to the edge of her world.

This was supposed to be her perfect family? Saroj looked from one forlorn face to the other and wondered. This was her family and yet, as she sat, all she really wanted was her husband back. If that part of her life would somehow repair itself, everything else, she believed, would follow suit.

After the rummy party, Saroj seriously started contemplating happiness and why it was elusive to her. She saw Amrita again, at Kohinoor, the Indian video and DVD store.

"Picking up one of my movies?" Amrita asked, seeing the DVD Saroj held. It was one of Amrita's old movies, one that her exhusband Pradeep Shankar directed.

"Yes, I saw it earlier, but just wanted to refresh my memory," Saroj said. She thought Amrita would make some reference to their conversation in Meera's guest bathroom, but the actress gushed about how wonderful it was to see her movies again and now available on DVD.

"It is so clear . . . unbelievable and now preserved," Amrita said, excited. "You tell me what you think about the movie, okay? *Ciao.*"

Ciao? Indians didn't say *ciao,* Saroj thought, throwing a disgusted look at Amrita Saxena's slender back as she left the store.

She didn't want to end up like that stupid actress, divorcing and marrying and divorcing and marrying to find happiness. Happiness was here, she had seen it, felt it, lived it. She just had to get it back, had to reach out and shake Avi out of his stupor. Their marriage had lost all semblance of a relationship. They were like roommates now, barely able to communicate about anything but time schedules. This was the dull, ugly side of marriage that Saroj was always confident she would never see. Just as the silverware she received from Avi's mother after their marriage caught tarnish, their marriage had lost luster as well. She'd been less careful with her marriage than she'd been with the silver plates and cutlery, which still shone.

But what if beneath the tarnish and the stains of apathy, there was nothing? Saroj felt that it was that subconscious fear that kept both of them from trying to repair their relationship. It had all started to fall apart at some time, and even if she could pinpoint that exact moment, how would it help solve the predicament she was in now?

After dinner, the kids, as Saroj still thought of them, and Vasu sat down to watch a Hindi movie. Girish made noise about missing some Spanish movie on the Independent Film Channel. The intellectual *laatsahab!*

"You can go home and see what you want to see," Shobha said as she sat cross-legged on the carpet by Vasu's legs. "We're going to watch Sunil Shetty light up the screen."

"With wet and half-naked young girls," Vasu reminded her and then glanced at Girish. "Are you sure you don't want to watch the movie?"

"You mean there will be nubile girls drenched from head to toe?" Girish asked sarcastically. "I think I'll pass."

"And they'll be wearing thin white saris so that you can see their titties," Shobha said with a broad grin and was immediately admonished by Saroj.

"What's wrong with the word *titties?*" Shobha instantly demanded. "It's not a bad word like . . . say . . ."

Devi started giggling softly.

"Don't even think it," Saroj cried out, but she was smiling. This was good, she thought happily. This family scene was right. Everything was in place. Wasn't it?

"Are you sure you don't want to watch nubile half-naked wet girls?" Saroj asked Avi, playfully falling in step with the mood in the house.

"When I have you, *janam,* why would I look at anyone else?" he said as he used to a long time ago when she would tease him about him leaving her for another woman.

Saroj's heart took a small leap, and recognition flared in Avi's eyes as well. Then Avi's expression shuttered again as he carted plates from the dining area to the kitchen sink.

As the opening credits started to roll with cheesy Hindi movie music in the background, Saroj decided to throw the first dart in the dark.

"Would you like to go for a walk after we do the dishes?" Saroj asked Avi and felt the same nervousness she had when she talked to him about marrying her all those years ago. But this was harder than that had been. She didn't have anything to lose then. Now everything was at stake.

"Walk?" Avi asked as if Saroj had spoken in an alien tongue.

"Yes, like we used to . . . remember, in Udhampur?" Saroj said as she gnawed on her lower lip, feeling as gauche as a teenager propositioning a boy she had a crush on. "It is nice and warm outside . . . and I thought . . . we don't have to . . ."

"No, no," Avi said, sounding just as uncomfortable. "Sure. A walk should be good. We could just walk by the park or something."

"Yes," Saroj said, her heart light.

.   .   .

Shobha watched him surreptitiously. He was sitting next to Vasu as if someone had put a gun to his head. He didn't like Hindi movies, the intellectual snob.

"This is not as bad as I thought it would be," Girish said, making an exasperated sound as a young Indian woman came onscreen wearing a thin red chiffon sari. And then predictably the skies above her rumbled with false thunder and rain started to fall, soaking her to the skin, displaying all her bodily assets.

"Oh my, they do leave nothing to imagination these days, don't they?" Vasu said when the actress leaned over in her dance routine. Her breasts were an eyeful.

"I thought they wore white when they did this rain song-and-dance business," Shobha complained. "I want white."

"I like red," Girish said. "And I must say that color and sari bring out the best in her."

The Hindi actress was singing in the rain now and Shobha was sure that if one looked carefully, one could count her pubic hairs, clearly visible through the thin, wet, red sari.

"Maybe if I wore that sari and stood under the shower it could do miracles for us," Shobha snapped at him for no reason except habit.

"Maybe . . . maybe not," Girish said and then turned his attention to Vasu. "In your days women had more class, didn't they, G'ma?"

Vasu looked from Shobha to Girish and then raised her eyebrows. "Are you asking about women in general or women in the movies?"

"In the movies," Girish said after waiting a long moment.

"It was not the same tits-and-ass show it is now, but I don't compare. There were good movies then and there were bad movies then, same as now," Vasu said. "Devi loves old black-and-white Hindi movies."

"Don't I know it," Girish said. "We went to San Francisco once when they were having a Guru Dutt film festival and saw *Pyaasa* and *Kagaz Ke Phool*. She sobbed all the way back from the city."

Devi made a face and shook her head.

"Yes you did," Girish said smugly. "Big tears and lots of sobbing and hiccupping."

"When was this?" Shobha asked as small hairs stood at attention on the back of her neck.

"Ah, some time ago," Girish said negligently.

"When?"

"How does it matter?" Girish said and then went back to discussing women in Indian cinema.

Shobha could feel the blood surge through her. He was so friendly, so much fun, so charming with Vasu and Devi, but as soon as they were alone he turned into a sarcastic devil.

Maybe she should have slept with Vladimir, maybe she should have slept with a billion other men while she was married to Mr. Sarcasm. Tears of frustration threatened to spill out of her eyes. Her marriage was over, she knew, but each time she re-realized it, it was a blow. And she still didn't know what to do about it. Should she just tell Girish to his face that it was over and turn her back on him?

She watched her parents go out for a walk and wondered if she and Girish would look like her parents if they stayed married. Would she have the same fucked-up marriage her parents did? Oh Lord, she didn't want to be her mother. She didn't even want to be her father. She just wanted to be happy. It sounded like such a simple thing to want but it was so elusive. Just happiness! They should make a fucking pill or something.

"I think I've had as much of this movie as I can take," Shobha said, standing up. "Maybe I'll go for a walk, too?"

"And I will join you," Vasu said, standing up.

"Then I guess Devi and I'll switch to the Independent Film Channel and enjoy a good Spanish movie," Girish said, taking charge of the TV remote. "If you like old Hindi movies, you'll love this," he told Devi.

For an instant Shobha thought that Devi would come along with them for a walk, but then her little sister smiled at her husband and settled back on the sofa.

It was a pleasant night. The cool winds from the bay had leveled some of the heat of the day. Shobha could smell her mother's night jasmine and feel the crunch of dew on the grass under her shoes.

"It's quiet," Shobha said.

"It's late," Vasu said and then took Shobha's hand in hers. "What's wrong?"

"My marriage is over," Shobha said and then glared at Vasu. "I can't believe I said that out loud."

"It has probably been over for a while," Vasu said, pity brimming in her eyes.

Because it annoyed Shobha to see that, she turned away from Vasu and started to walk down the stone path through the garden toward the sidewalk.

"If I could have children things would've been different," she said confidently.

"No," Vasu said, catching up with her. "And you know it. If you loved each other, not having children wouldn't matter. You would adopt, find another way."

"And he's cheated on me," Shobha said and felt the words slam through her heart.

"Oh." Vasu nodded. "Are you sure?"

"Yes."

Vasu shrugged. "Have you . . . have you?"

"Gone astray?" Shobha finished for Vasu and when she laughed, Shobha sighed. "No I have never cheated on him, but it has crossed my mind, several times."

"He looks very serious these days," Vasu said. "I think he is sad. Maybe he knows it, too, that your marriage is over, and like you is waiting for something to happen."

"Nothing's going to happen," Shobha said as she kicked a wayward pebble on the sidewalk. "Nothing, if we don't make it happen. But I'm scared of divorce, the legal implications of it, the life implications of it."

"You should talk to him," Vasu suggested. "Is this affecting your work?"

Shobha stopped and turned to face Vasu. "Oh yes. How did you guess? Don't tell me, you're clairvoyant, too."

"No, just a grandma," Vasu said as she touched a hand to Shobha's cheek.

"When Devi . . . did that thing, I got delayed in a product launch.

Nothing to do with her, but it happened and now it's going to happen again," Shobha said and then shrugged. "But for the first time I'm not obsessing about my job. I'm obsessing about my marriage and divorce."

"Do you want to fix things with Girish?"

"No," Shobha answered immediately. "God, this is mortifying, isn't it? We've been married five years and I so easily say that I don't want to be happy with him, I just want to be without him."

"He's a good man," Vasu said understandingly.

"And that does make it harder," Shobha agreed. "But he isn't all that nice to me. He can be a real asshole."

"I am sure you don't do anything to provoke the asshole in him," Vasu said with some amusement.

Shobha made a face and then laughed despite herself. "We've not been getting along ever since we got married. And now . . . now he's having an affair with someone else or he's had an affair with someone else."

"Are you sure, Shobha?"

"I found a pearl earring in his car," Shobha said and then shook her head. "I'm sure, regardless of the earring, I'm sure and it should break my heart and it does, but not for the reason I thought it would."

"Betrayal is difficult to deal with."

"He can't betray me, G'ma," Shobha said softly. "He and I never had that kind of a relationship."

Saroj wished she could grab Avi's hand as they walked slowly, silently. They had been walking for more than half an hour now and all they had talked about was Vikram's new grandson, whose pictures they recently saw, and how Avi's old company's stock was faring on the NASDAQ.

"It should be fall soon," Avi said looking up at the clear dark sky. It looked like a black sari with sparkles stuck on it.

"Yes," Saroj said uneasily. This was her last chance at making it right, at making Avi realize that they needed to get back to their life and their marriage or all would be lost.

"Did I tell you about my meeting Amrita Saxena again at the video store?" Saroj asked as she wondered how to broach the subject. This was not an easy conversation to have. How could she start? *Our marriage is failing and we need to fix it* would hardly do.

"Hmm," Avi mumbled, obviously not interested.

"She had so many divorces," Saroj said and grabbed Avi's hand. He didn't pull away, but neither did he respond by holding her hand in return. His hand just lay in hers, neither foe nor friend.

"Those movie types always do," Avi said.

"She told me that all she was doing was looking for happiness. She just wants to be happy, so she moves from man to man to find it," Saroj explained. "Isn't that what we all want, Avi, to be happy?"

Avi nodded.

"Are you happy?" Saroj asked as her heart thudded against her ribs. She was afraid he would lie and say he was, and she was petrified that he would tell her the truth that he wasn't.

"I don't know," Avi said instead. "I don't know what that means anymore, Saroj."

Saroj wished he had lied.

"Weren't we ever happy?" Saroj asked shakily.

Avi nodded and then turned to her and smiled, a big broad plastic smile. "We are still happy."

Saroj laughed with tension. "No, our youngest daughter attempted suicide and won't say a word now. Our older daughter and her husband don't get along at all and they can't have children. My mother is ill. You and I have become roommates. So no, Avi, we are not even close to being happy."

"Everyone has problems," Avi told her. "This isn't some Hindi movie, Saroj. Life is like this."

"And all of this would be easy to handle, and we could still find happiness, if you and I, if you and I could just talk, be friends again, lovers again," Saroj said, putting all her cards on the table.

Avi stopped walking and turned to face Saroj. "I don't know," he said honestly and Saroj could hear her heart break.

"We can make it work," she said, trying to keep a brave face. She wasn't going to lose him, not now, not after all these years and so much sharing.

"I feel that Devi had her miscarriage because of us," Avi said, his face twisting in pain. "I feel that because of what we did, God made her and Shobha pay for it."

"What did we do?" Saroj asked.

Avi shook his head. "It doesn't matter now. You and I . . . we're fine, Saroj. Things will get better once Devi starts talking and—"

"What did we do?" Saroj demanded, now angry that he was carrying a terrible guilt she knew nothing about inside him.

Avi sighed. "Remember after Shobha was born?"

Saroj nodded, still not sure, and then clarity came to her and she made an annoyed sound. "Avi," she cried out. "Shobha was three months old and I got pregnant again, what else could we do?"

Avi sighed again as he removed his hand from her hold. "I knew you would say something like this. That's why—"

"Something like this? What do you mean by that?" Saroj demanded.

"You are so bloody practical, Saroj. So righteous. You don't even stop to think that maybe it was a mistake. That baby you had aborted was a baby, our child, but you didn't even think about it. It was an automatic decision with you, wasn't it?" Avi's eyes were blazing with anger.

The old Saroj, the one who rehabilitated a wounded soldier, would've cajoled. The new Saroj, bitter after years of negligence, was spitting mad.

"We made the decision together," Saroj reminded him. "And in any case, the choice was *mine*. I would have to carry a baby. I would have to carry a baby while I had a three-month-old to take care of, alone. If you think that God is so stupid as to make our children pay for an inevitable decision of ours, then you should stop believing in this God and start believing in something intelligent."

"Lower your voice," Avi said as a light in a darkened house by the sidewalk came on. "Do you want the entire neighborhood to know?"

"Know what? That my husband is an idiot? Sure," Saroj said, turning around to go back home. "Wake up, Avi. Our marriage is in ruins. We have nothing left. If you are going to dig up old dirt and give ridiculous reasons for things that are happening now, then we might as well go our ways. I am not going to hang around bickering all day and night with you. I need a husband, a friend, a companion at this time as I have always. But now I am too old and too tired to put up with your nonsense. So if you want to continue believing in this stupid and vengeful God of yours, then do it someplace else."

Saroj started to walk away from him and then paused and turned around. "And in case you are wondering, I know the California laws and I take half of everything you have. Which means, I keep the house. You can live in some small, dingy condo somewhere."

She marched down the sidewalk, leaving an openmouthed Avi to stare after her. They fought bitterly and argued passionately, but usually Saroj was neither this eloquent nor this final in what she had to say. She felt rather proud of herself. As if she had won the marathon, even though it took a long time for her to get there.

She bumped into Shobha and Vasu five minutes from home. "What's wrong?" Shobha asked as she saw Saroj's face flashing anger.

"I am divorcing your father if he doesn't come to his senses," Saroj announced.

Vasu's eyebrows shot up. "What?"

"Do you know that he blames us . . . no, he just blames me, for Shobha not having a baby and Devi having a miscarriage?" Saroj said, as she let out some steam. "When you were three months old, I got pregnant again, so I had a D and C. I had to. I couldn't take care of you and be pregnant. Now that stupid man thinks that because of that, you and Devi are suffering."

Shobha stared at her mother for a moment. Saroj could see she was surprised, even a little shocked. Saroj waited for Shobha to say something mean and hurtful, but she was taken aback by her words.

"I haven't heard this much crap in a long time, and that, too, from Daddy," Shobha said seriously. "Didn't think Daddy was such a—"

"—moron?" Saroj finished for her.

"Well, since you're married to him you have the right to say so," Shobha said and then put her arm around Saroj. "So you put him in his place?"

"Oh yes," Saroj said smugly. "I told him I would take all his money and leave him in some apartment to die."

"Good for you," Vasu said and patted Saroj's cheek.

"I don't want a divorce," Saroj admitted sheepishly. "I hope he knows that. I was just angry. I just want him to wake up."

Shobha grinned. "I'm sure he knows, Mama. I'm sure he does."

LETTER FROM AVI TO SAROJ. WRITTEN ON A COMPUTER
AT THE SANTA CLARA KINKO'S ON EL CAMINO REAL.

Dear Saroj,

I have wondered what is deader than a dead relationship and then I have wondered if our relationship is indeed dead. I never gave divorce serious thought. I never thought about it because I didn't think that it would be acceptable to you. You and Shobha are so alike in this. You both want to succeed at everything you do. You wanted the perfect family, but I always knew things couldn't be that perfect when I had an arm missing. I have always wondered if you would stop loving me because one day you would wake up and see I was short one arm.

While I was working, I didn't worry about us, or even give us much thought. I know that you think I am to blame for this barren wasteland of a marriage, but you are not without guilt. You didn't do anything, either. You let me be the workaholic, you didn't change a thing, you didn't try to bring us closer. And what was I supposed to think?

I didn't want Shobha to have an arranged marriage, but you didn't listen to me and now look how unhappy she is. You made all the decisions at home and I let you. I regret it. I regret it so much. You, who always wanted a better relationship with your daughters, because you had a bad one with your mother, have done nothing to speak with your children. They still treat you like a stranger, sometimes like a tyrant.

There have been times, so many times that I have been tempted to leave, to never come back. But my children, I stayed for my children, always. They have been my priority, our priority, and it was easy to put them first, wasn't it, because we didn't want to have anything to do with each other. I know you resented my success because I didn't give you credit for it, but I never thought of giving you credit because you did nothing for my business. Vikram and I set up the company on our own, despite your and his wife's doubts. And you doubted me at every step. You always told me that we should never have come here, that this wouldn't work out. I could never come home and relax, never talk about my problems at work because the minute I did, you would talk about going back to India.

Here I had respect, my own business, money. Back in India I was nothing. I had nothing and no one gave a damn. I was just a one-armed soldier, and that's it. I wanted more, I wanted to be more. Now I am more. If your life didn't turn out the way you planned—hell, Saroj, that can't be my fault. We married each other, we didn't write each other's destinies. If you wanted a life then you should have gone and gotten one. Coming to me now and saying that you gave it all up for me is nonsense.

You gave it all up because you wanted to. You never wanted a career, never wanted to do anything but what you did. If you are dissatisfied with that, how can that be anyone else's fault but yours? Being a housewife is a choice you made and you have to live with it.

Divorce? I would be happy. The bitterness I carry inside me is not something I can throw at you all the time the way you throw yours at me. I don't have the energy to do so. I . . .

[END TEXT]

~⌒〇

Saroj waited for him in the living room. It had been three hours since she'd walked away from him. Three hours since she'd said the word *divorce*. And he was still not back. What if he didn't come back? How would he do this? Call and ask her to pack a bag for him? She'd be damned if she would pack him a bag. She would burn all his things, just the way that woman did to her husband's things in that movie with all those black girls.

Oh yes, she would burn everything and his Jeep. To hell with him! If he didn't want to come back, then that was his business.

The door finally opened at three AM. Saroj had been unable to close her eyes for more than a second to blink. She was watching the Sunil Shetty movie discarded by the kids to keep her mind clear of the biggest worry she created for herself.

As soon as Avi stepped in, Saroj rose from the sofa, ready to run to him and apologize, to beg him to take her back.

"I'm so sorry," he said before she could get a word out. "I'm so terribly sorry."

Saroj didn't move. She didn't have the courage to ask him what he was sorry about.

"I started writing a letter to you and I wrote and wrote and I realized that I was so bitter about the past, about everything, and that through the bitterness I couldn't see you, see us, how good we were, how good we can still be," Avi said sincerely.

Saroj sat down with relief. He wasn't going to leave.

"I hated it that I was to blame as well, so I put all the blame on you," he continued. "I didn't know how to go back and find those days in Udhampur and Jorhat so I didn't try to go back at all. I don't want a divorce, Saroj. I want another chance for both of us. To try and make this work. I think we can."

Saroj started crying, unable to get up and go to him.

She didn't realize he had moved so it was a surprise when she felt his arm around her.

"Don't cry," he said as he used to a long time ago.

"What if we can't make it right?" Saroj asked.

"We'll give it our best shot," Avi said as he tightened his hold on his wife.

"And that will be enough?"

"More than enough," he said confidently and Saroj believed him.

.   .   .

DEVI'S RECIPE
MAMA'S RASAM WITH MY PASTRY
The night Mama and Daddy made up

I watched them surreptitiously from the hallway. I have never seen Mama and Daddy make up quite like this. Actually I don't remember ever seeing them make up. They would usually just let the fight die and things would go back to normal. It was touching to see them talk to each other like this and it was a relief to know that one marriage around me was still on track. Regardless of the quibbles I have with Mama and how she runs her life, I can't imagine a world where Mama and Daddy are not together. Maybe love doesn't die, maybe it stays alive and sometimes gets neglected but it can be resurrected. I admire Mama's courage in shaking Daddy up. Things could've not worked out this way, yet Mama took a chance and it paid off. Now maybe they can be happy again, the way they used to be before Shobha and I were born. Maybe now Daddy will start appreciating her just as I have.

I admire Mama's ability to whip up rasam powder without a recipe. As I fiddle with food, I realize how important it is to pore over recipe books, watch cooking shows, and use your senses. But with Mama it's innate. She knows how much black peppercorn and how much cinnamon and how many cumin seeds it takes to make rasam powder. I wonder if after years of experience in the kitchen if I will be as blasé about dumping spices in a pan as Mama is. I hope I will.

Making the pastry was very simple. I just took some plain flour and mixed it with pieces of chilled butter and then when the flour was crumbly in texture I added ice-cold water and made dough. I didn't knead too much, just mixed and then put the dough in a freezer bag and left it in the fridge for a few hours, until it was time for dinner.

Rasam is so ridiculously simple to make that I have decided to make it every other day and drink it like soup. Leave some whole tamarind (Mama would die before she bought the easy-to-use concentrate) in hot water and let it soak. Then squeeze the pulp out and mix with warm *water. Throw the remaining tamarind out. Put regular* tadka *of mustard and curry leaves in hot oil. Add chopped tomatoes and cook for a while. Then add* rasam *powder and mix. Add the tamarind pulp and water and mix again.*

I poured the rasam *in ceramic soup bowls (which I bought at Cost Plus for this purpose). Then I rolled out the pastry dough into small circles, which I placed on top of the* rasam *and baked for a while, until the thin pastry was done.*

I thought it turned out very well, for just plain ol' rasam.

The Truth About Shobha

She had an office.

As a vice president, for the first time in her career in Silicon Valley, Shobha had an office. It didn't have a view of anything interesting, just the parking lot of the Chinese supermarket. Still, she had an office, a window, and in Silicon Valley that meant something.

As she swiveled around in the leather chair she'd custom-ordered for herself when she'd been promoted two years ago she realized that she'd made it and she'd also fucked it up.

Pavan, her product manager, just called to let her know that for the second time in six months they were going to be unable to launch a product on time. It was not a surprise. Everyone knew there would be a delay. Pavan's call just made it official.

She didn't even have the energy to be angry. This was a long time coming, probably ever since she got promoted. She wasn't ready for this responsibility. That was it.

Oh, to hell with it, she told herself. She was ready, she just fucked up. Everyone fucked up. It happened all the time. All the time!

For the past half an hour, since her boss's assistant called to schedule an appointment for eleven AM, Shobha had been contemplating how to handle the meeting. Mitchell, her boss, was never this formal, never had his assistant call her for a meeting. He usually stopped by her office, or sent a quick e-mail to arrange an impromptu chat. The officialness of it made Shobha realize that this was not some random meeting. This was *the* meeting, the one where she was going to be sent home packing.

Since Pavan told her about the impending delay, she'd been prepared. Just the other day she'd even cleared out her desk. Still, she felt the shivers of surprise course through her. She'd never been fired before!

Shobha looked at the hasty note she'd written when Mitchell's assistant called, which cleared that tiny doubt in her mind that maybe she'd just dreamed it up. She really did have a meeting at eleven AM with Mitchell in the Mount Doom conference room. It was not just a figment of her imagination.

The *Lord of the Rings* mania hadn't escaped the company, and when the new conference rooms emerged from rearranged cubicles, names naturally came from the legendary books. Mount Doom, Minas Tirith, Gondor, Mordor, Rivendell, and The Shire were the chosen names for the conference rooms. The three e-mail servers were Gandalf, Aragorn, and Legolas. The sturdy old legacy server was Bilbo and the unsteady server, which almost always crashed, was labeled Boromir. This was common practice in most IT companies. In Shobha's last company the servers were C-3PO, R2-D2, Darth Vader, and Yoda. The conference rooms were also not spared the *Star Wars* theme and were named Alderaan, Naboo, Tatooine, and Coruscant.

So it was actually almost cute that Mitchell set up *the* meeting in Mount Doom, not probably by design but availability.

"Hey, we're going to lunch at Hama Sushi, want to join us?" Leo popped his head into her office.

"Hmm," Shobha said vaguely.

"You look like your puppy got kicked," Leo remarked.

"I think I'm getting fired in about"—she looked at the clock on her computer and then at Leo—"fifteen minutes."

"Fired?" Leo stepped into her office. Shobha and Leo were friends. They'd started working at the company at the same time and had worked together on various teams.

"Fired or laid off?" Leo wanted it clarified. "Are we having lay-offs? My wife's pregnant with baby number three. This company can't be having layoffs."

"Fired," Shobha said, raising her hand to quiet him.

"Oh shit, I'm so sorry," Leo said. "You taking anyone else down with you?"

"I don't think so. They'll want Pavan to stay if I'm leaving," Shobha said as she chewed the inside of her bottom lip nervously.

"Good, because you probably can go without a job, thanks to professor husband at Stanford, but the rest of us have families, man," Leo said with a sad smile.

Ah, the husband, Shobha thought unhappily. Now what? Should she keep the husband because she had no income, no job, no career, no future, no babies, no nothing?

"So, what happened?" Leo prodded.

"Second delayed product launch and we didn't meet our num-bers last quarter. I think . . . no, I'm pretty sure I'm going to get blamed for it," Shobha said.

"If they didn't keep changing the product specs on you, you'd probably have the product out on time," Leo said, sounding as irri-tated as Shobha did with the executive staff.

"I know," Shobha muttered as she got up. "I already cleaned out my office. Shit . . . I've never been fired before."

"I'm not ashamed to tell you that it has happened to me a few times. And here's what you can learn from my experience, just don't cry, embarrasses the hell out of them. I should know. The first time, I bawled like a baby," Leo said, and patted Shobha's shoulder. "And you're a trouper, babe. I'll get the others together and we'll go drown your sorrows in sake at Hama Sushi."

"I'll need sake after Mitchell's little firing speech," Shobha said as she gave her office a last glance and walked toward the confer-ence room.

Mitchell was a nice guy. He was slightly roly-poly, more than a little bald, and had no idea a world existed beyond IT and the Oak-land Raiders. But he was a steady, stable sort of fellow who didn't take too many chances, and Shobha liked him because of all those reasons and disliked him for the same reasons as well. What made him good at keeping the company on safe ground also kept him from being able to take the big steps to change the direction and market cap of the company.

Mitchell wasn't alone in the conference room. Shobha kicked herself for not thinking about it. Mitchell was after all the nice guy. The director of human resources, Carol Miller, was with him, a broad smile on her *I'm-a-bimbo* face, to ensure all legalities were followed and that Mitchell did what he was supposed to do. Shobha couldn't stand the newly hired little perky, blond-haired, blue-eyed director.

"How are you doing?" Carol asked and Shobha nodded as she sat down.

A small smile splayed on her lips. She wasn't going to bawl like a baby, she was going to get a handsome compensation package as they kicked her out.

"I'm fine, Carol. Hello, Mitchell," Shobha said, feeling very much in control, like Demi Moore in *Disclosure* before they get her for entrapment.

"You know that things didn't work out last quarter," Mitchell said, then raised both his hands in the air, clapped once, and laid his hands on the lacquered wooden conference table.

"I'm aware that we didn't meet our numbers," Shobha said, calmly looking at Carol, who seemed a little jittery. Not a very experienced HR director, this one.

"We analyzed the situation and the numbers clearly show that if we'd launched PiSon on time last quarter we could've made it," Mitchell said, new confidence suffusing his voice. He'd hired and fired too many people to be nervous about this. But Shobha knew he liked her and maybe that was why he had a small scratch in his throat as he spoke.

"So, I'm the scapegoat," Shobha said, looking at Mitchell and then turning to face Carol, again with a smile. "The product was delayed for a lot of reasons. We're understaffed, you cut the budget one too many times, and I have lost too many good programmers. It leaves me with absolutely no room for anyone in my department to even fall sick. PiSon was also delayed because the specs were changed *after* they were frozen."

Mitchell nodded. "I know all that and we could do nothing about the specs change. Eric had an idea and . . ."

"So it's my fault that the CEO had a vision? A vision that came a little too late?" Shobha asked pointedly.

Mitchell shook his head. "And even if we let that matter slide. We are now in the same position again."

"You changed the specs again after the freeze," Shobha reminded him. She knew the decision was already made. All she had to do was make a good enough case so that they gave her a good "firing package." She never thought she'd see this day. She was angry as hell with the company. Corporate America had no loyalty. She had turned down offers from competitors in the past because she believed in her company, its products, and her career here, but now, it was over. They thought she was a liability and wanted her gone.

"Let's cut to the chase," Shobha said when Mitchell was about to speak. "You want me gone and I want to be gone as well. My office is packed and cleaned out. I can leave right now, no fuss, no mess. Pavan has all the documentation. He knows where we are on all the projects."

"Okay," Mitchell said, sounding only a little surprised.

"So what can you do for me?" Shobha asked, swallowing the ball of nervousness in her throat.

"If Pavan has everything . . ."

"I have another offer," Shobha lied easily. "Do you really think that I'd let things reach this point without shopping around?"

Mitchell nodded his head in agreement. It was reasonable that Shobha was interviewing with other companies. Mitchell knew she was frustrated with the new CEO and his habit of changing specs on products after the work on the product had already begun. When that conversation had taken place, Shobha hadn't thought she would be able to take advantage of it.

"Pavan, Vladimir, and maybe three or four others will leave with me if I ask them to," Shobha said clearly. "I will sign your noncompetitive agreement and not take them or anyone else with me, but I need to first know what you can do for me."

"Six weeks with benefits," Carol said, her tone resembling that of a schoolmarm. "Shobha, this is standard."

"Shove standard, Carol," Shobha said and turned her attention to Mitchell. "Well?"

"Six months with all benefits," Mitchell said without flinching. "Plus all the bonuses you would receive if you stayed."

"Mitchell," Carol cried out. "We haven't discussed this—"

"I cleared this with Eric," Mitchell said without even glancing at the perky HR director, and once he said the CEO's name, Carol didn't protest.

"All right then. Let's get the agreement in place and I'll go have lunch. Then I can be back and sign anything you want me to," Shobha said, standing up. "I had a hell of a time working with you, Mitchell."

"You need me as a reference, I'll be available anytime," Mitchell said, standing up as well. He offered Shobha a hand and she shook it. "This is not the end of your career."

"I know," Shobha said, even though she didn't quite believe it. Her compensation package would keep her out of financial trouble for a while, but would there be a job at the end of this ordeal? What if no one else hired her?

"So who are you going to be working for?" Mitchell asked.

"I'll send you an e-mail," Shobha said and walked out of Mount Doom.

"To the best engineer I have ever known." Pavan raised his glass of sake. "Hail to the mistress of code."

Everyone at the table raised their glasses as well.

"I'm going to miss you very much," Anne said, pushing her glasses up her nose. "Who am I going to go to the mall with during work hours?"

"I'm sure you'll find someone," Shobha said, pleasantly surprised. She'd made friends here, friends she didn't even know about. More than fifteen people had showed up at Leo's short-notice invitation, from all over the company.

"And she always filled out the right forms for mailing shit out, which you other guys never do," Damien the mailroom guy said, lifting a piece of teriyaki.

"Thanks, Damien," Shobha said as she folded her right hand into a fist and rested her mouth against it. She felt blubbery. Tears would fall soon. How bloody embarrassing.

"So what's next?" Vladimir asked. He was wearing a dark green polo shirt with Gap chinos, and Shobha felt a spark of interest flare inside her. He was still here, still interested, and she wasn't his boss anymore.

"I think I'll take a couple of months off," Shobha said, deciding what to do as she spoke. "Or I'll panic and start looking for another job tomorrow."

"If we all had Stanford professors as husbands we would wait a couple of months or so, too," Leo said with a grin. "So what does he think about your unemployed status?"

Oh God, Shobha realized, she hadn't even bothered to call Girish to tell him. It didn't even cross her mind. With most marriages on occasions like this, people called their spouses immediately, for support, to let them know that they would be a paycheck short at the end of the month. But Girish and she had had separate bank accounts all through their marriage. They had one joint account, which they used to pay the mortgage and for household expenses, but besides that neither depended on each other financially. Shobha didn't even know how much money Girish made anymore. In the beginning Saroj kept her up to date from information wheedled out of Girish's grandmother, but that was five years ago.

"He's fine with it," Shobha lied.

"What are you doing after lunch?" Vladimir, who was sitting next to her, whispered in her ear.

Shobha could feel the moisture of his breath on her ear and cheek. He smelled of sake and something else . . . adultery? Yes, that was what he smelled of. If she wasn't so sure that Girish had an extramarital affair, she would've tried to resist, but now, professionally and personally, she had no reason to refuse the hunk from Ukraine.

"Ah . . . I'm not sure," Shobha said as she licked her lips and turned to face Vladimir. "I was wondering . . ."

"Hey, Shobha," someone called out. "Speech, Shobha, speech."

"Yeah," everyone said, and soon spoons were being beaten on the table.

The moment was lost and Shobha jerked out of her trance. She smiled at everyone and stood up to say a few words.

No one was happy with her.

Even the good doctor was disappointed that Devi wasn't talking yet.

When Devi's friend Hilary had a baby she went through something similar. Hilary's daughter Laurie was fifteen months old when Hilary started to panic. All of Laurie's friends at day care were saying "Mummy" and "Daddy" and whatnot, while Laurie was still saying "coo" and "coo." Hilary was very disappointed that Laurie wasn't talking yet.

"Maybe she hasn't thought of anything really good to say," Devi suggested when Hilary was stressed out of her mind trying to determine why Laurie was behind in the speaking department.

Devi felt a little like Laurie. She didn't have anything to say, but her family, her friends, her doctor, everyone was unhappy with her because she couldn't just open her mouth and start letting those words fall out.

On their way home from the doctor's office, Vasu (who was Devi's chaperone for this appointment) and Devi stopped by Safeway to shop for dinner. Ever since Avi and Saroj stopped snapping at each other, Saroj was nagging to cook and Devi finally gave in.

Their sudden reconciliation felt a little weird, though they were still tempering it with steady arguments. Never having seen them so lovey-dovey, Devi wasn't sure if it was healthy to see her parents get so mushy. But it warmed her heart.

Saroj was set on making a wonderful for-Avi dinner. She was

starting out with her famous *aloo* grenades with her equally famous yogurt and tamarind sauce. She had clearly told Devi that she didn't need any funny things in her food, which she wanted cooked just the way Avi liked it.

Saroj truly believed that the way to a man's heart was through his stomach.

Devi opened a plastic bag and started filling it with crisp-looking green beans. She put the bag on the weighing machine and when the needle swayed to 2 LB, Devi tied the top of the bag and threw it into the shopping cart.

"Why do we have to buy organic milk only?" Vasu muttered as she looked through the milk area for Saroj's favorite, *Horizon* milk.

Vasu pulled out two of the red milk cartons and put them inside the cart.

"You are off kitchen duty today?" Vasu asked, and when Devi nodded sourly, she smiled. "Bored?"

Devi didn't respond but picked up a carton of plain yogurt, organic again, and put it inside the cart.

Yes, she was bored. She hadn't cooked in two days and she was bored stiff. Did her parents have to make up? And why did making up mean that she couldn't cook whatever the hell she wanted anymore? But it was hard for Devi to argue with her mother, who was obviously delighted with the idea of pleasing her husband. How old-fashioned, Devi thought irritably.

Now that she wasn't cooking she was forced to think about the future. She had been happy with her lunch–dinner routine, breakfast being a simple, cereal affair in the Veturi household. Until Girish brought it up that night he had to watch that stupid Spanish movie on the Independent Film Channel, Devi hadn't thought about the future.

After Shobha and Vasu had left for a walk, Girish had pounced on her as if she were fresh meat and he a starved flesh-eating carnivore.

"So, how long is this going to go on?" he'd asked bluntly.

Devi feigned ignorance and raised her eyebrows in query.

"This silent treatment," Girish said in irritation. "Did you think that if you didn't talk no one would have to know about the baby?"

He was sad, Devi could see that. She wanted to comfort him but he was Shobha's husband.

"You should've told me about the baby," Girish said wearily. "You should've at least let me know. Now what am I supposed to do?"

Devi got up, ready to leave. She didn't have to sit here and listen to Girish. Who the hell did he think he was anyway?

"Devi, you have to let me know," Girish pleaded, but she just shook her head. "You can't just shake your head. I need to know. I need you to tell me."

Devi closed her eyes and let out a sigh. She raised her hands in defeat and let them drop.

"And what about the rest of your life?" he questioned, standing up as she had. Facing her, looking down to meet her eye to eye.

Devi averted her glance and walked past him.

"How long, Devi, are you going to stay at Daddy's house and pretend the real world doesn't exist?" he demanded.

Devi increased her pace to reach her bedroom before Girish could say anything else, before she had to hear anything else. But she wasn't quick enough.

"You didn't die, Devi, like your baby did. Have the guts now to live," she heard him say right before she closed her door behind her. But she could still hear his voice loud and clear.

He hadn't come for dinner for two nights since then. Shobha didn't even bother to make an excuse, just said that she didn't know why Girish didn't want to come. It was a relief, Devi admitted, to not have him there, scrutinizing her lack of speech, lack of a planned future.

Saroj was humming as she carefully plucked out coriander from her herb pot when Vasu and Devi came into the kitchen, carrying four paper bags filled with groceries.

"Oh good," Saroj said, a lightness to her tone and face that hadn't been there for a long time. "Avi's bringing Vikram along for dinner. Megha is in Sacramento visiting her sister, so Avi thought it would be nice for Vikram to have some company."

Devi was relieved that Megha Auntie, the gossipy old hag, wasn't coming along to ask her how she was doing and assure her that everything would be okay if she let her parents take care of her. How would everything be okay? She wasn't talking and she had no future. There was nothing ahead and what was behind her she couldn't use for anything.

What would she do when this was over? When would this be over? And what was the "this" that needed to be over? She was in limbo and she didn't know how to extricate herself from her present situation so that she could start living her real life. The real life she'd known died when she tried to kill herself in that bathtub all those eons ago. She had to start a new real life and she had no idea how to.

"So, I thought we'll make bread *aloo* first with the chutney and then we'll make green beans with coconut, some *rasam* with plain *pappu*. What do you think, Mummy? A good Andhra dinner?"

"Yes," Vasu said.

"You want to help me mash these potatoes, Devi?"

Devi nodded eagerly. She'd do anything, anything at all to stop thinking about the future.

Girish was in his office when Shobha came home. She knocked on the door and leaned on the door frame.

"Hi," she said and he nodded, not looking up from the computer screen.

"I quit my job," Shobha announced.

That got his attention and he turned to look at her.

"Well . . . technically they made me quit," she added.

"Bummer," Girish said.

"I'm thinking of taking a couple of months off, vegetate, enjoy life before I start looking again," she told him as she walked into the office and sat down with a flop on the armchair by Girish's study table. This was his room; all things here belonged completely to Girish. He'd had these chairs, tables, rugs, bookshelves, everything before they were married.

"Okay," Girish said.

"You look depressed," Shobha said. She had been noticing it for a while now.

"I am depressed," Girish agreed.

"What happened?"

"Nothing and everything."

"Ah, the enigmatic Girish," Shobha said and blew out some air. "Happiness is a very strange and elusive emotion, don't you agree?"

"Being unhappy is not being depressed," Girish pointed out.

Shobha laughed. "But it is. If you are not happy, then you are unhappy and then you are depressed. That's why half the country is popping Prozac, Girish, because they are not happy, because they are depressed."

"You think I need Prozac?" Girish asked.

"Maybe . . . maybe what you need—" Shobha clamped her mouth shut midsentence as she realized what she was about to say.

"Maybe I need what?" Girish asked.

"Another wife. Maybe you need another wife," Shobha picked up her courage and told him.

If he was shocked, it didn't show. It didn't bother Shobha that he wasn't even surprised at her assessment. They had been married for a long time and badly for most of that time. This was an inevitable analysis. Good God, how had she let this happen to herself? She was supposed to have found a soul mate and all the trappings that went with it.

Girish was not her soul mate. They'd not managed to even become friends. They looked picture perfect and probably they had been slightly in love in the very beginning even though their tastes differed so much and they were so different. But they couldn't break the ice that had to be broken in arranged marriages. They couldn't step out of their shells and start accepting each other.

Gautami, one of Shobha's now ex-colleagues, had told her how hard it had been for her to get used to her husband. Gautami married the arranged way and came to the Bay Area from India. She couldn't get used to living with her husband, being with him, having sex with him. Everything was impossible, insurmountable. She kept going away to visit an older cousin and his family in Boston. It was on one of those trips she realized that she'd rather be anyplace than with her husband. It knocked the air out of her and she decided to stop running away and deal with her marriage right away. So she went back home, stopped visiting relatives in the various states of the U.S., and worked on her marriage.

When Shobha heard that story she realized that she'd never had that epiphany. She never woke up one moment and decided to fix her marriage. She had been trying to fix it on and off ever since she got married but after she found out she couldn't have children, there just didn't seem to be a point.

"Maybe I'm not the marrying type," Girish said.

"I know I'm not," Shobha said bitterly. "How did we both end up getting married to each other?"

Girish shrugged. "My grandmother met Saroj."

"What a twist of fate? Right?"

"Right. What's going on, Shobha?" Girish asked.

"There's this Ukrainian software programmer in my . . . well, ex-office. He's very sexy," Shobha said and smiled to herself. "I've wanted to have sex with him ever since I hired him, but I was afraid that I'd get into trouble with HR in the company."

"You weren't afraid you'd get into trouble with me?" Girish asked.

"No," Shobha replied honestly. "But I was curious what you'd think and say, if you'd find out that is."

Girish rocked on his office chair and grinned.

"At this point you should be asking me if I did sleep with this Ukrainian," Shobha reminded him, grinning back.

"Yes, I should," Girish said looking her in the eye, the grin gone. "But I won't."

"Because you may have to answer a similar question that I may pose?"

"Yes." He didn't lie.

Even though she'd guessed he had an extramarital affair, hearing him say it was shocking, and Shobha didn't have the courage to press the issue any further.

"I got an e-mail yesterday from John Waters," Girish said, changing the topic completely.

"Your classmate from Oxford? Balding guy, pretty black wife?"

"Yes," Girish nodded. "There's an opening there for a quantum mechanics position and they will offer it to me, if I say I'll accept."

"And?" This wasn't the first time he was getting an offer to work elsewhere, in another country.

"I think I'll take it," Girish said, looking at Shobha. "I think I need to."

Shobha nodded as she swallowed, the bile rising in her throat. Was it over? That easy?

"So, I get to keep the house, huh?" Shobha asked.

Girish laughed sadly and said, "If you want it."

"No thanks. I can't afford it. I don't have a job, remember?" She was close to being hysterical. There was a high pitch to her voice.

"Then we'll get rid of it, split the profit if there is any," Girish said.

"I'll call the real estate agent and have him put the house on the market," Shobha replied. "But I don't think there will be any profit, not with the economy going the way it is."

"That's okay, too."

"When do you leave?"

"Soon. Fall."

"So what's the procedure now? Lawyers . . . what?" Shobha asked, her heart heavy but her mind was starting to feel free, open, loose.

"I think we can just use a mediator because we . . . Are we going to fight over things?" Girish asked.

"No, though I'm taking all the carpets, no matter who bought them," Shobha announced, trying to lighten the mood.

"And I'll keep all the books," Girish said in the same spirit.

"Fair enough. But not the records. I take most of those. Anything else?"

Girish thought about it for a moment and shrugged. "I can't think of anything I'd want to go to war over. How about you?"

"No, nothing," Shobha agreed and then stood up. "I'm really sorry that it didn't work out."

"Me, too," Girish said, standing up as well.

They hugged tightly and then Shobha stepped away from him. "I think I'm going to stay with my parents for a while."

"Okay. I'll call your dad next week or so and talk to him," Girish said.

"Good, by then they'll all hate you because I'll put all the blame on you," Shobha said, but she was smiling. For once, she wasn't angry, just relieved.

"I . . . say good-bye to Devi for me," Girish said and he licked his lips. "I . . . I . . . just tell her I'm leaving, going to Oxford."

"Okay," Shobha said. "Anything else?"

"I'll talk to Vasu and Saroj as well," Girish said. "And we'll keep in touch."

"We'll have to until at least the legalities are cleared up," Shobha said.

Girish nodded and then bent his head to look at the floor. This was it, there was nothing more to say. It was finally over. It was all so civilized that it was almost indecent.

"I think I'll go and pack now," Shobha said when there was nothing more to say and left his study.

Half an hour later Shobha was driving down the interstate to her parents' house. She wondered with a broad smile what Saroj would think about having both her grown daughters home.

MAMA'S RECIPE
BREAD AND *ALOO* GRENADES WITH
TAMARIND-YOGURT CHUTNEY
The day Vikram Uncle came home for dinner

This is the easiest Indian dish to make in the world. But Mama insists that only she can make it well. I can't understand what the fuss is all about anyway. She boiled potatoes and peas, mashed them, added some salt, chili powder, garam masala, *and fresh coriander, and mixed everything well.*

Then she took day-old Wonder Bread, sliced the edges off, dipped the bread in water, and then squeezed the water out. She scooped some of the potato mixture and covered it with the bread in the shape of a grenade.

(Shobha and I came up with that name when we were small. We called them potato grenades and ate them with ketchup until we felt sick.)

Once the grenade is shaped, Mama deep-fried them in oil until they were crispy and golden.

The chutney is insanely simple as well. She took yogurt and mixed it with tamarind pulp, sugar, salt, and chaat masala.

As simple as it is, I have to admit Mama does a fine job of making those grenades. I could still eat a dozen with ketchup!

The Truth About Devi

Saroj looked questioningly at Shobha's black travel bag.

"What? I can't come and stay here for a while?" Shobha demanded belligerently. "My room is still my room, you know."

"No, I don't know," Saroj said and then looked at Vasu. "Do you know anything about this, Mummy?"

Vasu shook her head and looked at Shobha with questioning eyes, then at Devi who was sitting on the floor. A newspaper was spread on the carpet as Devi stripped strings off the green beans and dumped them in a bowl of water.

"Where's Daddy?" Shobha asked, looking around the living room.

"Out," Saroj said. "Where's Girish?"

"I'm not sure," Shobha answered. "We're going our separate ways."

Devi, who was putting a green bean in the steel bowl of water, made a sharp motion and spilled some water from the bowl.

"What does that mean?" Saroj asked, watching the water Devi spilled spread on the floor and carpet.

"I'm leaving him. We're leaving each other."

"You are getting a divorce." Saroj gasped the word *divorce,* her eyes ready to pop out of her head, and then she turned to face Vasu. "Mummy, this is your influence."

"They were never happy, Saroj," Vasu said sadly. Would no woman in her family ever find a man to keep her content?

"They didn't even try," Saroj said and then shook her head. "What bad have I done to both of you?" she demanded, looking from Devi who was sitting, shocked, on the floor, to Shobha who was standing with a cocky expression on her face. "She tries to kill herself and you leave your husband. And you are both here now. I see parents complain about how their children never come to see them. My kids, they come and live with me because one wanted to die and the other doesn't want her husband. So, what wrong did I ever do to you?"

Shobha shrugged and hooked her thumbs in the pockets of her jeans. "Mama, my marriage was over a long time ago, long before we decided to officially end it. In the meantime, Girish has been diddling around a little."

"What is this diddling you talk about?" Saroj asked. "Girish is a decent man."

"Who was fucking some woman with a pearl earring," Shobha said, almost shouting.

"Pearl earring? What nonsense is this?" Saroj looked accusingly at Vasu again. It was her fault. It had to be. Influencing her children in this way, ruining their lives.

"I found a pearl earring in Girish's car once. I knew then that he was seeing someone. Now he confirmed it," Shobha said and then sighed loudly, dramatically. "Look, Mama, my life is a mess right now. I'd think you'd want me to be here, to get support and love."

"You don't need support and love, you need a good whack on the head," Saroj said.

Shobha laughed. "And I have to stay here, we're selling the house, you see, and . . . I lost my job."

Saroj gasped. "What?"

Devi rested her head against the palm of her right hand and closed her eyes.

Vasu shook her head.

"How?" Saroj demanded.

"I screwed up and they fired me," Shobha said flatly.

"How do you get fired from your job? How? I don't know anyone who gets fired," Saroj said angrily. "Shobha, this is unacceptable."

"That's what I thought when they asked me to quit. I work and work and work and then they fuck me over," Shobha said casually and pulled out a pack of Marlboro Reds from her jeans pocket. "If you don't mind, I'll go and smoke outside."

"Smoke?" Saroj could barely form the words now. As Shobha left the living room, she spluttered with rage, her accusations all centered on Vasu.

"How am I to blame?" Vasu demanded. "*You* got them married and I don't smoke, never did."

"All your fault, Mummy," Saroj said, convinced. "All of it. You ruined my life."

"I ruined your life?" Vasu seemed flabbergasted. "Your life is your own. You are fifty-three years old, you are responsible for your own life."

Devi came outside and found Shobha smoking a cigarette, sitting on the stairs.

Devi sat next to her, her jean-clad leg brushed against Shobha's.

"Want one?" Shobha asked, holding up the pack of cigarettes. Devi took one and lit it with the lighter her sister gave her.

"I wasn't going to smoke, but I had to fill up with gas and I saw the cigarettes at the gas station. I'm thinking of smoking and drinking all night," Shobha said, not sounding as cocky about her divorce and joblessness as she had inside the house.

They smoked companionably for a while. After they crushed the first cigarettes on the cobblestones, they lit two more. It was nice to just sit there, smoke a cigarette, and not bother about the women inside, mother and daughter, fighting over who ruined whose life.

"That pearl earring, that was mine," Devi said, speaking very quickly, the words merging into one another. She then immediately put the cigarette to her lips and inhaled.

"I know," Shobha said.

The smoke cluttering up Devi's chest moved, and she coughed

violently, dropping her half-smoked cigarette between lax fingers. Tears were streaming down from her red eyes by the time the chok- ing, smoky sensation passed.

"You okay?" Shobha asked when Devi could breathe again.

"No," Devi said, her voice scratchy. "What you do mean you know?"

"Of course I know," Shobha retorted and threw the cigarette she was smoking on the cobblestones. "Do you think I'm stupid?"

"Oh hell." Devi sighed. "I'm the stupid one, Shobha."

Shobha shrugged. "I saw the other earring in your jewelry box . . . but I was suspecting. I'm not blind."

"I feel like I should be on Ricki Lake or Jenny Jones," Devi said in self-disgust.

"In the 'I slept with my sister's husband' episode?" Shobha asked coldly.

"Yes," Devi admitted. "But it would be the 'I slept with my sis- ter's husband, got pregnant, lost the baby, and attempted suicide' episode."

"Fuck," Shobha said and blew out some air. "I didn't know . . . I didn't think that the baby . . . I just didn't think. No wonder he's so messed up."

They both fell silent and contemplated what they'd just learned.

"I don't know how to feel about this," Shobha finally said.

"Why not just be angry? That's your safety-net emotion," Devi suggested.

"But who am I supposed to be angry with? You? Or Girish? Or myself?" Shobha said and sighed deeply. "When I first thought that you and he . . . I told myself I was crazy. But then it was like a bad whodunit novel unraveling."

"And now that you know?"

Shobha shrugged and crushed the cigarette butt lying on the stones in front of her under the heel of her boot.

"Do you hate me?" Devi asked, tears filling her voice.

Shobha didn't look up for a long moment and then shook her head.

"I thought you'd hate me if you ever found out," Devi said shak- ily, almost hysterical. "So, do you, Shobha?"

Shobha looked up then, faced Devi.

"I don't know how I feel, but I don't hate you," she said carefully. "For once I'm not sure what to feel and how to deal with this."

"Hating me would be easy, wouldn't it?"

Shobha smiled. "Being angry would be easy and yeah, hating both of you would be so easy. But I'm not and I don't and . . . fuck, Devi, of all the people in the world, Girish?"

"I want to apologize but I'm not sure what the apology should be for," Devi said. "I did you wrong. I betrayed you. I should've never slept with Girish. But now I don't know if saying sorry is enough."

Shobha buried her face in her hands and took a deep breath.

"You know," Shobha said, looking up and putting her hand on Devi's shoulder, "he and I never ripped up the sheets. It never happened."

Devi nodded and then waited for Shobha to say more.

"We never fell in love, we never became friends, we didn't even become roommates like all those pathetic arranged-marriage couples do. I can't understand why you'd want him," Shobha said honestly. "He was boring. You said so yourself. He . . . I can't understand why you and he would want to . . . I mean, why?"

Devi raised both her eyebrows and sighed. "If you're looking for a blow-by-blow account . . ."

"No," Shobha cried out. "No, please God, no."

"I don't know," Devi said desperately. "It just happened one day and then it happened another day and another. It was like watching a terrible car accident. You stay enthralled and you can't look away."

"Oh, there was that much passion?" Shobha asked caustically.

"I don't know," Devi repeated. "I'm so sorry that your marriage failed. I'm sorry that I slept with your husband. I'm sorry I got pregnant . . . that was an accident, a stupid accident, and I'm sorry . . ."

"My marriage didn't fail because of you," Shobha said quietly. "It failed because it was wrong from the start. I can't really blame you or him for . . . what the hell, Devi, Girish is a dud in bed."

Devi shrugged.

"Oh, and he was great with you? Is that it?" Shobha asked.

Devi shrugged again.

"What, silence mode again?"

"I can't . . . What do you want to know?"

Shobha grinned all of a sudden. "So he was something in bed with you, wasn't he?"

Devi heard the teasing note in Shobha's voice and cocked an eyebrow at her.

"Good old Girish. Who would've thought," Shobha said, amusement filling her voice.

"He felt very guilty," Devi said because she thought it was important Shobha knew.

"With his sense of justice and morality, I'm sure he did," Shobha said and then added after a pause, "I'm sorry about the baby."

"Yeah, that was shit luck," Devi agreed.

"Do you ever feel relieved that you lost the baby?"

Devi took a deep breath and then blew out some air. "For the longest time I was just in shock. I was so happy to be pregnant and then it was over and I didn't know what to do. I didn't tell anyone. By then Girish and I decided that it was over . . . God." She paused as the enormity of her confession hit her again. "He was your husband, Shobha. Hell! What we did was wrong, so bloody wrong."

Shobha nodded. "Yeah, it was wrong. But shit happens, you know."

Devi shook her head. She couldn't quite believe that Shobha wasn't yelling the place down, telling Saroj and Vasu of this ultimate deception. This kind of betrayal ruined families, ended relationships. When Shobha told them that she was getting a divorce, Devi knew the time to hide was over.

"I thought you didn't like Girish," Shobha said, shaking her head. "You were so anti-him. You didn't like the idea of our arranged marriage, of him being a boring professor. So what the fuck happened?"

Devi chewed on her lower lip as she debated what she could say, what would sound the most dignified. "I think I always had a crush on him. He was different from the guys I dated. He was steady, polite, opened the door, pulled out the chair. He was always nice to me. It didn't matter to him that I wasn't successful, the way Daddy is, you are."

"I just got fired and my husband dumped me. I don't know how much of a success I am," Shobha reminded her sister. "Who'd have thought? You and Girish sitting in a tree, K-I-S-S-I-N-G."

"Are you sure you're okay?" Devi asked, a new paralyzing fear coursing through her because there was a hitch to Shobha's voice as if she would crack any minute and the real Shobha would emerge. "I mean are you now just pretending to be okay but you are soon going to start yelling at me and hating me?"

Shobha sighed. "Lord, Devi. I'm not into those dramatics. I just don't fucking get it. You've always slept around with . . . well, everything that has a penis. I just don't understand why with Girish and why Girish with you?"

"Did you just call me a slut?"

"You slept with my husband," Shobha said pointedly. "How can you take umbrage at me for calling you a slut? You are a slut, a sister-husband-sleeping slut."

"I can't really argue with that," Devi said, admitting defeat. "Are you going to use this for the rest of our lives to win fights?"

"Oh yes," Shobha said smugly. "And to borrow clothes and perfume and whatever else I want. I mean," she snickered, "you slept with my husband, I can't lose ever again with you."

"You're counting on me feeling guilty forever?"

"Oh yes."

"What if I don't?" Devi demanded.

"Oh, I'll make sure you do," Shobha said and then smiled, her first real smile in a long time, a smile that came out of feeling some happiness. "I'm glad you're talking, tyke."

Devi nodded. "I guess now I have to go inside and talk to the others as well, huh?"

"You don't have to tell them about Girish," Shobha said softly. "I won't, if you don't want me to, either. This could be our secret."

"Just like we never told Mama who broke her pink glass vase?" Devi asked, remembering the incident that was almost two decades old. Even then Shobha hadn't told on her. She never was a tattletale.

"How come we have secrets like the broken glass vase but we could never get close?" Shobha wondered aloud.

Devi nodded. "I've thought about it myself."

They both fell silent for a while and then Shobha turned to face Devi.

"And now that you're talking, what's with all that damn cooking?" Shobha asked seriously.

Devi lifted her shoulders slowly, her hands in the air. "Who knows?" she said with a smile.

"It wasn't meant to happen," Devi told Dr. Berkley the next week during her session. "Usually, we try not to sleep with our sister's husbands, you know?"

Dr. Berkley nodded with a smile. Devi could see she was relieved her patient was finally talking.

Everyone was relieved that she was finally talking. Saroj asked so many questions. Devi answered a handful. Avi kept saying he was so thrilled and Vasu, she just held on to Devi, big unshed tears in her eyes.

Devi hadn't told them about the baby, the father of the baby, or any part of that sordid tale. It was not easy to tell them even though she was talking again.

The first few times she had resented coming to see Dr. Berkley, but this time she had so much to talk about that she'd hardly been able to wait.

She and Avi came half an hour early and wore down the soft beige rug in the lounge pacing. Dr. Berkley's assistant kept looking at her cautiously and at the glass wall behind her, as if worried Devi would jump through the glass of the fourth-story office.

Now that she was talking, Devi wondered how long she'd need to come to Dr. Berkley. There was comfort in seeing a shrink because you attempted suicide. It made you believe that something was wrong in the upper story and the doctor was fixing it. But if everything was all right and she was talking again, then Devi knew she had to get back to life and living. She wasn't ready.

Her mother was nudging her, asking her what she planned to do next. Her father hadn't said anything but he kept talking about the job market and how the economy looked like it was going to get better. Shobha hadn't said anything and Devi thought it was because she herself was spending her afternoons watching Oprah with Saroj when she should be looking for a new job. Vasu kept saying that Devi should take her time and find out what was in her heart before rushing into anything.

Even Girish had tried to drag her out of her silence and push her into a new life when they had been alone in her parents' house watching, or rather pretending to watch, some Spanish movie on the IFC.

"He's gone," Devi said sadly. "He was supposed to go to Oxford this fall for a new job. He already left. He told Shobha it was to find a place to live and get settled."

"Did you want him to speak with you before he left?" Dr. Berkley asked.

Devi nodded. "He just told Shobha to tell me that he was leaving and that's it." She smiled with tears in her eyes. "Of all the men in the world I could fall in love with and there are a lot of men in the world, why the hell did it have to be Shobha's husband?"

Dr. Berkley nodded sympathetically.

"I feel like Humphrey Bogart in *Casablanca*. You know? Of all the bars and et cetera, et cetera in the world, she walks into mine? I had so many choices, so many other assholes to sleep with, and . . ." Devi was once again at a loss of words.

"Would you want to pursue a relationship with him?"

Devi groaned. "I can't even think about that. I'm so nervous about telling my parents, my grandmother about this. Though I have to say, Shobha took it . . . well, she didn't react the way I'd thought she would."

"But you still told her," Dr. Berkley pointed out.

"I had to," Devi said. "I had no choice."

"Why?"

"I didn't want her not to know," Devi said, trying to explain. "I couldn't let her get divorced without at least knowing who Girish cheated on her with. I thought she'd go berserk, instead she said she knew. She knew all along. I wish she'd gone berserk. She said she didn't know how she felt about this. I'm scared that when she does know how she feels, she's going to hate me."

Guilt was a constant companion. There was a lot of guilt, as if purchased in wholesale to save money. There was guilt for having not spoken for days, for having slept with Girish, for having gotten pregnant, for having lost the baby, for not having told anyone about the baby or losing it, for . . . it was like a huge mountain, resting on her head.

"I thought that once I started talking everything would become easy and it would all be clear," Devi told Dr. Berkley.

"And it isn't like that?" Dr. Berkley asked.

Devi shook her head. "No, it's all the same, now I can just tell everyone how much it is the same."

Vasu figured it out. It wasn't very hard if you'd been watching carefully. Saroj hadn't and Vasu decided to leave the woman in her delusional world as they both chopped tomatoes for the tomato pickle, one of Avi's favorites. Vasu was comforted that Saroj and Avi had talked about their problems and were trying to solve them.

"I can't believe Girish had an affair," Saroj announced, unable, obviously, to comprehend what had taken place right under her nose.

"Some things just happen," Vasu said carefully. Knowing the truth was a burden. She had to now be extra careful to ensure that Saroj didn't trip on it as she had.

Saroj made a clicking sound with her tongue and sat down on one of the dining chairs. She was uneasy, her impatience obvious. It was difficult to see her daughters' lives fall apart. Vasu knew because it was just as difficult to see her granddaughters' lives fall apart. Technically both Shobha and Devi were in a better place, but at their age one expected them to be settled with lives of their own, not coming home to Mama and Daddy after they either try to kill themselves and/or lose their jobs and leave their adulterous husbands.

Devi was with her doctor. Avi had taken her, as Vasu was feeling "uneasy." Saroj immediately pounced on that word and demanded that Vasu see a doctor. But at her age, what choice did she have but to feel uneasy? She was over seventy. She had a fragile heart. She had lost the man she loved, and her favorite granddaughter had attempted suicide. Vasu would've wondered what was wrong with her if she weren't feeling uneasy. At this point, when life was behind her, she knew what lay ahead: more uneasiness.

"And Shobha is going to be a divorcée. Your influence, Mummy," Saroj declared as she ran her sharp knife through the ripe and lush tomato.

Vasu smiled. "Your father was nothing like Girish. He was not very well balanced. Sweet one minute, a monster the next."

"I don't remember him being like that," Saroj said, as always leaping to her forgotten father's defense.

"You don't remember anything," Vasu said teasingly. "That doesn't mean none of it is true."

"I was five years old, Mummy, not an infant," Saroj told her.

Vasu wiped her hand, which had become wet from the tomatoes, on her light gray cotton sari's *pallu*. "Do you remember the night we spent in Captain Faizal's house?"

"They had a yellow cat," Saroj said, remembering. "And a cuckoo clock."

She remembers the cuckoo clock but doesn't remember why we had to spend the night there, Vasu thought in amusement. The human brain was an amazing sieve. Certain memories stayed, others evaporated.

"And they had no children," Saroj said, piling all the tomatoes into the blender.

"Yes," Vasu said. "Do you remember why we stayed the night there?"

Saroj added chili powder to the tomatoes in the blender, along with a big spoon of pureed tamarind. She whizzed the blender as she thought about it, her forehead creased. She stopped the blender and shook her head.

"No. Why did we stay there that night?" Saroj asked.

Vasu opened her mouth to tell her but decided against it. What would the point be? Saroj wouldn't believe and even if she did, what would it achieve? If she had good memories of her father, then so be it. All her life Vasu struggled with anger, even jealousy that Saroj should think nicely of Ramakant. Why? The man was a bad husband, a terrible father, didn't earn a proper living, slapped her around, yet her own daughter claimed she loved him, remembered him fondly.

"Do you remember the doll with the blue eyes that he got for me when he went to Calcutta?" Saroj said, her eyes brightening. "I called her Lathika. I wonder what happened to the doll."

"Still in storage," Vasu said. "When you come to India, you can look through the boxes in the spare bedroom. They are full of your . . . our old things."

"I should have brought them along," Saroj said and sighed. She turned the gas stove on and put a wok on the fire. It was an old wok, one she had brought along with her all those years ago when she'd moved from India. Even though she'd managed to bring many things along, she'd left just as many behind. "I should have given that doll to Devi and Shobha to play with when they were kids."

"You can save it for your grandchildren," Vasu said.

Saroj smacked her lips disapprovingly and poured peanut oil into the wok. "What grandchildren, Mummy? Shobha can't have babies and Devi . . . well . . ."

"Devi will have children and who knows, Shobha may adopt," Vasu told her, raising her voice to be heard over the sizzle of the mustard and fenugreek seeds Saroj dropped into the hot oil.

"How can an adopted child be our own?" Saroj asked as she stirred the seeds so that they didn't burn. "Not our blood, not ours at all."

Vasu didn't argue. Saroj was set in her ways and at fifty-three years of age, it was too late to change her.

"But if she adopts, then, a baby is a baby, right, Mummy?" Saroj said and poured the oil and fried seeds into the tomato mixture. "And we'll love the baby. Hard not to love babies."

As Saroj prattled on about babies and booties, mixing together all the ingredients of the tomato pickle, Vasu tried to ignore the pressure building inside her. She had to talk to everyone tonight, she decided, she had to go back to India. If the time to go had come, she wanted to go in India, not here in "the white pit" as Saroj called it.

"Was it good, Devi?" Avi asked as he drove them both back from Dr. Berkley's office. "Does it help at all?"

Devi nodded and then realized that she could speak again, so she said, "Yes."

After having not spoken for almost four weeks, it was hard to speak, to use her voice again. It was almost tempting to go back to the days of no words.

"So, what are we having for dinner?" Avi asked, unsure of what to say to his daughter.

"Mama is on a cooking rampage. *Dosas* tonight with *sambhar* and fresh tomato pickle," Devi told him.

"She's cooking like there is no tomorrow," Avi agreed.

"Just like I was," Devi said and grinned. "I miss the cooking, but Mama lets me help, so that helps."

Avi smiled and nodded.

"I couldn't believe it. When Saroj called and told me, I couldn't believe it," he said after a short silence.

Devi didn't feign ignorance; she knew what her father was talking about. He hadn't said anything, hadn't talked about the "incident," until now.

"I couldn't understand why you'd want to . . ." His words broke away as he tried to explain his confusion. "But I understand the feeling."

"You do?" Devi asked, surprised.

"Of course I do," Avi said and raised his prosthetic arm. "When I woke up without the arm, I was angry, shocked, disoriented. I yelled at the doctor. I'd rather have died. My entire battalion was dead, my commanding officer was dead, my friends were dead. I was alive . . . with no arm."

"You tried to kill yourself?" Devi asked, shocked.

Avi sighed and then shook his head. "Didn't have the guts. But I did try to drink myself to death. I even thought about getting a gun from Quarter Guard and shooting myself dead. I thought about dri-ving into a wall. I thought about jumping off a cliff. Plenty of those in the Himalayas."

"But you didn't," Devi pointed out, feeling small and insignifi-cant in front of her father. He'd lost so much, an arm, all his friends, and he'd still managed to live while she'd given up when she had so much to live for.

"No, I didn't, because Saroj came inside my room and beat the bad thoughts away," he said with a small smile. "I was lucky that she came when she did."

"And she was lucky that she could pull you out of that room," Devi said.

"Yeah, we both got damn lucky," Avi said with a big grin.

They drove silently for a while and then Avi stopped the car at a red light. He turned to look at Devi.

"Do you have plans for the future?" he asked.

Devi laughed. "Girish was asking me the same thing a few days ago."

"That son of a bitch," Avi said and then slammed his hand on the steering wheel.

"Daddy!"

"He cheats on my little girl? And then . . . how dare he?" Avi said angrily and slammed his foot on the accelerator as the light changed.

"You told Shobha that you supported her," Devi reminded him.

"Of course I support her," Avi said. "They weren't happy, I know that, but still, he cheats on her? The bastard!"

Devi turned her head to look out of the window. She leaned over and made a wet patch with her breath on it.

"He had the decency to call me and apologize. Why apologize to me? It wasn't my marriage he fucked around with," Avi said, his lan-guage veering from the straight and narrow.

Devi made a mark on the wet patch with her forefinger.

"Has Shobha talked to you?" he asked.

"Yes," Devi said and looked up from the wet patch. "She seems relieved about the divorce. They were so unhappy together. It wasn't meant to be, Daddy."

"I know." Avi sighed as he slid the Jeep into his driveway. "Still, divorce? That's a big deal for me. I wanted my children happy."

"I'm happy," Devi offered brightly.

Avi looked at her for a moment and then nodded. "And it makes *me* very happy to hear that."

Devi smiled and then took a deep breath before she got ready to ask her father for help.

"I need a favor, Daddy."

Just a few months ago she'd have bitten her tongue off rather than say those words. All her life she had wanted to be a great career woman without her father's help, without anyone's help. She wanted to be at level with her father without any assistance from him. Now she knew that this was not a competition. She didn't have to one-up her daddy. She had to realize what made her happy and pursue it.

"Anything," Avi said without hesitation.

"I need you to put me through school again," Devi said.

Avi raised both his eyebrows.

"I'm looking into going to a culinary school," she told him, and he nodded appreciatively. "I think I should give that a shot."

"I say go for it."

"Really?"

"Absolutely."

"Thanks, Daddy," Devi said and then threw her arms around her father over the gear shift and the controls of the Jeep.

~‿◞

MAMA'S RECIPE
DOSA WITH SAMBHAR
The day I decided my future

Mama refused to let me make the dosas. *I suggested that it would be more fun to try making savory crêpes to go with the* sambhar *and pickle but she vetoed the idea.*

She took the overnight-soaked rice and urad dal *and ground them to a paste in the food processor. Then she added some baking soda and salt* to the mixture and let it sit for a while. She took the mixture, which had now swelled a little, and stirred it thoroughly.

Taking a ladleful of the dough, she spread it rather expertly on a hot cast-iron pan and let it cook. No one, and I mean no one, can made dosas *as paper-thin as Mama can. It's the way she does it. A ladleful goes on the pan and then she uses the round base of the ladle to spread the mixture in a circle.*

For the sambhar, Mama cooked thoor dal *with salt in the pressure cooker. In a separate saucepan, she fried mustard seeds along with asafetida and turmeric. She added green beans, pearl onions, tomatoes, and sweet potatoes to the oil and fried them for a while. She then poured in a mixture of tamarind water with* sambhar *powder (which Mama obviously made at home by frying a lot of whole spices together and then grinding them). After that she added the cooked* dal *plus some water and let it all simmer for a while.*

My memories of Sunday mornings of eating hot dosas *with* sambhar *and pickle are vivid. I'm glad that I'm living here again so that I can learn to appreciate the one thing that I never did learn to do before: Mama's impeccable south Indian cooking.*

For Once, Then, Something

Shobha woke up early. A little too early. But once she was awake she couldn't go back to sleep. She watched the alarm clock in her old childhood room change from two AM to three AM and then to four AM. Tired of watching the flicker of the red LCDs, she decided to give up on trying to sleep and got out of bed. Her room, she thought as she turned the bedside lamp on.

This was where she'd grown up. They had moved to the house when Shobha was eight years old. Saroj didn't want to give the girls separate rooms; she worried that they'd get scared at night. Devi said she wouldn't mind sharing a room but Shobha was eight, belligerent, and wanted her own room. And she got it two years later, after long fights, arguments, and tantrums. Even after Shobha left for college, Saroj didn't change the room, not really. She'd added a few things here and there but the room was the same, the single bed was still uncomfortable and her black-and-white posters of Humphrey Bogart (a crush in her teens) and Lauren Bacall were still where she'd left them.

She'd dreamed of MIT and Harvard and big business schools in this room. But she'd ended up at Cal getting an engineering degree and when it came time to go to business school, she went back to Cal. It was in the Bay Area and convenient. Even now she regretted not getting into MIT for her undergrad. It had been a slam to the ego, such a failure, but she'd covered it up by convincing herself that she'd always wanted to go to Cal anyway. It was closer to home, it was in a familiar area, and it was a very good school.

It was a warm night, even though it was almost August. Fall had threatened to come but now didn't seem imminent; still, in California one didn't have to worry or wait for the seasons. Maybe she needed to move, she wondered seriously. She lived too close to her parents, her childhood. Maybe she needed to move to someplace where the seasons changed, the weather altered. Spring and summer were looked forward to after the chill of winter and the quiet cool of the fall was welcomed after the heat of the summer. Even as she thought it, she knew she couldn't leave. She was a Californian, she couldn't live anywhere else. She could probably go on vacation, on a project, but she would always live here. And there were advantages to living near her parents' home. Whenever she got fired and divorced again she knew she'd have a place to crash.

When Shobha came to the living room, her hair mussed, her eyes a little sleepy, she found Avi sitting on the sofa watching television. The sound was muted and a black-and-white movie was unfolding.

"So you figured out how to whistle yet?" Shobha asked as she slid onto the sofa next to her father.

"Yep, you put your lips together and blow," Avi said, trying to imitate Lauren Bacall.

"You can't watch Humphrey Bogart with the sound turned off," Shobha admonished him. "Can you imagine just reading *here's looking at you, kid* from the closed captioning and not hearing Bogie actually say it?"

Avi shrugged. "I didn't want to wake up Vasu just because I couldn't sleep," he said, inclining his head toward the adjoining guest room.

"G'ma sleeps like a log," Shobha said. "Once I tried to wake her up because I had a bad dream and wanted to sleep with her. I shook her and called out to her, nothing, she was dead to the world."

"When was this?"

"Ah . . . we were visiting her in Hyderabad. You and Mummy had gone for some wedding. The *muhurat* was at some ungodly hour, two in the morning I think," Shobha said, remembering. "I think it was Prabhat Uncle's wedding."

"Vasu's grown old now, she doesn't sleep that well anymore," Avi said. "And Prabhat didn't get married in India. He got married in New York. Remember that horrible trip? We missed the connecting flight in Chicago—"

"—and had to spend the night at the airport." Shobha nodded. "Mama was not a happy camper."

"And then the bastard got divorced seven years later," Avi said and then made a sound. "I'm sorry."

"What? Now you can't say the words *suicide* and *divorce* in front of your daughters?" Shobha demanded sarcastically.

Avi laughed self-consciously. "I hurt for you."

"Don't," Shobha told him. "I'm happy that we're apart. It's better this way. I can start living my own life, alone, and he can start living his. We were never meant to be married. We never got along, always argued. We got married but never became a couple."

"Still, I feel responsible," Avi said. "I should've fought harder with your mother and you. After living all your life here in America you're simply not suited for arranged marriage and neither was he."

Shobha shook her head. "Prabhat Uncle had a love marriage and he got divorced, but you and Mama are still married. Vikram Uncle and Megha Auntie had an arranged marriage and they're still married, happily for the most part, right? It's a luck of the draw, whether you fall in love or walk into it the arranged way."

"You have a point," Avi conceded. "But I can't help blaming myself."

"It's done with," Shobha said sharply. "I'm happy. Isn't she gorgeous?" she asked suddenly, looking at the woman on television.

Avi nodded.

"I think women in these old black-and-white movies simply looked better because we couldn't see them in full color," Shobha said, staring at the television screen. "I've seen Lauren Bacall in color and she doesn't look anywhere as hot as she does here. What the hell am I going to do?"

Avi didn't bat an eyelid at her change of topics.

"About what?"

"Everything," Shobha said in frustration. "Girish just left so I have to make sure the house sells and I have to divide all our stuff, pack it, and ship it."

"But you offered to do all of this," Avi pointed out.

Shobha grinned then and nodded. Girish had seemed in such a rush to leave the country that she didn't press for his help in getting rid of the house, making sure the packers packed everything and shipped it to the right places. This was the easiest divorce in the history of divorces. They'd lived such separate lives that now there were no intertwining material things for them to argue over.

"And then there is the whole job situation," Shobha said, feeling embarrassed. Her father was a successful entrepreneur, while she was currently unemployed. She'd never started her own business, had never wanted to, she'd always wanted to be CEO of someone else's company, and now she'd been fired.

"You'll find something soon. Good people always do," Avi said carelessly.

"Do you know what the job market is like these days?" Shobha asked, incredulous that he couldn't see the perilous situation her career was in.

Avi nodded. "Yeah, yeah, I know. But if you're good, you're good. I told Vikram and he already wanted me to ask you if you want to work for Sentinel."

Sentinel was the company that Vikram Uncle and her father started all those years ago. The company was still alive, though it had merged with another company ten years ago. It was after the merger that Vikram Uncle and Avi had both started to feel the pinch of working in someone else's company, and a few years later they'd both accepted positions on the board and left the day-to-day duties to the next generation. Vikram Uncle continued to talk about a second start-up, but Avi said he was too old and too tired to start all over again.

"I don't want to work for your company," Shobha said uneasily. "I'll manage."

"I can make a few calls to make your life easy if you like, but I really don't think it'll be necessary," Avi said, his demeanor indicating clearly to Shobha that he thought there would be no problem in her finding another equivalent job.

"I thought you'd be ashamed of me," Shobha said, surprised, even a little confused. Her father was the one person she had been afraid of facing because she thought she had disappointed him the most. She couldn't imagine him feeling any pride in her after what happened.

"Why?" Avi asked, now looking confused. "You're a VP at your age. I'm incredibly proud of you."

"I got fired. I'm not a VP anymore."

"Bullshit," Avi said and put an arm around Shobha. "The job business—don't take it personally. Every time the shit hits the fan someone's head rolls. This time it was yours, next time you'll be firing your scapegoat. That's business. What I feel bad about is Girish. I can't believe he cheated on you, and I don't know what to do now that I know he did."

Shobha made a sound of disbelief. There was no way she wanted to have this discussion with her father. He had no idea how close to home this whole adultery business was and how interconnected it was with the first domino to fall: Devi.

"I thought about cheating on him," Shobha said, not wanting to put all the blame on Girish. It wouldn't be fair. "I mean I really did."

"But you did not cheat on him," Avi said angrily.

"Would it be okay with you, then, if Mama fantasized about other men?" Shobha demanded.

"The idea doesn't have appeal," Avi remarked. "But still . . . the son of a bitch."

"And I thought you always liked him," Shobha said and cuddled closer to her father.

"As a man I still like him, but as my little girl's daddy, I could break that boy's kneecaps," Avi said. He kissed her forehead and rocked her gently. "Are you sure you're okay?" he asked.

"Yes, Daddy," Shobha said and closed her eyes. "I think I've never been better, but you're free to follow up on the kneecaps threat, as long as I can watch of course."

~◯

LETTER FROM AVI TO SHOBHA

Dear Shobha,

Divorce? That word has an ugly taste, doesn't it? Just a few days ago your mother threatened me with that word and scared the life out of me. I was afraid she'd pack my bags and throw them out; worse, burn them and tell me to get lost. I'm Indian enough and in love enough that divorce scares me, maybe even disgusts me a little.

So when my little girl tells me that she's divorcing her no-good husband, I want to break that boy's legs and put him on a platter and serve it to her.

But I know Girish and I know you. If I didn't know Girish, I'd happily blame him and sit back while I made sure he burned for his sins. But I know him, and knowing him I know that a man like him would never break a commitment this serious unless something drastic happened.

And I know you. I know that you would never fail at anything unless something terrible happened.

I realized just now that maybe this was for the best. I thought about what I would do if Saroj cheated on me or what Saroj would do if I cheated on her. For all her small temper tantrums, Saroj would probably very calmly get a gun and put a bullet in between my eyes. I can't say I wouldn't do the same. But you, you are so blasé about this, smoking a cigarette, getting drunk on my good whiskey with Devi, acting like it is party time, that I wonder if maybe it really is party time for you. You seem to be laughing loudly enough. But I wonder.

There is a song from this old movie called Arth where a man asks a woman, "You are smiling so much, there must be a deep pain that you're hiding." I wonder what your deep pains are and I wonder how I have failed you.

I have always been so proud of you. You are so easy to be proud of. When you became VP, I strutted around like a peacock telling everyone who'd listen that my daughter was a vice president at the age of thirty.

And even now, I am proud of you. You decided to give up your un-happy life and search for a new, happy one. And I will be there, standing right behind you, whether you like it or not, to make damn sure you find that happy life.

I should have fought harder with Saroj, with you, against that damn arranged marriage. This time I will, this time I will be the hard-ass par-ent and not let you make any more mistakes.

As for Girish, I'd still like to break that boy's legs!

I love you, Shobha.
Daddy

~~~

It was early in the morning when Vasu woke up to a small knock on the door. She didn't sleep well anymore; small sounds woke her up. Not like the old days when she was young and slept like the dead. When death was close people didn't sleep as soundly, worried that it would snap them up when their eyes were closed.

"Come in," Vasu whispered, her throat feeling tight after having just woken up. She reached for the glass of water she always kept at her bedside and soaked her parched tongue and throat.

She had to go back to India, she thought as she coughed a little. The dryness of the Bay Area was sucking the energy out of her. She had to go back, she thought again, and decided to talk to everyone in the morning.

"G'ma, it's me," Devi said as she came inside, wearing a white T-shirt with the logo of one of her ex-companies and the tagline THIS ISN'T YOUR GRANDFATHER'S DOT.COM printed on it, big and bold in black.

"Are you okay?" Vasu sat up immediately.

"I just wanted a snuggle," Devi said as she got under the covers.

Vasu smiled and nodded. "It has been a long time since you wanted a snuggle."

"It has been a long time since I woke up this early after having slept through the night," Devi said and leaned against Vasu.

"Are you feeling okay?"

"Perfect."

Vasu wet her lips and then squeezed Devi against her. This was her flesh and blood and she felt her heart warm at the closeness.

"I love you," Vasu said. She didn't often say things like this, she was a private person, not usually open with her affections, but with Devi all defenses were down. She was the granddaughter who always slipped through.

"I love you, too," Devi responded, her tone childlike.

They fell silent for a while and Devi was dozing off when Vasu spoke, almost silently, almost in a whisper.

"I know," Vasu said and Devi raised her head. For an instant there was confusion and then there was understanding. "I know," Vasu repeated and Devi sighed, leaning her head back against her grandmother's shoulder.

"I should've known that you'd know," Devi said wearily.

"I could see," Vasu sadly. "And it broke my heart. I know how hard it is to love another woman's husband."

"It was not just another woman, it was my sister," Devi pointed out.

Vasu nodded. "Hmm, I know. I knew Shekhar's wife quite well before we started . . . what should I call it? Our friendship? Our affair?"

"Isn't there that Hindi song, *pyaar ko pyaar he rehane do, rishtoen ka ilzaam na do,* maybe we should abide by it," Devi suggested.

It was one of Vasu's favorite Hindi songs and she'd introduced Devi to it. It made her happy that Devi remembered it and joyous that Devi was alive to remember it. If Saroj had been a little late, the songs, the love, the memories, everything Devi had within her would be buried along with her. It would've been such a terrible waste.

"Let love be love, let's not accuse it with a name," Devi translated. "I'd like to see that movie again. It was one of the good Hindi movies."

"Yes," Vasu agreed. "Maybe you can come with me when I go back and spend some time with me. We could watch Hindi movies, take long walks, and eat roadside food. What do you think?"

"I'm thinking about going back to school," Devi told her, "and I want to start as soon as they'll let me."

"School?"

"Yes," Devi said and smiled. "I want to go to culinary school."

"Are you sure?" Vasu frowned. She wasn't sure if Devi should make a career out of a hobby that helped her resolve her feelings after the "incident."

"Yes," Devi said and then asked hastily, "Why? You think it's a mistake?"

"No, no," Vasu said immediately. She believed in letting people make their own mistakes. She wasn't one to offer advice and interfere in other people's lives even if the other person was her own granddaughter. That was the difference between Saroj and her: Saroj didn't respect others the way Vasu did.

"How did you deal with Shekhar Uncle's wife after you starting seeing him?" Devi asked curiously.

"I didn't," Vasu said. "Anu never spoke with me again and I couldn't go to her and apologize. I loved Shekhar, what would I apologize for?"

Vasu never wanted to be involved with a married man or any other man after her husband committed suicide. It was almost three years after Ramakant died that she was posted to Poona. Shekhar was the commanding officer, a colonel, then. Already an old man by all Indian standards. But he was handsome, riveting. He was forty-eight years to her thirty-one and had the well-deserved reputation of being a rake. Every place he was transferred to he had an affair and there were rumors, gossip, a broken heart, usually not his.

The last broken heart had been that of a nurse, who'd left the army for civilian life. It was rumored that she'd been pregnant and an abortion was arranged for at a civilian hospital. Later on Vasu found out that there'd been no pregnancy and no abortion. In the fashion of all good rumors, this one also had nothing to do with the truth.

"The first time I saw him was at the party they threw for me when I was posted to Poona," Vasu said, a dreamy smile on her face. "He was wearing his dress uniform because he had come from a meeting with the Chief of Staff. I thought he looked so good and so important. But I heard that he slept around and that Anu kept track and made life for the woman miserable after the affair was over."

"I thought you said she was nice," Devi said.

"She was," Vasu said with a laugh. "She was just taking some revenge in the only way she could. At that party, Anu came to me and started talking to me, and I was drawn to her. She is very beautiful, and very charming."

"But Shekhar Uncle never loved her, right?"

Vasu smacked her lips together. "He did. He loved her."

"And he loved you?"

"Yes. He loved us both. He couldn't leave her, he couldn't leave me," Vasu said flatly. It was fact. She hated it that he couldn't leave Anu to be with her. That their relationship would always be on the wrong side of society. But when love slammed into her with full force she hadn't been able to stop herself.

"It was all right," Vasu said, keeping the bitterness she could still feel out of her voice. "We met when we could, we shared, we loved. We wrote long letters, we talked on the phone. We went away alone on vacation."

"But he had a wife," Devi said. She couldn't accept that Girish was married, especially to Shobha, not that it would've made any difference if he were married to someone else. She'd ended the relationship because sanity finally claimed her. He was married to her sister and Devi couldn't be their home wrecker. On the other hand she couldn't, she wouldn't, continue to love and have a clandestine relationship with a married man. No matter how much she sympathized with her grandmother, for herself she'd decided that it wouldn't matter how deep the love, how strong the feeling.

"Yes, he had a wife and we were in love," Vasu said. "But that isn't enough for you, is it?"

"You say it like it's a bad thing." Devi sat up, angry with her grandmother for judging her. Love wasn't enough because it never

was enough. Not everyone could just live on the boundaries of society like Vasu had and drag everyone who cared for her along. For the
first time in her life, Devi understood why Saroj and Vasu didn't get
along.

"For some love is just not enough. For me it was," Vasu said unable to comprehend Devi's defensiveness.

"Love is never enough just as it is," Devi said, getting out of
Vasu's bed. "I couldn't hurt Shobha and Mama and Daddy and you.
I love all of you, too, and that love superseded this love because I
wanted to protect my family and continue to be part of it. That
doesn't mean I feel less love or that my love is smaller than yours."

Vasu sat up in the bed. "I didn't mean it like that."

"Yes, you did," Devi said. "You did, G'ma."

Vasu wanted to deny it again but realized she said exactly that. In
defending herself for what she did she'd attacked Devi.

"No, that's not what I meant," she lied. "I love you, Devi."

"I know," Devi said and then smiled. "I love you, too, G'ma. But
this is why Mama and you don't get along. Don't you see, she always knew that you cared more for Shekhar Uncle than you did for
her."

It was as if a curtain had been raised and everything behind it revealed. Vasu felt a familiar tightening in her chest and bitterness
rose into her throat. All her life she'd believed that Saroj hated her
because she'd divorced Ramakant, but now Vasu was being forced
to admit that Saroj hated her for not loving her enough. Vasu loved
Shekhar the most. She neglected her child for that man. She ignored society and she let the world fall around her as long as she
could be with him, on *his* terms.

Had he loved her enough? If he loved her more than he had,
would he have left his wife and married her? Oh, what was the point
of this? Life was too short already and Shekhar was dead.

"I love Saroj," Vasu said sincerely. "I just loved him more."

Devi nodded and then leaned over to kiss Vasu on the cheek.
"That's okay. I won't tell anyone."

Vasu felt tears in her eyes. "I hurt her very much."

"Don't worry, she hurt you right back," Devi said, not wanting to aggravate the matter. "And she can nag with the best of them. So I think you're pretty even."

A searing pain shot through Vasu's arm as she tried to respond to Devi teasingly. Vasu collapsed on the bed, her hand dramatically clutching her left breast. Devi cried out for help as she ran toward the telephone to dial 911.

When Saroj first heard Devi's call for help there was a paralyzing moment when Saroj saw a bathtub and her bleeding daughter lying in it.

As she waited in the lounge of yet another emergency room, her second one this summer, Saroj truly started to contemplate her mother's death. Until now she'd never imagined the old lady would die. She was infallible, always healthy, always on the go. Now she lay in a hospital bed while doctors performed tests to see how bad the paralysis was.

Vasu had had a massive heart attack that had led to a stroke. It was too early to say anything, but the doctors didn't think that Vasu would be able to walk again, and since she hadn't shown any signs of waking up they were suspecting a "hemorrhagic stroke," which the doctor explained was bleeding in Vasu's brain.

Saroj wished she'd nagged more, forced Vasu to see a doctor here in the United States where doctors didn't buy their degrees as they were sometimes rumored to do in India.

Would she die? Would it all end today? Her first thought was that all the years of bitterness and anger she'd felt for Vasu were a waste. After her death, what would Saroj complain about and to whom? No, no, Saroj told herself as her eyes kept watch at the revolving door that led to the rooms in one of which her mother lay, Vasu wouldn't die. She'd pull through. That's what tough women did, they pulled through, and God knew Vasu was tough.

Saroj remembered the time when Vasu called from India and with no tears told Saroj that Shekhar was dead. The cancer had eaten away his body, and thankfully it all ended before the pain became intolerable and he a parody of what he used to be.

"You should come here right away," Saroj instructed her mother then. "No point living in India anymore. He's gone and you should come and live here with us."

"But that's not my home, Saroj. I don't live here because of Shekhar, I live here because this is my home," Vasu had explained patiently.

Saroj wondered then if she'd be half as sane if Avi died before she did. Would she able to even talk coherently? Saroj knew how Vasu felt about *that man*. There was no doubt in Saroj's mind that all the love Vasu had inside her, she gave to that man, every last iota of it. There was nothing left for anyone else. Oh, she loved Devi and Shobha, but that was a different, once-a-year kind of love. And that was how often they met, and rarely for more than six to eight weeks at a time.

Saroj had felt admiration and resentment for Vasu then. How could that woman still stay strong after Shekhar? Did nothing crush her? she'd thought.

Now she wished she'd been kinder, more tolerant. Vasu could die and then what? Then, nothing, she admonished herself. How did it matter now that Vasu left Saroj's father? How did it matter that Vasu fell in love with a married man? How did it matter that ever since then Saroj never topped her mother's priority list? If she died now, all that would be the past and Saroj would be left with a bitterness and no mother.

Avi put his arm around Saroj as she leaned her head back and closed her eyes. A guilt-ridden Devi was pacing the floor while Shobha stood by a window staring down at the parking lot below.

"Devi, can't you sit down? You are giving me a headache, walking up and down like that," Saroj said.

"I did this to her." Devi repeated what she'd been saying on and off all day. "I told her . . . damn it, I was hard on her and then she goes and has a stroke. I did this to her."

"No, you didn't," Saroj said even as she was tempted to blame someone, anyone, so that the accused could make it right and Vasu would somehow live. But she was being reasonable and knew that no one was to blame. As Vasu had said so many times, she was old and old people died.

"I was harsh," Devi said and sat down next to Saroj. "I didn't mean to be, Mama."

"I know, *beta,*" Saroj said and took Devi's hand in hers. "Mummy has been sick for a long time now. And since *he* died, she hasn't been all there."

And that was a fact. Vasu had lost a lot of her vitality after Shekhar passed away. She outwardly remained the same but Saroj could now look back and see that small things had changed. There was less laughter, less happiness in Vasu, something that hadn't happened when her husband committed suicide. Saroj couldn't hold that against Vasu now as she would've just a while ago, before Devi, before she realized how ephemeral everything in life, including life itself, was.

"I told her she was selfish," Devi confessed. "Well, not in those words but words to that effect. I told her that she loved Shekhar Uncle more than anyone else and that was wrong. I told her she only thought of herself and no one else."

"She's not lying there because you said those things to her," Avi said firmly. "Saroj has said those same things to her several times but she never had a stroke before. She had a stroke because she is sick, has been for a while."

Shobha walked toward her family and sat down beside Avi. "How long do we have to wait here until they find out what the fuck happened?"

"Shobha, language," Saroj muttered.

"She had a stroke," Devi said, "and it's my fault."

"So what's next on the agenda? You're going to try the bathtub stunt again because you're feeling guilty?" Shobha demanded.

Saroj gasped, Avi groaned, and Devi stuck her tongue out at Shobha. "Fuck you."

"Wonderful, I have two daughters who need their mouths rinsed all the time," Saroj complained.

"She started it," Devi said childishly.

"She started it," Shobha mimicked. "Lord, Devi, grow up. We don't say who started it, we try to be smart enough to—"

"Shh," Saroj said. "Your grandmother could die in there."

"That old bird? Nah, she won't," Shobha said and rested her forehead against her father's shoulder.

"Are you sure?" Devi asked.

"Positive," Shobha said, "So don't go find a bathtub, okay?"

"Very funny," Devi retorted.

She had seen it in movies, heard about it on all those stupid talk shows Saroj watched, and the feeling was eerily similar. There was a light at the end of the tunnel, even though Vasu knew that it was the CT scan at work, it comforted her to know that death was close and it brought light with it. There was no coherence to her thoughts, she knew that as well. People and emotions were hopping around in her brain. Thoughts came and left unbidden.

She'd seen Shekhar and then she saw Ramakant. She hoped she wouldn't meet Ramakant on the other side. He would be gravely unhappy that she did everything she could to poison their daughter's mind against him, and he would be smug that she hadn't succeeded.

Then Anu, Shekhar's wife, came strolling in, wearing a white sari, saying that she had the right to wear it, not Vasu. Vasu retorted by saying that she didn't want to wear a white sari and the color really didn't suit Anu, either.

When Anu left, Geeta came, her closest friend, and she smiled. "It'll be okay," she said, and then there was darkness.

The CT scan was probably over and they were taking her elsewhere, away from the light. Her mind revolted against being drawn away from the light and just as that happened there were bright lights within her, she could feel her heart slow, pace itself to the world she was entering.

She wished Saroj would come by and talk to her before she had to leave because she knew her time was here. She had to go. She could feel it all the way inside her where the small sparks of light were playing, trying to stimulate her heart, which was slowing down making her free, unfettered.

She wanted to say she was sorry to Saroj for not loving her enough.

The sparks started to die away and Vasu felt her heart stop and then everything turned white and she slipped into oblivion.

~⌇

DEVI'S RECIPE
REGRET
The day G'ma died

Regret is the heaviest thing to carry; it is heavier than guilt, than memories, than life itself. Regret is this heavy thing that I carry inside of me.

I wish I was kinder. I wish I didn't tell her the truth. I wish I didn't rush to defend myself. I wish I admitted my love was less strong than hers. I wish she lived. I wish she didn't die because of what I said because regret is this heavy thing that I carry inside of me.

Death is final. Beyond it, nothing lies. No dreams, no future, no tomorrow. Death is ultimate and with death comes regret. The regret that life didn't turn out the way we wanted. That death came too early. Death is inevitable. Death lives in all our tomorrows. And along with death lives regret, this heavy thing that I carry inside of me.

Saying good-bye is never easy to someone who is already gone. How do I say good-bye to the dead? How will she know that I let her go? But I don't want to say good-bye, I want to get her back. Why say good-bye when I can't mean it? Why carry that regret as well, because regret is this heavy thing that I carry inside of me.

Some love deeply, some love forever. My love for her is beyond tomorrow, beyond today, and beyond forever. I will always remember her, always mark the day she came and the day she left. She will forever be inside of me, along with regret, which will not be as heavy because she will be there as well, easing this heavy load inside of me.

Thicker Than Blood

Dear Devi,

A long time ago I asked Avi how he stays so calm, no matter what happens around him. He told me he wrote letters. Letters he never sends to the recipient. Just vent it all out, he said, tell the truth because there are no consequences.

I usually don't write letters, so this one is very difficult to write and because it is so difficult to write, I might just have to send it to you. I mean, I put all this effort into this, I've got to let you have a look at it, right? I can see you reading this line now and thinking, He's still joking, the world has gone upside down and he's still joking.

I thought I'd tell Avi when I called him from here that the woman I cheated on Shobha with was you. Then he said that he wanted to break my kneecaps and I chickened out. If you tell him could you give me a head start? I like my kneecaps.

Yeah, I can see you now, nodding and sighing, thinking that I'm still joking.

I met an old friend here, a professor of mine. I told her about you, Shobha, the whole mess. She's not a therapist but I'm thinking of asking *about her hours. According to her I'm an asshole (she's not really a therapist because they are not supposed to call their patients names) and that I should go on my knees and beg forgiveness from you, Shobha, Avi, Vasu, and last but not the least Saroj, who will probably take her rolling pin and give me two (or maybe more) good ones.*

And I'm to blame. I was the married one, the one with the marital vows. But what is a man supposed to do when he falls in love with his wife's sister? Isn't there some bad Hindi movie with this theme? And what happens in the end of that movie? The unmarried sister sacrifices all and leaves the man to his wife? None of that worked here. Shobha and I couldn't stay together as we couldn't continue the farce, not after finding out all that we did. So your sacrifice and mine got us nowhere because at the end of the bloody day, I'm here in Oxford wondering what the hell happened.

I wish we could start again, from the beginning, the very beginning, before I married Shobha. I wish you and I could meet again, on a date, as two strangers, but then I'm probably not your type. I have seen the men you've dated, all of them look like jocks and here I am, a skinny Indian professor with glasses and a wife. I wonder what you saw in me. I know what I saw in you, the whole damn world. I saw my world and then you turned and looked at me, how was I supposed to resist that?

I didn't pay much attention to you for a long time. You were just Shobha's sister whom she bitched and moaned about. Personally, I think she was jealous that you got to have great sex with different men while she was stuck with her sexless wonder: me.

But Shobha is a rock. She was the rock in my life for the years we were married. I was convinced that no matter how bad things were, our marriage wouldn't end. I thought that if we could still stay under the same roof and stand each other day after day, it would be enough. And she put up with everything I threw her way. But it wasn't enough.

And I agree with Shobha that if we'd had a child, things would've worked out. Well, that pain runs deep, as does the pain of losing our baby. Now I wonder how I could've done what I did to Shobha. How could I have betrayed her trust, your trust, everyone's trust? And then I console myself thinking that I didn't do it alone, that you were a willing accomplice. It is a small comfort, actually, it's no comfort at all.

I feel like a walking mass of pain, unable to understand my actions, yet feeling little remorse, which makes me feel guiltier. This is a vicious cycle I can't break free of.

But I wanted you to know that whatever it was that happened between us was, is, important and treasured. And that I know there's nothing we can do about it. I can't come back to what was and you can't leave what is.

So, good-bye and I wish you a long and happy life with a wonderful man and a houseful of children. (I know you're thinking that I'm just being polite and I don't mean any of this, and I don't. I wish we could make it and no matter how generous I try to be, I can't.)

Girish

Devi never really overcame the guilt, Shobha never got over not saying good-bye, and Saroj was ridden with regret that Vasu left before she could tell her she loved her and that she was sorry that she couldn't be the daughter Vasu wanted.

Vasu had never been too sentimental about death and didn't have any elaborate desires, just some simple ones. She told this to Avi after Shekhar's funeral. She'd been frustrated by how much religion was involved with his death when during his life he'd been less religious than her. At least Vasu believed in God, even if it wasn't a specific God. Shekhar had never even pretended to have anything to do with the great unknown. She felt after his death his family made a farce out of his life.

"They had so many *pujas* and nonsense, fifth-day ceremony and eleventh-day ceremony, it was just too much," Vasu complained vehemently. "And Anu . . . they broke her bangles and cut some of her hair off. Barbaric!"

"At least they didn't shave her hair off," Avi reminded her consolingly.

"She wouldn't permit that," Vasu said confidently. "She is religious but not a fanatic. When I die, Avi, I don't want all this religious nonsense. No ceremony, no *puja,* no nothing. I don't want anyone to come and look at my dead body. What's to see?"

"People like to pay their respects to the dead," Avi said.

Vasu made a clicking sound. "More nonsense. If you have to give someone respect, give it to them when they are alive, they will value it, why bother after they are dead."

Avi was amused at how passionate she seemed about the matter. Vasu frowned at him when she saw the silent laughter in his face. "At my age this is relevant, Avinash. And I want it to be simple. I will die in India so they will keep the body waiting until you get there, so get there fast because—"

"Why are you sure you will die in India? You spend a lot of time here, you could die here. What do I do then?" Avi asked then, interrupting her.

"I will die there because I live there," Vasu said in exasperation, "and so you'd better show up quickly otherwise they will let my body disintegrate and the idea of all those bacteria and maggots . . . I don't think you will want to deal with that."

"Yes, ma'am," Avi said as if Vasu were an army general.

"And I want to be cremated, simply, no priest and no nonsense. Just burn the body, no matter where I die, here or in India, and take the ashes and drop them in the ocean by Vaisakh," Vasu instructed him. "And no one gets to *view* the body. That is just perverse."

"Aye, aye, ma'am." Avi laughed softly.

Then, he couldn't have imagined that she would die; it had seemed such a remote possibility. This woman who was fit, healthy, and competent wouldn't die, couldn't die. It was unfathomable. But she was dead, gone. There was a hole in everyone's lives, a hole as big as Vasu.

Saroj looked at the brass urn perched on the dining table with incredulous eyes. That was Vasu? It seemed bizarre that a walking, talking, criticizing Vasu was now in a silent brass urn.

"Mama, what are you doing up so early?" Devi asked as she came into the dining area. The clock on the microwave said the time was four forty-two AM.

"Can't sleep," Saroj said, not looking away from the urn. "She is in there. She is dead and I can't understand that."

"Oh, Mama." Devi leaned down and gave Saroj a hug.

"I hated her," Saroj said harshly, a sob tied in with the anger. "I hated her so much. And now I realize that I never hated her. I always loved her."

"She knew," Devi said, pulling a chair close to Saroj.

"Do you think you hate me?" Saroj asked, and Devi stopped in midair as she was sitting down. Her bottom fell on the chair suddenly as she snapped out of her surprise.

"What?"

"Do you also think you hate me? The way I thought I hated Mummy?"

Devi blinked and then shook her head. "No, I don't hate you. I think you're a pain in the ass at times, but I don't hate you."

"I wanted my relationship with my daughters to be different. Closer, you know, like they have in movies and . . ." Saroj sniffled and wiped her tears with the back of her hands.

"Mama, when times are tough, both your daughters are in your house. How can you say we don't have a close relationship? We're both here. We never doubted that we can come here whenever we want to and especially whenever we need to," Devi said.

Saroj sucked in a deep breath and then shook her head. "I don't remember, you know, never can, all that she said about my father."

"That's okay," Devi said. "She shouldn't have pushed you to remember. But she hated him and she wanted you to hate him."

"And that just made me think he was better than he was." Saroj snickered. "Poor Mummy never could convince me he was a bad husband and a bad father."

"It doesn't matter, Mama," Devi said. "She said she loved you, she told me that before the heart attack."

"She did?" Saroj was surprised. Vasu was not one to talk openly about her feelings.

"Yes," Devi said.

Saroj smiled unevenly as her face convulsed and then she broke into fresh tears. Devi held her, tears falling from her eyes as well as she rubbed her face against Saroj's hair.

Saroj pulled away slowly and wiped Devi's tears with both her hands. "When I saw you in that bathtub, my heart stopped beating.

I was so scared that I had lost you. And then you wouldn't talk and I thought I had lost you anyway."

Devi shook her head and wiped the tears rolling down her cheeks. She'd been crying on and off for the past week since Vasu died of the heart attack she'd had in the guest room. They'd hoped that she would come out of it but even as the doctors performed tests on Vasu to see what her condition was, she'd had another heart attack and then passed away.

"I was scared," Devi told her. "Really scared, Mama."

"What for?"

"I didn't know what to do. I lost my baby and my job and my life was going nowhere. I was scared and the baby . . . I thought that since God took so much away from me he'd let me keep the baby, but then the baby died and I just . . ." Devi shrugged and let her words trail away. "And after that there didn't seem much point in living. But you saved me, Mama. Thank you."

"And then you came home and started cooking." Saroj laughed even as tears filled her eyes. "We were so shocked that you were cooking the way you were. I thought you were crazy, dropped a few nuts and bolts somewhere."

Devi licked her lips. "I'm planning on going to culinary school after we come back from India."

Saroj's first reaction was to object. Her daughter a cook? It was one thing to cook in one's home, but to cook in a hotel or some other place for strangers? But Devi looked so happy that she reined back that thought. If it made her daughter happy then it must be the right thing for her to do.

"And who's going to pay for all this?" Saroj demanded.

"Daddy said he'd pay for it all," Devi said. "You don't mind, do you?"

"No, our money is your money," Saroj said and laughed a little. "Sitting here with you makes me happy. I can't believe I can feel happy. Everything is going wrong. Everything. And I can still laugh. Isn't that amazing?"

"Yes," Devi said. "It's terrific."

"What's terrific?" A sleepy Shobha asked as she came into the kitchen. "Can't you two be quiet for a while? It's five in the fucking morning and you're making a ruckus."

She sat down on the other side of Saroj at the dining table and put her head on the table. "I want to sleep, I'm even sleepy, but I can't sleep. I keep tossing and turning."

"That is how God is punishing you for divorcing your husband," Saroj said, getting up from her chair. "*Chai?*" she asked her daughters, who nodded.

"I'm not divorcing him, we're divorcing each other. There's a difference," Shobha pointed out. "Shit, is that G'ma?" she asked, looking at the brass urn.

"Yup," Devi said.

"Gives me the creeps having her here," Shobha said and then grinned. "But also feels right to have her here, doesn't it? A whole G'ma now in a small little pot."

"Mama, put *elaichi* in my *chai*," Devi instructed.

"And lots of sugar in mine, and no cardamom, please," Shobha piped in.

Saroj folded her hands into fists and rested them against her waist. "Does this look like a hotel to you both? One wants *elaichi* and the other doesn't. I will make it one way and you can drink it or not."

"Please, Mama," Shobha pleaded sleepily and then looked at Devi. "Why can't you go whip up some *chai*, Miss Culinary School?"

"Because I reserve my talents for five-star restaurants only," Devi quipped.

Saroj looked at her daughters bicker and smiled. Yes, it was right to have Vasu here. In the old days the first night of Vasu's visit would be spent here; four women, spanning three generations, would gossip, nag, and fight. Oh, all the time she'd wasted being angry at Vasu, at Avi, at Devi, at Shobha. It was so unnecessary. She wished she'd had this epiphany before Vasu died, but realized that if Vasu were still alive, everything, especially how she felt about her, would be unchanged.

"So, what're you planning to do, stay unemployed and divorced?" Devi asked Shobha.

"First, there's the trip to India to dispense of G'ma in the Bay of

Bengal. And then maybe I'll seduce this Ukrainian programmer I hired in my ex-company," Shobha said with a gleeful smile because she knew that talk like this would evoke a strong reaction from her mother.

"*Chee-chee*, Shobha, you talk like a cheap loose woman," Saroj said on cue.

"But he's a nice guy, Mama. Speaks with an accent. I wonder if he does other things with an accent," Shobha said, grinning at Devi.

"I once dated a Turkish guy," Devi joined in, "and he was—"

"I will pour *chai* over both your heads if you talk about things like this," Saroj said as she placed two cups of tea in front of them. "Yours has *elaichi*, and four spoons of sugar in yours," she told Devi and Shobha.

"Come on, Mama, didn't you have any crushes while you were growing up?" Shobha asked. They'd had this flavor of a conversation several times. Usually Saroj told them that good Indian girls didn't indulge in nonsense like this.

"Once," Saroj admitted finally, and both Shobha and Devi gave out a hoot of laughter. Saroj smiled cockily and sipped her tea. "He was my classmate in college. Very handsome. His name was Jitan and I was madly in love with him."

"So what happened?" Devi asked.

"Nothing," Saroj said casually. "In those days not much happened to good girls."

"Right," Shobha muttered, drinking her oversweet tea. "And that's how you lassoed Daddy? By being a good girl?"

"Of course," Saroj said with a naughty smile. "You can achieve a lot by being a good girl."

"I was a good girl and I ended up with Girish," Shobha muttered.

"And he was a good man," Saroj reminded her.

"Yes, he was," Shobha said, looking at Devi.

"And decent," Saroj said. "He called and said he was sorry about Vasu and apologized for the divorce. I understand you both can't be together but that doesn't make him bad. What do you think, Devi?"

"About what?" Devi all but choked on her cardamom tea.

"About Girish," Shobha supplied sweetly. "You know, there are some good culinary schools in Europe, maybe some near Oxford. You could nail the art of English cuisine."

Devi's mouth turned mutinously and she tried to shush her sister by kicking her under the table.

"And you could hook up with Girish as well. It's not like you know a lot of people in England," Shobha continued cheerfully, ignoring Devi.

"Why go all the way there? And she doesn't have to *hook* up with Girish. Geeta Auntie's brother lives in London, he'll take care of her," Saroj said confidently. "I've heard of a good school here in Napa and that will be just fit for her."

"Yes, it will be fit if they'll have me," Devi said and then looked pointedly at Shobha. "But who knows, maybe I *will* end up in Oxford for some other reason."

"Ah," was all Shobha said before burying her nose in her cup of tea.

"What ah?" Saroj asked suspiciously.

"Nothing," Devi said quickly and this time succeeded in silencing Shobha by kicking her under the table. "Isn't it nice to sit here like this? All of us," she said in an effort to divert Saroj's attention.

"Yes," Saroj said, looking at the brass urn on the table.

"Very nice," Shobha agreed with a broad smile. "So, Devi, aren't you glad you didn't die in the bathtub and miss these wonderfully nice moments?"

"Shobha!" Saroj cried out and Devi started laughing.

Avi woke up because of all the noise. When he didn't see Saroj next to him in bed, he immediately worried that she was crying again. The sorrow of losing Vasu ran deep, and it tore at him that he could do nothing to ease either his pain or the pain of his wife and daughters.

He quietly tiptoed into the kitchen. He could hear Shobha, Devi, and Saroj. He was afraid he'd find them mourning. So he stood out of their line of vision, not wanting to intrude on their sorrow.

Dawn was breaking outside, spilling into the dining area from the large French windows behind the dining table. He could, if he turned just a little to the right, see the silhouettes of three women, stark against the white walls. In the unclear light of dawn, it looked as if they were holding hands and then he heard the rich sound of laughter.

Serving Crazy
with Curry

A Reader's Guide

AMULYA MALLADI

A Conversation with
Amulya Malladi

Devi Veturi, the protagonist of Serving Crazy with Curry, *and Amulya Malladi met at an indiscriminate time and place to have this conversation. In the middle of the conversation things went a little crazy as Shobha, Saroj, and even Vasu showed up to chat (accuse?).*

Devi: In the first version of this book, which you titled *Thicker than Blood,* I die and then my sister, Shobha, becomes the protagonist. What happened? How did I live?

Amulya: Well, you did die in the first version. I wrote about two hundred pages of that book and then realized that it wouldn't work. I couldn't sleep at night and feel content about how the book was falling into place, so I knew that it needed to be scrapped. I scrapped it and went back and wrote it again and again and again. That suicide scene where you slit your wrists has been written innumerable times. But then, one day, it struck me that you'd live, you'd stop speaking and you'd start cooking weird food. And the title of the book would be *Serving Crazy with Curry.* It all just fell into place . . . like magic.

I have a question for you. Why did you try to commit suicide? Someone who read the book said to me that this kind of bad stuff happens to lots of people and lots of people don't kill themselves.

Devi: Lots of people are not me. I think it's important to remember that my emotions and my feelings are different from everyone else's. You are probably strong enough to deal with a loss of career, loss of a baby, loss of a man in your life, and loss of self-respect, but I wasn't. And like I said, it was not just a careless thought, it was planned. I really wanted to die. I couldn't see any reason to live. Imagine this: You hate going to sleep every night because tomorrow is going to be the same empty day and when you finally go to sleep you hate waking up because it's going to be the same crappy day. I think after a while you reach a point where you can't see the light at the end of the tunnel and it all becomes pointless.

Amulya: But now you're smart enough to know that killing yourself was not such a bright idea.

Devi: It's not fair to call it a stupid idea. It was what it was and it seemed like a good idea then. I can't go back and live my life. I can only live forward. If I had to do it again, I hope I wouldn't try to kill myself but I can't be sure of that.

Amulya: Now, the whole Girish business; were you really in love with him? Or did you sleep with him because he was Shobha's and that would be a nice "F*** you" to your sister?

Devi: I would never use language like that. That's Shobha's style.
    But yeah, I think it was a little of both. I was in love with Girish and even though I knew I could never let Shobha find out about us, there was a small perverse pleasure in sleeping with her husband. But when I told her the truth there was no pleasure, perverse or otherwise. I was terrified of losing Shobha and I realized that I didn't love Girish enough to lose my family. They were more important.

Amulya: I have to know, why the cooking?

Devi: I'd like to know as well. Since you wrote it in, why don't you tell me?

Amulya: Hmm . . . well, I think you started cooking all that fusion cuisine because you wanted to do something that was different, yet you wanted to hold on to what was. You wouldn't speak, so you used food as a communicating medium. You expressed your feelings through it, joy, fear, boredom, anger . . . all of that.

Devi: You mean, since I stopped speaking as a result of my traumatic experience, I had to do something, and cooking was it?

Amulya: Absolutely! A budding hobby that I think will make a fabulous profession for you.

Devi: I love to cook. The smell, the texture, the taste . . . everything. Do you cook?

Amulya: I think you like to cook because I like to cook. Also, another reason why you were cooking like a veteran chef was because the kitchen had always been Saroj's domain and your trying to take that domain away from her was a subconscious effort on your part to tell her that you can control your life since you can control her kitchen. You were asking her to back off. She saved your life but you didn't want her to take control of it now that you were alive. And speaking of Saroj . . . I'd like to talk to you about your mother.

Devi (sighs): Do we have to?

Amulya: Well, I thought you all made up, nice and neat in the end.

Devi: Your end is not my end and we didn't make up nice and neat. Well, we're on better terms than we used to be . . . but she's still a pain in the ass.

Saroj: Mind your language, Devi. Talking about your mother like this, you should be ashamed.

Devi: This is a private conversation, Mama, you can't just barge in.

Saroj: There are no private conversations for you. After pulling a stunt like that in your bathtub, do you really think we're going to let you talk to anyone you feel like without knowing what you're talking about?

Devi: Oh, Lord! Here she goes again.

Saroj: One thing I want to make clear. I am not a terrible mother or a terrible cook. You kept saying that all the time, Amulya, and it hurt my feelings.

Amulya: I . . . I . . . am sorry . . . ah, well, so, how are you doing since your mother passed away?

Saroj (shrugs): It is very hard to lose a mother . . . a parent. Now I remember her with great joy, but I also know that if she was alive I would still be despising her.

Amulya: Do you think Shobha and Devi will always have mixed feelings about you?

Saroj: Why should they? I have been a good mother. My mother was never around, I have always been around. They have no reason to dislike me or have mixed feelings about me.

Amulya: And how are things with Avi?

Saroj (smiles): Wonderful. I didn't know about the letters, you know. I wish I had known what he was going through, I wish . . . maybe if I had known, I would have been different. I don't know. But I am happy my marriage survived. I look at Shobha . . . so many boyfriends since the divorce . . .

Shobha (comes in and interrupts): Don't exaggerate, Mama. Just one. I have just one boyfriend and have had only one, this one, since Girish.

Amulya: Vladimir?

Shobha (laughs and shakes her head): Hell no! A guy who hits on a married woman is not a very nice guy. Actually, this is someone I met through my new job. I got hired as a director at Microsoft, did I tell you? It's wonderful working there and I met him at this breakfast meeting. He works for MSNBC and . . . we clicked.

Saroj: Clicked? My foot. He is some foreigner, from Scotland or Ireland or something.

Shobha: He's Italian. He has the accent, you know, gives me the goose bumps. Mama just doesn't get it.

Saroj: I do get it. You leave your good husband and sleep around like a loose woman. No shame, Shobha, you have no shame.

Amulya: Well, looks like things are pretty much back to normal.

Shobha: Of course. Did you really think things would change?

Devi: I've got to go, a seminar at school. Jamie Oliver is coming. I'm so excited about seeing him.

Amulya: So, things are going well at the culinary school?

Devi: Fabulous! I already have three job offers for when I graduate next summer, one right here, one in Atlanta, and one . . . in Europe.

Shobha: Ask her where in Europe.

Devi: I'm *not* leaving the U.S.

Amulya: No plans to go to Oxford?

Saroj: Why should she go to Oxford? She has a job in San Francisco. She will take that.

Devi: I'll probably go to Atlanta. I don't know. I haven't made any decisions. Look, I really have to go now.

Amulya: It was nice talking to all of you.

Saroj: You make sure you clear it up that I am a good cook and a good mother.

Shobha: She will, Mama, she will.

[Everyone leaves.]

Amulya: Whew! Odd to have a conversation with people I created. Very odd! Maybe I need to get some help.

Vasu: Before you do that, maybe you and I should talk.

Amulya: You're dead.

Vasu: Sure. But then none of us really exist and you're still chatting away with us. So does it really matter that I am dead?

Amulya: Okay. What do you want to talk about?

Vasu: I think you misunderstood me. I loved Shekhar, yes, but I also loved Saroj, very much.

Amulya: Not just as much.

Vasu: But I loved Devi more than anyone else. I thought about it and realized that you made a mistake. You show me as this selfish woman . . .

Amulya: Never selfish. You were a woman with screwed up priorities, but you were never selfish.

Vasu (smiles): That is something then. I don't want people to think that I don't have the capacity to love. I loved my daughter, my grand-daughters, Avi, even Girish. I loved them all. But I also loved Shekhar.

Amulya: I understand. You held the family together in many ways. I think Saroj wouldn't have fought to make things work with Avi if you hadn't been her mother. Devi would've broken Shobha's heart and her parents' if she hadn't known what it meant to love a married man through you.

Vasu: I guess I gave them the good with the bad. So, does Devi have a new man in her life?

Amulya (grins): I think she's still mooning over her sister's ex-husband.

Vasu (smiles back): They will make a lovely couple. She will love him madly and he will adore her . . . maybe they will get together; have children, the nice house . . . everything.

Amulya: I'd like that. It would be scandalous enough and it would burn Saroj's ass.

Vasu (laughs): Well, thanks for the chat. I better get going. And as a doctor, my recommendation would be for you to get some help. It isn't healthy, Amulya, to talk with characters in your books, dead or alive.

Reading Group Questions
and Topics for Discussion

1. Why does Malladi choose to open the book by discussing the "day it would happen," specifically delineating Devi's plans for suicide? What tone does this choice lend to the narrative? Why do you think the author presents Devi's decision-making process, instead of opening the book with the suicide attempt itself?

2. What does Devi's list of reasons to live and die indicate about her values and the problems she faces? Why do you think she commits suicide?

3. Saroj admits that she often "thinks of leaving her family without warning" (p. 15). What holds Saroj back, but propels Devi forward? How are the two women more similar than either of them would like to admit?

4. How is Saroj traumatized by the discovery of Devi's almost-lifeless body? How does she present her role in foiling the suicide attempt as an accomplishment? Why does Saroj shift the focus to be "all about her"?

5. What is Saroj's attitude toward each of her daughters? How does she project her own unhappiness upon them? How does each woman deal with the prospect of failure?

6. The comparison between Shobha and Devi literally begins at birth. How does this constant assessment influence each woman's conception of herself? How does it color their relationship with one another? Why does Saroj value Shobha for being "easier"?

7. "Instead [they] stood as adversaries," Saroj says of her marriage (p. 25). Why has her marriage with Avi crumbled? How are other interfamilial relationships similarly adversarial?

8. How does the relationship between Saroj and her mother, Vasu, compare with the rapport Saroj has with her own daughters? Why does Saroj resent her mother? What is her attitude toward her father?

9. Why does Devi decide to stop talking? How does this decision mirror the actions she took as a small child? In which ways does her silence liberate her, and how does it hold her back?

10. Why doesn't Malladi disclose what happened to Avi's arm at the beginning of the book? How does his disability inform his behavior and influence his choices, particularly the decision to come to America?

11. At first, what about Avi is so endearing to Saroj, and vice versa? How have they both changed since the early years of their marriage?

12. "Life is so much fun," writes Avi in an unsent letter to Devi (p. 69). How has each character in *Serving Crazy with Curry* fallen away from embracing the good things in life? Who comes closest to reclaiming a sense of joy in the book?

13. Much to her mother's dismay, Devi takes over cooking duties from Saroj after she moves back in. What does the kitchen repre-

sent to both mother and daughter? Why does Devi start to cook? Do you think that she's always wanted to? How is it a collaborative process for each of them, and how is each proprietary over the act?

14. How is adjusting to the United States difficult for Saroj? Does Avi feel the same way? In which ways are their children traditionally "Indian," and how do they identify more with their American contemporaries?

15. Why does Saroj blame America for all her problems? How does she idealize India? How does she embrace all things traditional, from the relationship she wants with her son-in-law to the food she cooks?

16. In which ways do Shobha's feminist beliefs belie her feelings about love? How is she a risk-taker, and in which ways would she prefer to play it safe? How does Shobha's firing jar her "perfect world"? What about this event spurs her to break up her marriage?

17. How is Vasu a loving woman? In which ways is she selfish, especially in regard to her family? What does she value the most in life?

18. Vasu refers to Saroj's photographs as depicting a "contrived family." What comprises Saroj's vision of a perfect family unit, and how does this dream differ from reality? How is Vasu's conception of family more unconventional, and how has this both strengthened and weakened her family bonds?

19. How do the characters in the book identify themselves by what they do, and by what they have accomplished or stand to accomplish? How do each of them react when they are at loose ends occupationally? Why doesn't Saroj work? Do you think she regrets the decision to not finish her education?

20. How does Saroj become a more sympathetic character as the novel unfolds? What do you learn about her that makes her less of a one-dimensional "nag," as Devi classifies her? Why does Saroj confront Avi about the problems in their marriage? What does this accomplish?

21. Were you surprised to learn of Devi's miscarriage? How does her family react to the news? Do you think she could have told them about it before she tried to commit suicide? Why or why not?

22. Were you surprised to learn that the father of Devi's baby was Girish? What do you think might have happened if she had carried the baby to term?

23. Are you surprised by Shobha's reaction to Devi's affair with Girish? Do you think Shobha's attitude will change over time, or have the sisters really breached a chasm in their relationship?

24. Do you think that Devi will ever tell the rest of her family about her affair with Girish? In which ways are Shobha and Girish well suited for one another? Devi and Girish?

25. How is writing cathartic for Avi and for Devi? Why does Devi write down the ingredients of her recipes? Is this just a cookbook journal or is it more?

26. What do you think will happen after the story ends, especially in the unfolding of relationships? Do you think that there's any chance of a Devi-Girish pairing? Why or why not?

AMULYA MALLADI is the author of *A Breath of Fresh Air* and *The Mango Season*. She lives on the island of Mors in Denmark with her family. You can contact her at www.amulyamalladi.com.